BAD GIRLS
don't die

BAD GIRLS
don't die

katie alender

HYPERION
NEW YORK

For Christopher

Text copyright © 2009 by Katie Alender

All rights reserved. Published by Hyperion, an imprint of Disney Book Group. No part of this book may be reproduced or transmitted in any form or by any means, electronic or mechanical, including photocopying, recording, or by any information storage and retrieval system, without written permission from the publisher. For information address Hyperion, 114 Fifth Avenue, New York, New York 10011-5690.

Printed in the United States of America
First Hyperion paperback edition, 2010
10 9 8 7 6
V475-2873-0-13200
ISBN 978-1-4231-0877-1

Library of Congress Cataloging-in-Publication Data on file.
This book is set in 12-point Garamond 3.
Designed by Elizabeth H. Clark
Visit www.un-requiredreading.com

SUSTAINABLE
FORESTRY
INITIATIVE
Certified Chain of Custody
Promoting Sustainable Forestry
www.sfiprogram.org
SFI-01054
The SFI label applies to the text stock

Acknowledgments

I'd like to extend my gratitude to a lot of people who, one way or another, helped make this book happen.

Matthew "Matt" Elblonk, agent extraordinaire, for his passion for the project, and for placing it in the hands of other people who had passion for it (as well as helping me make sense of the publishing experience and listening to me ramble about my dog).

My husband, Chris, who believed in me enough that I suddenly believed in myself.

My loving family—Mom, Dad, Helen, Juli, George, and Ali; and the Alenders.

My beta readers from Eta Phi Tau, and my beta-beta reader, Amber Dubois.

My dog show peeps Cricket Wheeler and Dana Langford, and all the folks at Painless—best day job ever! The old team from JP Kids LA, who taught me how to collaborate (all of whom, I hope, understand the significance of Alexis's street address).

Eve Metlis and Tina (Gregory) McFarland, for helping me understand true friendship.

All of my wonderful friends, who encourage me and put up with me even though I never respond to evites.

And finally, because this is how we do things in Hollywood:

EDITED BY
Margaret Cardillo
Arianne Lewin

It was a privilege.

I STOOD PERFECTLY STILL, looking up at the house and the dark sky beyond it.

A band of mist drifted away from the moon, making way for the next set of clouds—what I hoped would be the picturesque backdrop I'd been waiting for.

The camera, a twenty-five-year-old Nikon FM2n, thirty bucks at a garage sale, waited patiently on the tripod.

I didn't know how long I'd been outside—it felt like hours, although I was probably like a subject in one of those science experiments where they tell you to ring a bell after an hour and most people make it for, like, twelve minutes. For a split second I thought about giving up for the night. There was always tomorrow.

But suddenly everything around me seemed to get one shade brighter. The moon came pouring through a wispy haze of vapor that looked like a tattered veil draped behind the house.

In other words, it was perfect.

Photographs taken in very low light need a long exposure—longer than most people, me included, can stand still—so I used a little device with a squeezy bulb and a cord that screws into the camera. I pressed the bulb, heard the click as the shutter lifted, and started counting. When I reached ten, I let go of the bulb. The shutter closed.

I repeated this a few more times, at one point adjusting the focal length so that the house itself was out of focus and the giant oak in the front yard was sharply defined. I didn't take very many pictures—when you use real film (and pay for it yourself), you just can't shoot as much as you want.

After a few minutes the clouds had melted together and the effect was back to being kind of blah. Even a house like ours—an ancient one with carved shingles, creaky overhangs, and an enormous stained-glass bay window—needed the right setting.

Now that my attention was diverted from the photographs, the spookiness of the scene hit me. Suddenly, standing outside all by myself, an easy target for any random maniac, seemed very foolish. My breathing turned shallow and my hands trembled as I snapped the lens cap into place. I was tempted to grab the whole setup and run for the house, but something inside me refused to give in to the fear. So with slow, deliberate motions, I removed the camera from the tripod and unscrewed the little plate that holds it in place. I slipped the camera strap around my neck and started winding the remote shutter around my hand.

Snap.

I swung my head around, looking for the source of the noise.

Deep breath. It was just a bird, or a squirrel, or one of the cats my sister insists on feeding even though it's going to give our mother a hissy fit . . . no pun intended.

Shuffle shuffle.

"Heeeeere, kitty," I said softly. "Heeeeeere, kitty kitty kitty . . ."

Snap, pop.

"Present yourself, kitty," I said, a little louder.

A head popped out from behind the trunk of the oak tree.

My heart did three backflips before I recognized the honey-colored hair of my little sister, Kasey.

"Present yourself?" Kasey asked. "Sergeant Meow, reporting for duty."

I tried to think of something biting to say, but I still hadn't caught my breath. I swatted her on the arm and swallowed a huge gulp of air.

She stared at the camera for a few seconds, her lips

pressed together in the almost-frown that had recently become her default expression. She shifted her weight from one foot to the other and back, her fingers lightly playing with the sleeves of our mom's ancient Surrey High T-shirt that she'd inherited as a pajama top.

"How long have you been out here?"

Kasey shrugged, looked at her watch. "A while."

"What time is it?"

"Three sixteen."

Seriously? I'd been outside for three hours. I guess I'd rock that bell-ringing experiment.

Kasey trails along behind me all the time when I'm out taking pictures. She stands near the camera and watches what I'm watching, but she claims she doesn't get it—doesn't know why something's worth photographing.

I've tried to teach her, but she's actually kind of hopeless. When we started, her pictures looked like bad vacation snapshots, and after five exhausting hours, they were *worse*—because now she was trying to be artsy. A lot of blobs and blurs and pictures with no life of their own.

I told her not to worry, that maybe her true talents would emerge when she was older.

What else could I tell her? That I can't imagine the feeling of walking through the world without being able to see the lines and shapes and balance of seemingly normal objects? That when I'm at school, I feel lonely for my camera as if it were a friend (which I don't have any of at school, so it makes sense)?

"What are you taking pictures of? I don't see anything," she said.

"I would explain, but it's three a.m.," I said. "I'll show you when I develop the film, okay?"

She nodded and yawned.

I took another look up at the house.

There was a soft glow peeking through the branches that shaded our bedroom windows.

"Oh, crap . . ." I said. "Kase, which room is that light coming from?"

If Mom was wandering around, turning on lights, then she knew Kasey wasn't inside, and then it was a pretty short road to figuring out that I was gone too. And that meant trouble.

No putting yourself or Kasey in strange and/or potentially dangerous situations to take pictures was the latest incarnation of the rule that had once upon a time been, *Don't go on the roof.* With every fresh misstep, the rule evolved—*No taking pictures of retail merchandise; No taking pictures on other people's property; Don't use Kasey as a decoy to get photos of people who don't want to be photographed.* I was fairly sure that pretty soon it would just be *Put the camera down, sit on the sofa, and don't move.*

Even with a parental tantrum looming, the

photographer in me couldn't ignore something so cool-looking. It's like the way a hunter will see an exotic animal and want its head on his wall, only less gross; when I see something visually interesting, I want to take a picture of it so badly it's almost like a craving. Instinctively I uncapped the lens and raised the camera to my eye.

"It's not *my* room," Kasey said. "It's not yours either."

"Set up the tripod," I said, waving to the spot where it lay on the ground. Then I turned my attention to the light.

It was a soft glow, pale gold, and Kasey was right—it wasn't coming from either of our rooms.

It didn't actually seem to be originating from *inside* the house at all.

I couldn't wait for the tripod—I held the camera as steady as possible, bending my knees and bracing my body and taking a deep breath and holding it—and pressed down the shutter.

After a few seconds I let go, then took another picture, and another.

"Ready," Kasey said, handing me the little plate to screw on to the camera.

As quickly as I could, I attached the camera to the tripod, then put my eye to the viewfinder.

The light was gone.

We waited a few more minutes, but it never

returned. Finally, I capped the lens and folded up the tripod. Kasey watched me, glancing up every few seconds to see if the light was back. Our eyes met at one point, and I had to swallow hard.

What was it? Where had it come from? Why did it turn off? Neither of us asked the questions out loud.

But we were both thinking them.

We marched silently through the side yard. Fortunately, the October nights were cool enough that the many, many ginormous spiders that usually populated that part of the yard were gone. I walked in front, though, just in case. Kasey was a freaker-outer, and we didn't need any bloodcurdling screams advertising our location.

I turned back to check on her, stopping so abruptly that she ran right into me.

"Spider?" she asked, panic in her voice.

I shook my head. I was looking past her into the front yard, at the spot where we'd been standing just twenty seconds earlier.

It was lit up by the same faint glow we'd seen in the tree.

And it actually seemed to be . . . growing.

"What?" Kasey whispered.

"Uh . . ." If my sister saw it, she would spaz. I looked right at her and smiled. "Nothing."

Out of the corner of my eye, I got a sense of the light

growing larger—and then I realized it wasn't getting bigger—

—It was getting *closer*.

It was following us.

"You know, I might have seen a *little* spider," I said.

"Go. Now. Move," Kasey said, pushing on my back.

I let her go ahead of me through the back door as I cast one final glance behind us. There was no glow. Either it had disappeared, or it hadn't rounded the corner yet.

We slipped into stealth mode to climb the stairs from the foyer to the second floor, skipping the third, eighth, and eleventh steps, all of which squeaked loudly enough to wake the dead, and then Kasey waved a little good-bye and ducked into her bedroom.

I set the tripod on the floor and the camera on the dresser, and exhaustion overwhelmed me. I changed into a long T-shirt and crawled into bed, telling myself that it had just been a swarm of curious fireflies.

I mean, it *had* to be. There wasn't any other explanation.

The last thing I saw before I fell asleep was the faintest trace of a glow on the spindly branches of the oak tree outside my window.

Curious fireflies, I told myself sleepily. So curious that they'd found a way to follow us upstairs without actually coming into the house.

2

BACK LEFT CORNER OF THE LIBRARY, underneath the study desks.

You have to be willing to sit on the floor, but that's a small price to pay for the perfect instead-of-class hangout: zero student traffic, lots of legroom, and complete invisibility to the librarian.

"Excuse me, Alexis."

Tragically, it was *not* invisible to the principal.

"What class are you cutting this fine fall day, Miss Warren?"

I stood up out of the library carrel and grabbed my bag. "History. But technically, I'm not cutting a *class*."

The corner of Mrs. Ames's mouth twisted up into an almost-smile, and she cleared her throat. This was promising—this was "My day hasn't taken a nosedive yet, so this is kind of amusing," *not* "I've had it up to here." When you spend as much time around the principal as I do, you get to know her idiosyncrasies.

"And why does history not qualify as a class?" As she spoke, Mrs. Ames adjusted the straw beach hat she'd worn for Hat Day—day one of the officially most annoying time of the entire school year, Homecoming Week. The hat clashed horribly with her beige blazer, but I knew way better than to comment.

We walked out of the library. As nice as it would be to pretend we were having a pleasant stroll, I knew where we were headed. And I knew what phone number she would be calling when we got there. And I knew what meeting my mother would be pulled out of to talk to her daughter's principal—again. And I knew exactly which classroom to report to for Saturday detention—and not the fun '80s-movie kind of Saturday detention—the incredibly boring kind that makes you want to stab yourself in the eye with a pencil. (At least then you'd get to leave.)

I sighed. "They're in the gym. Decorating for the banquet."

If there was a bright side to this whole thing, it was that I still got to miss decorating the stupid gym for the stupid alumni Homecoming banquet. Another detention, big deal. I hadn't had a free Saturday since August.

But Mrs. Ames is no dummy. "Ah," she said, and stared right into my eyes. "Well, I'll tell you what—why don't we sweep this incident under the rug and get you back to class so you can help out?"

I shot her a look. She gave me an innocent smile.

We started down the hallway that led to the gym.

"How many times is this now, Alexis?"

"This month?"

"This year."

I puffed air out of my mouth to blow the wispy pink hairs away from my face.

"Twelve, Alexis," she said. "Twelve skipped classes—that I know of—not to mention a number of other small incidents."

The way she said *small incidents* was a very clear reminder that some of the incidents weren't small. I, personally, don't see what's so criminal about giving honest feedback to a student teacher who should clearly quit while she's ahead, or having an anti-fashion show outside the gym during the choir's annual fashion show. But I guess that's just me.

"Let me tell you, Miss Warren, there's been some pressure to avoid handing out Saturday detentions like lollipops. There's a big trend in the district toward suspension right now."

Suspension.

I dug my fingernails lightly into the palm of my hand. Somehow *suspension* sounded way worse than *detention*. Detention happens to everybody. Suspension, though—that's for the sociopaths.

I wasn't a hundred percent sure I was ready to take that leap.

She sighed as we started walking again. "You know I think you have a lot of potential, Alexis. Your test scores are very high, and it's clear that you can do well, if you want to."

She went off into a lecture about how nobody can make my choices but me. I nodded, but I was only half listening. The word *suspension* was still buzzing around in my head like an angry bee.

We reached the gym.

The entire history class was spread out around the gym working on stupid, meaningless tasks for the stupid, meaningless banquet, and every head turned to look at us. I held my chin high and shot a couple of disdainful looks around. The kids I made eye contact with went back to their work.

Mrs. Anderson, who happens to be the dumbest teacher ever (and I'm not just saying that, it's true—it took her four tries to pronounce "aborigines"), came hustling over.

"Well, what have we here?" she asked. "Alexis, what a nice surprise. I assume you're on your way to the main office."

Mrs. Ames frowned. "No. Miss Warren and I have just been chatting, so I hope you'll excuse her tardiness.

I'm going to leave her in your capable hands, Mrs. Anderson."

She said *capable hands* a lot like she'd said *small incidents*.

"Wonderful," Mrs. Anderson replied.

Mrs. Ames looked down at me. "I'm sure you'll put your best effort into your work today, Alexis."

Oh, totally.

But Mrs. Anderson wasn't ready to let the torment end. She clapped her hands together. "Alexis! You must have forgotten that today is Hat Day! Silly girl, pink hair isn't a hat! Luckily, we have some backups—" She turned and called over her shoulder. "Jeremy! Bring that box over here!"

A boy who'd been assembling really ugly centerpieces out of fake flowers and wicker baskets reluctantly picked up a medium-size cardboard box and started toward us.

No way. I would wear a dancing banana fruit basket on my head before I would let one of those disgusting things touch my scalp.

Jeremy tripped and dropped the box. Hats went flying everywhere.

Nice.

"How thoughtful of you, Mrs. Anderson," Mrs. Ames said, as Jeremy crawled around gathering up baseball caps and colorful sombreros. "But I don't think Alexis is the Hat Day type."

Case closed. Mrs. Ames headed out of the gym.

Mrs. Anderson turned to me, all the peppy rah-rah gone from her voice. "What to do with dear Alexis?" she asked, scanning the room. "Why don't you . . ."

As long as I was far away from Mrs. Anderson, I'd be fine.

". . . go help Pepper."

Pepper?!

"She's not even *in* this class," I protested.

Mrs. Anderson looked triumphant. "Well, Alexis, *all* of the cheerleaders are helping out today. So why don't you check in with Pepper and tell her you'll be thrilled to do anything she needs."

Thrilled is not the word I would choose.

"It's not straight!" Pepper said. Her flaming orange hair was mostly tucked under a ridiculous floppy magenta beret, but one stray lock looped down and covered her left eye. She glared at me with the right eye.

I heaved a huge sigh. "Pepper. I swear. The banner. Is straight."

We'd been on opposite sides of a plastic WELCOME HOME, ALUMNI! banner for probably five minutes, and every time we had it in place, Pepper backtracked and decided it wasn't good enough.

"It doesn't *look* right," she whined.

"That's because you're looking at it with only one eye," I said. "You have no depth perception."

She sniffed and rolled her eye.

Let's get something clear: Pepper Laird is a cheerleader. As such, she is used to bouncing in place and holding her arms in the air for long periods of time.

I, Alexis, am not a cheerleader. In fact, I'm sort of an anti-cheerleader. So while Pepper is out there working on her biceps and triceps and glutes, I am slumping under the bleachers with the rest of the outcasts.

But no way was I going to admit to Pepper that I couldn't take it. I dropped my half of the banner. "Forget it," I said. My arms burned as blood poured back through the veins. "This is moronic. I'm not going to do this."

"We *have* to!" Pepper said. "And you have to help, or I'll tell Mrs. Anderson."

Oh, she definitely would. And then I'd have to face Mrs. Ames for the second time that day. And her goodwill and ability to see a shred of potential in me would probably be all used up.

I settled for doing some arm stretches and making a very angry noise in Pepper's direction.

"You *freak*," she said.

This was not a new concept to me.

"You and your stupid pink hair"—not new either—
"and your whole freaky family."

That part was new.

Because whatever forces separated Pepper and me in
the suffocating world of Surrey High School, one thing
bound us together, and that was family. Sisters, to be specific. Kasey had been best friends with Pepper's sister,
Mimi, since fourth grade. They were the kind of friends
who argue more often than they don't, but they were still
glued together.

"Grow up," I said. "Leave my family alone."

Pepper stood up straighter. "As long as your schizoid
sister leaves *Mimi* alone, I'm fine with that arrangement."

Confusion must have overtaken annoyance in my
expression.

"Her *arm*," Pepper said.

Mimi had broken her arm at our house, about a
month before, but it was an accident. She'd been running
down the hall and slipped on a rug as she turned into
Kasey's room. That kind of thing just happens.

Although, come to think of it, we hadn't seen much
of Mimi lately.

"Yeah, so?"

"*Your* sister broke *my* sister's arm," Pepper said.

"Oh, please."

"Mimi told me the whole story. She won't tell our

mom because she says she feels bad for Kasey. But I think she's afraid because your little sister is a violent maniac."

Okay, so I'm not popular and friendly and I don't have any friends. But I wasn't about to let someone stand there and talk smack about my baby sister—who, yes, is sensitive, but, no, is not a violent maniac.

I took a step toward Pepper. She flinched, but she didn't back away.

"Face it, Alexis. Kasey is a whack job." She narrowed her eyes. "All my sister tried to do was touch one of her stupid dolls. . . ."

Pepper went on ranting, but I wasn't paying attention. I didn't back down, but suddenly I didn't feel like fighting about it either.

Because that one word—*dolls*—seemed too right.

A lot of people are avid collectors of things you or I would consider stupid, or at least silly—rocks with googly eyes glued to them and seashells for feet. Candles shaped like animals or mythical creatures.

For Kasey, it was dolls.

I don't even remember when it started. Years ago. Long enough for Kasey, using her meager allowance, every dime of birthday or Christmas money, and who knows what else, to amass dozens of dolls.

And if my sister were ever capable of hurting someone, it would be to protect her precious collection.

Pepper grabbed her end of the banner. "Let's just do this so I can get away from you," she said.

"The feeling is mutual," I said.

We hoisted the banner once again.

"Stop—it's perfect," said a voice. I turned to see who had spoken.

Oh, great.

Megan Wiley, poised, self-assured, cocaptain of varsity cheerleading, even though she's just a sophomore—oh, and my own personal nemesis, more on that in a sec—studied our sign, then sauntered over with a hammer and nails. She hammered both sides into the wall without another word.

Here's the deal:

I speak up in class, I get sent to the office. Megan speaks up in class, she's a "strong, assertive model student." I post a few flyers saying that the vending machines on school property are a sign that our school district has sold out to the corporate-industrial establishment, I get (what else?) Saturday detention. Megan starts a campaign to serve local foods in the lunchroom (oh, and could we *pleeeeeease* maybe get rid of the soda machines?) and the local newspaper does a write-up about her.

She's like me, only not. Not like me at all. She's the golden girl and I'm . . . tarnished.

So forgive me if I hate her a little.

Pepper stalked off while I scanned the gym for a seat that would hide me from the roving eye of Mrs. Anderson, then paused and turned back around to look at the sign (which was, mercifully, straight).

"HOME IS WHERE THE HEART IS."
SURREY ALUMNI
HOMECOMING SCHOLARSHIP BANQUET
WELCOME HOME, ALUMNI!

A few feet away, Megan was looking at it too. Our eyes met.

"I'm not sure I'd give money at a fund-raiser if they couldn't bother to have it someplace nicer than a high school gym," she said, turning away before I could answer. Her gaze lingered on the canvas, and I suddenly noticed that she was almost not even wearing a hat. Just a devil-horn headband left over from last Halloween.

"Mm," I said, and walked away.

I guess, in her own way, Megan really is different from the rest of them.

But I still hate her.

3

ONCE UPON A TIME, I had a best friend. Her name was Beth Goldberg. Beth and I got in lots of trouble together, but back then, people called it "mischief" and went a little easy on us. Apparently, when it's two people, it's quirky and funny, but when it's a person doing the same stuff on her own, it's rebellious and antisocial.

I'd always assumed that Beth and I would be friends forever. But then in the middle of eighth grade, the Goldbergs went through the World's Nastiest Divorce.

Beth went a little nuts.

I don't blame her. When her dad got involved with his twenty-one-year-old dental hygienist, Beth got involved with the junk-food aisle at the grocery store. She carried processed snack cakes around the way toddlers carry teddy bears. She gained, like, twenty pounds, but I didn't think it was a big deal. I figured she'd get back to her usual weight once the shock wore off.

Unfortunately, I wasn't the only person who noticed.

May 14 was "Fun and Fit Day" at Surrey Middle School, so the gym was full of booths set up by local health clubs and doctors and dentists and sports leagues, all trying to entice us not to end up as couch potatoes. That part was fine. What wasn't fine was when the whole school sat down to watch the eighth-grade cheerleaders' program on physical fitness.

They had a PowerPoint presentation, and it started out okay, if a little stupid. . . . Finding their misspelled words made it kind of fun, actually: "veggetables" and "carbhohydrytes," and don't forget to eat plenty of "protene." Beth and I sat there and laughed. Good times.

Then came the next segment. You know those DO and DON'T pages in fashion magazines? Like, "DO try belting your hideous $900 fuchsia sweater with a ridiculous $400 belt" and "DON'T leave the house with your underwear on the outside of your pants."

The cheerleaders did that—only they used pictures of kids from our school.

"DO exercise regularly"—insert photo of several cheerleaders looking really pretty as they pretend to lift weights.

"DON'T sit on the sidelines in gym class."

The picture that went with this one had a black bar over the kid's eyes, just like in a magazine, but everyone could tell it was Javier Delgado, who'd been overweight since kindergarten.

That's when most people started laughing nervously.

And that's when Beth and I *stopped* laughing.

"DO eat lots of fresh produce." A shot of Kira Conroy and Megan Wiley daintily eating a salad outside the lunchroom.

"DON'T go back for seconds in the lunch line."

And there it was.

A picture of Beth.

Yeah, there was a black bar over her face, but it was obviously her. She had her favorite rainbow-striped sweater on—the really expensive one from Nordstrom, the one she loved to wear even if it was tight and sometimes rode up a little to show off her new Twinkie stomach.

Beth didn't want to come back to school after that. She got out of her mom's car a minute before first bell, ate lunch in the main office, and got special permission to leave five minutes before final bell. Probably because Mrs. Goldberg and Javier Delgado's mom threatened to sue the pants off the school board.

The cheerleaders got a slap on the wrist. A bunch of us started a petition to keep the high school from letting them on the junior varsity squad. We had hundreds of signatures, including a lot from teachers and parents. The

JV coach at Surrey High agreed and barred the whole team from tryouts.

But then the *varsity* cheerleaders decided to stand up for their sisters. And they invited just about the whole troupe to skip JV and join their team.

That was right around when Beth and her mom put their house on the market and started packing up to move to Florida.

So now, not only did my best friend leave, but the cheerleaders and their mindless followers assumed *I* was personally responsible for the petition (which, yeah, I was) and started being openly rude to me—shutting doors in my face, leaving nasty notes on my desk and in my locker, making fun of me when I could obviously hear them.

That's when I began keeping really quiet in class, and finding ways to show the other kids I wasn't afraid of them—like staring them straight in the eye when they looked at me, taking a step toward them when they talked to me, or walking right up to them and getting in their personal space if I heard them say my name. Saying the meanest things I could think of whenever I had the chance—repeating rumors, embellishing them. I found out that Kira Conroy had been arrested for shoplifting at the mall, and made sure everybody knew about it. The girl who'd had five beers on New Year's Eve and peed her pants, the girl who tripped and fell off the stage at the Miss Teen California pageant—I shared those stories the moment I heard them.

All's fair in war, right?

So suddenly I wasn't a nobody anymore.

I was a somebody.

Somebody everyone was afraid of.

Since Megan Wiley was the captain of the cheerleaders, the school withheld her Student of the Year award. Seeing how she's always been star of the student body and undisputed queen of the cheerleaders, I can only imagine the whole Fun-and-Fit presentation was her idea in the first place. And it's not like she'd break formation and say otherwise, even if it wasn't.

Beth and her mom moved the Saturday after the last week of school. We tried to stay in touch—we really did. But I guess going to a ritzy private school changes your priorities. All I know is that we swore we'd talk once a week, and it took about three months for that plan to dissolve into nothing. When Beth started talking about going on the Zone diet and wanting a Prada purse (pardon me, *bag*), I knew that was the beginning of the end. And when I dyed my hair pink last year, it was the end of the end. So.

Since Beth left, I haven't really had a best friend.

I guess I don't have any real friends at all.

I mean, there's Kasey. She's thirteen—two years younger—so if you believe the greeting card commercials, we should have this special bond or something. We get along all right, but once she hit middle school, I started to feel less like her friend and more like her security blanket.

There was a time when we used to hang out—Kasey, me, Beth, even Mimi—goofing off and watching movies. But gradually, my formerly funny and cool sister morphed into a neurotic, oversensitive, doll-obsessed mess. Now our vibe is pretty much "big bad sister protecting timid little sister." So until the greeting card companies start making cards that say "YOU'VE ALWAYS BEEN THERE WHEN I WAS EITHER SCARED OR BORED," our relationship doesn't measure up to Hallmark's standards.

There's one group I hang out with at school, but their attitude is getting tiresome. My secret name for them is the Doom Squad. Everyone assumes they're morbid and strange, so they do their best to live up to the hype. Some of them are really nice, and I think they could be okay . . . if they would just stop trying so hard.

I mean, just because you don't want to be a cookie-cutter clone doesn't mean you have to wear a spiky collar and dress like a vampire wannabe. In the first place, I'm too lazy to put that much effort into my appearance, and in the second place, I'm really paranoid about wearing nonmatching blacks, so I usually end up in jeans and a T-shirt.

After history, I stopped by my locker. Lydia Small, who might as well be the Doom Squad poster child, wandered up and rested her forehead on the locker next to mine. She spends a lot of time and energy trying to give people the impression that she's too emo and gothic to be interested in anything. Still, I did notice she was wearing a wedding veil that she'd shredded and glued a bunch of plastic spiders on to.

Lydia is rude and overbearing and pretentious, and to be honest, there are actually several people I'd rather hang out with than her. But she's the one who always seems to appear out of thin air. And because of her big old attitude, people tend to do what she says. So when she walks over at lunch and says, "Move, worm," to whoever's sitting next to me, they move.

In spite of my misgivings, Lydia and I had been hanging out a little lately, going to see movies, people-watching at the mall, ending up next to each other at lunch. She was drawn to me, like a moth to a porch light. In fact, sometimes I suspected it was my ambivalence about her that made her so eager to hang out.

She wasn't best friend material, but I was getting used to having her around.

"You won't believe what Pepper Laird just said to me," I said. Lydia was quiet for a second. I waited for her to say something sympathetic.

"*Ugh,*" she said. A fair start. As I drew in a breath to elaborate, Lydia widened her eyes. "Sabrina Woodburn dyed her hair *black*. Who does she think she is, Morticia Addams? She's in *marching band* . . . What a wannabe."

"Weren't you in Glee Club until the middle of last year?" I asked.

Lydia sputtered. "That's *totally* different."

"Sure," I said. "Keep telling yourself that."

Now, see, if somebody talked to me that way, I would tell them exactly where they could put their opinion, and then I would assume the friendship was over. But Lydia just pouted and looped her arm through mine.

We started walking toward homeroom together. As we passed a group of cheerleaders, Lydia stuck her tongue out at them and clicked her tongue piercing against her teeth.

They drew back in a scandalized herd. "Oh, that is *so* mature," one girl said.

As we kept walking, the crowd seemed to thin a little. I spotted Megan Wiley leaning up against a locker, talking seriously to a girl in a pink cowboy hat who was crying so hard her mascara ran down her cheeks. The girl was Emily Rosen. I had Spanish with her. She was nice.

I planned to drag Lydia right past without stopping, but she saw the tears and came to a screeching halt.

"Heeey, Em!" she called.

"What are you doing?" I asked under my breath, as both Megan and Emily looked at us.

"I hear you had a *big night* with Rory Henderson," Lydia said sweetly. "Gonna have to give that promise ring back to your daddy, huh?"

Emily's face froze for a moment, and then she was bawling again. I clamped a hand on Lydia's arm as Megan shot a dirty look in our direction.

The only thing that saved us was the swaggering arrival of Rory Henderson himself. Rory's only popular because his dad is a rich lawyer and his mom used to be the weather girl on channel twelve. He's not really good-looking, and his entourage is made up of goons who laugh at everything he says, even though none of it is funny.

"Hi, Rory, you big stud!" Lydia cooed, and he gave her a half-second of a smile. She dissolved into giggles. Out of the corner of my eye, I could see Megan glaring.

"God, Lydia, you're so obnoxious!" I hissed.

Lydia laughed her I-don't-care-about-anything laugh. "I know, right?"

"You didn't have to say that to Emily." Emily was genuinely sweet, the kind of girl who would offer you her notes if you were absent.

"She deserves it," Lydia said, all la-di-da. "Look, she's buddy-buddy with Wiley."

I turned to look back at Emily and Megan, but the first thing I saw was Rory.

He stood motionless, staring across the hall at something; a second later, I realized it was Megan he was staring at, only it was really the other way around. *She* was staring at *him*, and from the look of things, he wasn't all that wild about it. His ruddy cheeks paled, and he cast a nervous look at the kids around him.

"I don't know, Rory," Megan said. Her voice was low, but it carried perfectly. Everyone within twenty feet was watching and listening. "It seems really unlikely that any of what you said is true. I mean, considering what Jessica told us after prom last year . . . ? About things going . . . downhill?"

Jessica Xiong, an eleventh grader on the varsity squad, smiled brightly and waved.

Then, in unison, the cheerleaders laughed their tinkly little laughs, which made everyone else laugh too.

Huge rosy patches flooded Rory's face. He ducked his head and practically ran off down the hall, his crew following in disgrace.

Lydia dragged me away. "Oh my God, you should hear what he's telling everyone she did last night. It's nasty. . . . I'm sick of cheerleaders. They're so shrill!"

If there were a shrill contest, the Doom Squad would probably take the gold medal. At least silver. But I didn't say so to Lydia. She'd just take it as a compliment.

I happen to know that Lydia was not only in Glee Club last year, but she played Dorothy in *The Wizard of Oz* in eighth grade, and she used to blog under the alias BRDWYDIVA about all the Broadway shows she wanted to see and all the actors she wanted to meet. Then *whoosh*, she changed pretty much overnight into the spider-veiled Princess of Doom.

That's the pathetic thing about high school. Everyone tries so hard to be something they aren't. It's gotten so I don't know who I *am*, so how can I even try to be who I am, much less someone I'm *not*?

My problem is that I don't even fit in with the misfits.

I don't fit in anywhere.

So there I was, walking next to Lydia, who was waving her arms around and telling a story way more dramatically than she needed to, when a door opened right into my forehead and knocked me down.

Just like that. And when I say down, I mean, like, down for the count. I landed on my butt, which I suppose is better than landing on the back of one's skull, if one has to choose—but it still sucked.

I sat there for a second, thinking I was all alone in a very dark room that smelled like pennies, and then I started to hear voices all around me, and my vision came back.

Lydia crouched to my left, staring at me, and on the right a teacher was trying his best to take charge of the situation, and in front of me was a guy with blond hair and glasses.

My first thought was: he's really cute. His curly blond hair, his big, worried, blue eyes.

My second thought was: wait, I know that curly hair and those big blue eyes.

I closed my eyes again, and my head started to hurt.

The teacher, a tweed-clad staple of the history department, took hold of my hand and patted it a few times. "Try to stay awake . . . you could have a concussion."

Not like closing your eyes helps the pain anyway. I opened them without complaint.

He was still there, looking at me. I don't mean the history teacher. I mean *him*.

Carter Blume.

"Do you know your name?" the teacher asked.

Okay, I understand that it's standard first-aid procedure to ask this question, but if you *do* happen to know your name, it's really annoying to be asked. I nodded and started to answer.

"Her name is Alexis!" Lydia shrieked helpfully. "Oh my God, Alexis, are you okay?"

I squinted. "I'm fine." Her shouting was making my headache worse.

"Alexis Warren," Carter said.

I stared at him, and after a second he smiled.

"I'm the guilty door-opener," he said. "Very sorry." He stuck his hand out, and it didn't occur to me right away that he actually wanted me to shake it, like we were a pair of old men or something. I just looked blankly at his hand until he laughed and pulled it back.

Lydia tried to haul me to my feet. The teacher helped her, and Carter hovered behind them.

"Haven't you done enough?" Lydia spat at him. "Why don't you go back to the Young Republicans?"

He ignored her.

"I am *so* sorry," he said, looking into my eyes.

Careful, Alexis. I looked away. Not that there was any danger of me actually liking someone like Carter. I mean, so what if his eyes were really sparkly? And who cared if his blond curls looked as soft as a baby's hair?

He was not my type. In fact, I didn't have a type. Not that I was looking to date college guys, but I'd always operated under the assumption that my Prince Charming wasn't among the available choices at Surrey High.

I realized I'd been kind of staring at him, but thankfully the late bell rang, interrupting the moment.

"You should go to the clinic," the teacher said. "Check in with the nurse."

"Can I come too?" Lydia asked frantically. "I'm her best friend."

No you're not, I thought.

"I think she'll be fine on her own," he said.

"I should go with her, Mr. Daley," Carter said. "It's my fault. . . . I won't be gone long."

The teacher shot him a suspicious look, but nodded. "Five minutes."

Lydia breathed out through her nose and looked at her watch. "I guess I have to go to class, Alexis. . . ." It was a clear prompt for me to invite her along.

"Yeah, okay," I said. "See you later."

The teacher ducked into his classroom and Lydia trudged away. I was alone with my assailant.

"This really isn't necessary," I said. "I can get there without help."

"My pleasure," he said.

4

It all started in September of last year.

There used to be this show, *Surrey Survey*, that was broadcast once a week during homeroom, run by a couple of A/V nerds.

I was on the last episode ever to air.

It was a show about student government elections. The A/V guys were in my Spanish class, and while we were talking one day, they told me their next show was about elections. I said the whole concept of student government was a sham and a farce and a popularity/beauty contest. All the candidates claimed to be committed to change, to making things better, but I suggested that the A/V nerds do a hidden-camera setup and ask the front-runners why they were *really* running. So they did. When the nonhidden camera was running, the answers were textbook—helping the school, getting involved, taking a stand, blah blah blah.

When that camera was off and just the hidden one was rolling, that's when the real reasons came out. Motives as varied as "the faculty sponsor is hot" to "you get to skip class whenever you want" to "Tim MacNamara's parents always buy beer when he has meetings at his house."

When the guys asked me (on camera) who I'd be voting for, I told the truth, which was that I didn't give a flying *bleep* (that's how it came out on air, at least) who the candidates were or what they stood for, and neither did anyone else in the school.

I also suggested that, just for fun, everyone who was sick of the pretty people using school elections to perpetuate the social dominance of their tyrannical clique should make a point of voting for a person they'd never heard of.

I wasn't really serious. I just thought I was being . . . you know, funny.

But I guess people have different definitions of funny. I hadn't counted on them using all of that footage of me condemning my fellow students as the basis for the entire segment. I was just a freshman, the girl with the bright pink hair, nobody to get excited about.

That was the day *Surrey Survey* got the ax.

It was also the day I made my second appearance on the cheerleaders' Public Enemy #1 list.

Because the front-runner for Student Council VP was Pepper Laird.

And she lost the election to the new kid nobody had ever heard of—Carter Blume. Pepper may have been knocked off her throne, but Carter's popularity soared. Soon he was the pack leader of the preps—the buttoned-up speech-and-debate-obsessed clones. Preps are like cheerleaders, only with less jumping.

I had no idea how easy it would be to create a monster—in fact, I had created two monsters. Carter and myself. Suddenly, the freshman anonymity that had softened the public's image of me was blasted away, and once again, I was That Girl.

So.

I started to walk toward the clinic. He came wandering after me.

"So, okay," he said at last. "Clearly you have no idea who I am."

"Clearly."

He wanted me to ask. He was dying for me to ask.

He held open the clinic door for me. The nurse was standing at the counter behind her desk, trying to fish the last cotton ball out of a jar. "Be right there," she said, without looking at us. Then she disappeared behind the curtain.

I planted myself in one of the guest chairs, and Carter sat next to me.

He leaned over and spoke in a confidential tone. "Are you proficient in the Heimlich maneuver?"

It took me a second to realize he was reading from

one of the posters on the opposite wall. "No," I said. "Sorry to say."

I looked at the next poster over, a cartoon about helping your friends fend off depression. A little cartoon girl was looking at her friend and asking, HOW ABOUT YOU, DO YOU EVER FEEL LIKE HURTING YOURSELF? "How about you, do you ever feel like hurting yourself?"

He paused and let out a half-laugh. "Well . . . only on turkey tetrazzini day."

"I don't think they serve that here."

"Right," he said. "Lucky me."

He didn't say anything else. Neither did I.

The nurse came bustling out.

"Carter!" she said. "Are you hurt?"

"No . . . I'm just here to make sure Miss Warren gets the level of care she needs," he said.

He was totally flirting with the nurse, and she was lapping it up.

"And I thought chivalry was dead!" she replied.

He stood. "Maybe it is. I opened a door into her head."

"Oh, well, I'm sure it was probably an accident," the nurse said absently, sitting down at her computer. "What was the name?"

"Warren," Carter said, looking right at me.

Forget this. Not about to let him stand around and play hero, I went to the desk, moving closer to the nurse so that Carter had to edge away. "Alexis Warren."

She asked a couple more questions, and I kept shifting so that eventually Carter was completely blocked from the desk. Out of the corner of my eye, I saw him take a self-conscious step backward and felt a pang of guilt.

"I should get to class," Carter said. He patted a stack of papers on the desk and leaned down a tiny bit toward the nurse. "I've done my civic duty."

Civic duty? Was he just using me as a cog in the oppressive machinery of the white male hierarchy? A line on his college application? Part three of a Boy Scout badge?

To think I almost felt sorry for him. All so he could enjoy the smug satisfaction of being a good citizen, get into a fancy university, become a lawyer, and help sleazy rich guys dump toxic waste wherever they felt like it.

He looked at me. "If there's anything I can—"

"There's not," I said.

The breezy look on his face faltered.

"Stop." My head was starting to throb, and my mood was souring by the moment. "I can take care of myself."

Everyone was quiet. The second hand on the old wall clock was the only sound.

"Just go to class," I said.

"You're the boss," he said, touching his finger to his forehead in a tiny salute.

Then he disappeared.

5

ON MY WALK HOME FROM SCHOOL I heard a car horn and looked around for the honker, even though not once in my entire high school career had someone honked for me.

The responsible party was Carter Blume, in all his J. Crew glory, driving a shiny green Prius. He pulled up next to me, and the passenger window rolled down with a happy hum.

"Can I give you a ride home?" he asked.

I leaned down to look at him across the car, but didn't answer.

He shifted into park. "Hi," he said. "How's the skull?"

"I have a bump," I said. "But I got some sweet aspirin out of the deal."

"Seems like they'd at least let you sleep through one class when you've been knocked in the head"—he paused—"by an evil Young Republican."

"They like it when kids get minor head injuries. They think it builds character."

He nodded. "Glad to see I didn't knock any of the pink out of your hair."

I reached up to brush a strand of hair off my forehead and winced when I touched the lump.

"Please let me drive you home," he said again. "It's really the least I can do."

"You mean it's Section Four of your 'How to Be a Good Citizen' handbook?"

He scrunched up his forehead.

"Don't worry," I said. "You've completely fulfilled your *civic duty*."

His eyes widened. "No—that was a joke. You didn't think I really *meant* it, did you?"

I didn't answer.

"Trust me," he said, raising his eyebrows. "There are a lot easier ways to serve my community than dealing with you."

Hmmph. Young Republicans have weird senses of humor.

"As a personal favor," he said. "Please let me drive you home."

All right, then. Fine.

I sighed and opened the door. "You're the boss."

"What if your friend sees you?" he asked. "Are

you willing to deal with the consequences?"

"Oh, please. I am not afraid of the Doom Squad," I said.

"That's an excellent name for them," Carter said, smiling. "Maybe we can arrange a rumble between the Young Republicans and the Doom Squad." He shifted into drive. "So where do you live?"

I pointed down the street. "Three houses down, the one with the yellow shutters."

He laughed. "I guess I have bad timing."

"Yeah, well," I said. "You seemed pretty determined. I hated to disappoint you."

He pulled into my driveway and put the car in park again.

"Wow," he said, looking up at the house.

Our house is pretty cool, I must admit. It's the oldest house on the block—probably the oldest one in town. It's big and ornate, with elaborate details everywhere—not just shingles, but little scalloped pieces of wood, and not just columns holding things up, but arches connecting the columns—that kind of thing.

The oak tree in the front yard adds to the effect. It's enormous and gnarled; it hangs over the house like an overprotective boyfriend. It's lush and vivid in the summer, tangled and bare in the winter. In the fall it turns from green to red to yellow to brown so fast you hardly have time to notice, but right now it was one-third yellow, one-third brown, and one-third bare.

My sister actually flipped out the day we moved in, eight years ago. She thought our parents had somehow bought the haunted house from Disneyland and transplanted it to Surrey. She spent the whole day screaming. Mom even thought there might be something in the air that was causing her physical pain. But no, as is always the case with Kasey, it was purely mental.

Trying to appease Kasey's fear, my parents repainted the house's exterior with a sunny yellow-and-white color scheme, but it didn't really cut down on the overall spooky look. We get huge crowds at Halloween.

Sadly for me, the coolness is diminished by the fact that my family lives here.

"Home sweet home," I said.

"It's where the heart is," Carter said, craning his neck to see out the top of the windshield. "This is quite a house."

I bent down to pick up my bag off the floor. "Yes, it is."

"It's kind of a mess," he said.

I dropped my bag and bumped the back of my head on the glove compartment. "Excuse me?"

"I mean, it's really a jumble of architectural techniques." He pointed to the bay window. "That window is Gothic, and the shingle detailing is all Queen

Anne, which *kind of* go together, but the columns on the front porch are neoclassical, which is just plain . . . wrong."

Silence.

"Really?" I said coolly. But to be honest, inside I was kind of "lights and sirens."

I narrowed my eyes and shot him a glare, just so he wouldn't suspect anything.

"Yeah, I mean, whoever built this house just kind of picked random elements from all of those styles." He squinted up at the top of the house. "And don't get me started on the mansard roof. That's pure Second Empire."

I stared at him.

"My mom's an architect," he said, shrugging.

I slumped back in my seat. I really, really, really hate to admit it, but I was sort-of-kind-of-maybe the *tiniest* bit intrigued. It wasn't often you met kids my age with an appreciation for architecture.

"I'm Carter Blume, by the way," he said.

"Yeah, I know."

"Oh." He sat in confused silence for a few seconds. "Can I ask you a very serious question?"

"I'd rather you didn't," I said.

He stared straight into my eyes. "If you were an animal, what animal would you be?"

Wait, what? "Wait, what?"

"It's a classic icebreaker."

"If I were an *animal* . . . ?"

He faked a sigh and checked an imaginary watch. "Your inability to answer the question doesn't bode well for—"

"I refuse to answer that," I said. "On the grounds that it's probably the stupidest thing I've ever been asked."

He stared at me, frowning. "I hear your subconscious saying *monkey*."

"Right," I said. "Monkey."

"Are you mad at me for knocking you over with the door today?"

"Yeah, I'm furious," I said in a monotone, rolling my eyes.

He faked a grimace. "I need to be more careful. Do you—"

"My turn," I said. "Are you really a Young Republican?"

"Would that matter?"

I thought about it for a second. "I don't know."

"Well, I'm not. I'm not in any political party. I speak for myself."

Interesting answer. And suddenly the car felt like it was a hundred degrees, and I would have liked maybe three more bucket seats between us.

"I have to go," I said. "Thanks for the lift."

"Your shutters are goldenrod, not yellow," he replied. "See you tomorrow?"

"I doubt it!" I said, but I could feel my lips betray me with a hint of a smile. I ducked my head and turned away.

The front walk felt like marshmallows beneath my feet as I tried to get to the porch, knowing he was watching every self-conscious step I took. When I reached the stoop, I turned back to look at him. He took his eyes off the roof and looked at me.

"It's a mess," he called, "but I kind of like it."

Then he honked and waved and drove off.

I walked through the front door feeling a little dizzy. I stopped in the foyer and looked around.

Architectural jumble. Well, maybe he had a point. The entryway was even more ornate than the outside of the house—the wide stairway spilling out only a few feet from the front door, the high ceiling with crisscrossing arches, and wood-paneled walls with intricately carved details, like cherubic faces and squirrels and birds and sprays of flowers. It looked like a fairy tale had exploded all over the walls.

Straight ahead was the hall that led back to the living room. To the right was the kitchen, and just past that, the dining room. To my left was a sitting room that nobody ever sat in.

What did Carter know, anyway? I went up the long, straight staircase to the dark hall of bedrooms.

Mine was the first one on the left. I went inside and flopped onto the bed, my eyes sweeping the plaster molding for signs of architectural failure.

I had to stop thinking about Carter Blume.

Part of me wanted to develop the pictures from the previous night, but my eyelids started to feel like they were being pulled shut. I gave up and closed them, the delicious promise of a nap settling over me like a blanket.

I don't know how long I'd been asleep when I heard my sister's voice.

"Now, Arabella," she said. "Don't be a pig. You have to share."

A pause.

"I know it fits you perfectly, but she's new and she doesn't have anything to wear. Think what she's been through. Don't you care about her feelings?"

Another pause. I pressed my hands against my head.

"But what if we have company again? You know Sar—"

I couldn't take it. I reached up and thumped on the wall with my fist.

A minute later there was a tiny tap-tap-tap on my door, and Kasey popped her head into the room.

"I didn't know you were home," she said. Her eyes were wide.

I traced the outline of the bump on my forehead. "Why are you talking to your dolls, Kasey?"

"I'm not," she protested.

"You know you're *thirteen*, right?"

"That's *not* what I was doing!"

"It's just a little crazy, that's all."

"I am not crazy, Alexis! You're so *rude*!" She slammed my door and stomped back to her room.

I tried to go back to sleep, but I felt a little bad. So I got up and knocked on Kasey's door.

She opened it a crack. "I'm writing a story and I was just working on the dialogue!" she said, before I could apologize.

She backed away from the door, and I followed her inside.

It had been a while since I'd been in her room. She's too worried that I'll break something. Even our mother isn't supposed to go in there, according to Kasey. If *I* banned my parents from *my* bedroom, they'd assume I was operating an international drug cartel, but Kasey's always been the well-behaved daughter, so she gets away with it.

I stared at the dolls, which were lined up on the built-in shelves like a sinister chorus. There wasn't room for all of them—there were more in an old cabinet squeezed between the bed and the window, and half the closet was filled with them too.

Kasey had rag dolls, porcelain dolls, talking dolls, peeing dolls, baby dolls, dolls in elaborate costumes, and dolls stripped down to their pantaloons (like the poor new girl, whichever one she was). Some were so old and used that their soft, smooth cheeks had been worn to a shine. Some were brand new. Some were half bald. Some were pristine.

But they were all creepy. It was the only quality they shared.

I was dying to photograph some of them, but that was just unheard of. Impossible.

Kasey seemed to realize for the first time that I'd entered the forbidden zone.

"Let's go talk somewhere else," she said, trying to sound chipper.

"You're utterly transparent," I said.

But I let her guide me out into the hallway and back to my room. We both flopped backward on my bed, and she grabbed my old blue teddy bear, Mr. Teeth, and started tossing him into the air.

"How was school?" she asked, in the tone of voice that means she wants something.

"Fantastic," I answered. "How about for you?"

She hugged the bear tight to her chest. "Not so great."

"No? What happened?"

She shrugged and yawned. "Don't want to talk about it."

"Okay." Let's see, a half-hour whinefest about the middle school cafeteria running out of pudding versus peace and quiet? I didn't press for details.

"Hey, Lexi," she said, her voice small and hopeful. "Did you do an ancestor report in eighth grade?"

"Don't remember."

"Everybody does one."

"Then yeah, I guess."

"Do you still have it?"

"I must," I said. I'm a pack rat, like my mom. Thankfully I'm also obsessively neat, like my dad. I even have file cabinets of my very own. (*Thanks, Santa!*) "I wouldn't have thrown it away. Why do you ask?"

"I have to do one," she said. "And it's hard."

"When's it due?"

"Tomorrow."

"Kasey!" I said, sitting up. "You always do this!" Every couple of months, it seemed, the whole household was thrown into chaos because of some academic crisis caused by Kasey's poor planning.

I thought she might cry. "I know, but I can't help it."

"That's a cop-out. You could. If you tried."

She pulled Mr. Teeth tightly across her face. "I know. I know. *I know, I know, I know, I know, I know*—"

"God, stop!" I said, grabbing the bear away. This was the way most of her weird moody spells started—she'd get all wound up about nothing.

She closed her eyes and sighed. "You don't have to help me."

"Seriously, tomorrow?"

She nodded. She looked completely miserable all of a sudden. Her face had gone all splotchy, and her blue eyes were bright like she might start crying.

Kasey's in eighth grade. That means she has less than a year to pull herself together enough to survive being my sister at Surrey High.

She's supersmart, but it's the kind of smart that makes you think she's going to end up a mad scientist. She can read something in a book and remember it exactly. She can't see scary movies because she'll remember all the scary parts perfectly and have nightmares for months. I'm smart too, but I'm more like "take the toaster apart and put it back together and, lo and behold, it still works" smart.

"I'll help you, I guess," I said. "You can't just not turn one in."

She made a gurgly sighing noise. "Oh, thank you."

"You should try to plan ahead next time."

She sniffed. "Who are you, Mom?"

I whomped her with Mr. Teeth.

"Is it in your files?" she asked, popping up off the bed. "Can I look?"

"I'll find it for you," I said. "Later. Right now I need a nap."

"Yay, yay, yay," she said, dancing out into the hallway.

One second, the weight of the world. The next, lighter than air.

Must be nice.

A thought occurred to me. "Hey, Kase, come back," I called. "I heard the stupidest thing today."

She reappeared in the doorway, looking at me curiously.

"It's dumb," I said. "It's silly . . . it's just something Pepper Laird said."

Her eyes were still wide, but a deep crease spread over her forehead.

"When Mimi broke her arm, that was an accident, right?"

Kasey was quiet for a moment.

I swallowed hard. "I mean, Pepper's totally stupid, I just thought I'd ask."

"They're *both* stupid," Kasey said. "Stupid Pepper and stupid Mimi."

"Right," I said. "So you aren't friends with Mimi anymore?"

Kasey scooped Mr. Teeth off the bed and threw him

at the headboard. "Mimi Laird is a fathead liar! She has no idea what she's talking about! She's just clumsy. She's a *liar*. A clumsy liar."

"Calm down, Kase," I said. "Forget it. I believe you."

"I hate Mimi, and I hate her stupid sister!" Kasey said, running out and slamming the door. The whole house shook.

I guess that could have gone better.

I settled back onto my pillow and let my eyes close, lulled by the sound of the blinds rattling in the wind.

I dreamed I was standing on an island in a swamp full of alligators. I could see their backs floating in the water, like logs. And then I saw Kasey swimming toward me, blissfully unaware of the predators that surrounded her. So I pulled out a rifle and shot any alligator that got close to her. Then Kasey was with me on the island, braiding my hair and singing me Christmas carols. And a battered doll in a ripped petticoat came out of the water and walked over to us, but Kasey couldn't see her. And the doll pointed at Kasey and looked at me and said, *Your sister is crazy.*

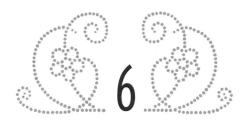

AH, DINNER AT THE WARREN HOME. At best, an adventure
in awkward silence, punctuated by the occasional screech
of a fork on a plate. At worst, an apocalypse. That night
it seemed like we might be in for an easy ride.

I was in the kitchen when Dad showed up with
Chinese food from the Golden Happy Family restaurant,
which is like a huge joke. I doubt they would let us eat
their food if they knew how far we were from being a
golden happy family.

"Hey," he said.

"Hey," I said, turning away.

Dad and I used to do all the father-daughter groups
and camping trips and all that. But as I got older we
stopped hanging out. Sometimes it feels like he'd rather
spend all his time watching football and forget he even
has a family. But every once in a while I miss the stuff we
used to do together. He'd always made me laugh.

Lately he had this permanent sad-dog expression
on his face, like he wished we could still be buddies or

something—and I was pretty sure he didn't know he was doing it. I couldn't even look at him. Like now, I stared at the floor instead.

"I talked them into extra fortune cookies," he said.

I didn't want to see the "please be my friend" look in his eyes.

"Great," I said, and ducked out of the kitchen. He stood there with his briefcase in his hand, his jacket draped over his arm. It was like a little knife stabbing me in the heart, to think I was hurting his feelings.

Oh well.

"Where's Mom?" Kasey asked, slinking into the dining room and sitting in her usual chair.

Dad set the containers of food down in front of us. "Off saving the world from a critical stapler shortage."

I stabbed my fork into a piece of pepper beef. For some reason it doesn't bother me when Kasey and I talk about our mom, but when Dad does it, it feels . . . wrong. He's supposed to defend her, not make fun of her.

Mom is a district manager for a big office supply company. She's been trying to make the jump to vice president for, like, two years. Which means she's *always* at the office—and when she's not, she's grouchy because she can't stop worrying about being at the office.

We spooned our food out in silence. Kasey's plate was

mostly rice, with the tiniest bit of kung pao chicken. She hates spicy food, but the rest of us eat it, and as usual, she just lets everybody steamroll her. It's like she thinks we won't like her anymore if she says what she really thinks. Or that our parents will think she's "bad"—bad like me.

We always eat our fortune cookies first. I unwrapped mine and broke it in half, then read the slip out loud:

"'Home is where the heart is.'"

Kasey shrugged, unimpressed, and unfolded hers. "'You are a very trusting person.'" She balled it up and tossed it over her shoulder.

"These aren't even fortunes," Dad said. "They're just sayings." He cracked his cookie open and looked at the little paper. "'Neither a borrower nor a lender be.'"

The front door slammed. Mom's heels clack-clacked past us down the hall as she dumped her briefcase in the living room. She came back, sat down, and started serving herself.

"Well, look who's on time," Dad said. He picked up a fortune cookie and pretended to nod. "'Confucius say: paper clips more important than family.'"

Mom dropped her spoon with a clatter. "Darrell, please don't start with me tonight."

Dad shrugged and went back to his food.

"I get to go see the Homecoming parade on Friday," Kasey said.

"That's interesting," Dad said, completely uninterested. "Who's Surrey playing in the game?"

All eyes on me.

"Oh, please," I said. "You're kidding, right? Like I care."

"It wouldn't hurt you to show a little school spirit," Mom said. As if she were a fan of high school football. Mom can take a simple observation, such as saying that it wouldn't hurt for a person to show a little school spirit, and say it in such a way that she might as well be saying, "It wouldn't hurt you to stop clubbing those baby seals."

"I think they're playing West Hardy," Kasey chirped. "Aren't they?"

"I have no idea," I said, even though there were about a hundred trees' worth of "Go Eagles! Beat the West Hardy Wolverines!" posters plastered around campus.

"Are you going to the dance?" Mom asked. Somewhere deep down inside she held on to the hope that one night I'd show up with my brown hair back, a pack of preppy friends in tow, and turn into Teen Princess Barbie, homecoming court, star tennis player . . . like she'd been in high school.

"Oh, yeah," I said. "My only problem is trying to decide who to go with—the captain of the football team or Zac Efron."

"If you went, I bet you could be the Homecoming Queen," Kasey said.

I almost said something rude, but then I saw her shining eyes and how a hint of a smile turned her lips up at the corners. She really meant it.

"I'd need a fairy godmother," I said. Kasey laughed.

"You'd need a miracle," Mom said down to her plate. Then she glanced up in surprise. If we were on a sitcom, she would have said, "Oh, did I say that OUT LOUD?" and the canned laughter would have kicked in.

Silence sank over us. The only sounds were chewing and Mom's knife sawing through her chicken. My mother uses a knife and fork on foods that were never meant to be eaten that way. I personally think a psychologist would have a lot to say about it.

"Kasey, I don't think a plateful of rice is an acceptable meal," Mom said suddenly.

Kasey ducked her head down as Mom spooned a heaping serving of spicy beef onto her plate.

"She doesn't like that stuff," I said.

"This has nothing to do with you, Alexis," Mom said.

"Tell her you don't want it, Kasey," I said.

Kasey was tracing figure eights in her food. She clearly didn't have the least intention of eating any, but she didn't protest.

Mom let the subject drop. I think she felt like she'd done her motherly duty, and now she could go on with her life.

She stuck a final forkful into her mouth and pushed her chair away from the table.

"Sorry to eat and run," she said. "I just have a bunch of reports to look over. We have a consultant coming in tomorrow, and I need to brush up on some quarterlies out of the sales department." She says this stuff as if it means anything to us. "I'll be in my bedroom. Knock if there's an emergency."

"Mommy," Kasey said suddenly. "I need to talk to you."

Mom looked only slightly concerned. "Is everything okay?"

"I need help with a project." Kasey stared down at her food. "It's for school."

"Can we talk about it later this week?"

"*No,*" Kasey whined. "I don't have very much time."

Mom sighed. "Look, Kase, I'm totally swamped. Maybe Alexis can help you."

"Hey!" I said. "I have my own stuff to do."

"But it's extra credit," Kasey said. The Holy Grail of middle school academics.

"Then your father can help you."

Dad was reading the sports page by this point. He looked up, bewildered. "What? I'm going to Jim's to watch baseball tonight."

"Dad didn't grow up in Surrey," Kasey said. "It needs to be someone who grew up in Surrey."

Mom looked around helplessly. "I don't know what to say, sweetie. I wish you'd come to me sooner. You should have sent me an e-mail."

"Nobody likes me," Kasey said, staring down at her plate, which was overflowing with food she couldn't eat.

"Don't be silly," Dad said in his best "Dad" voice. Then he looked at his watch. "Better hit the road. Don't wait up."

He hopped out of his chair, kissed Kasey on the top of her head, and patted me on the shoulder, which made me squirm. The only thing worse than parents who don't pay any attention to you is parents who pat you on the shoulder on their way out the door.

He didn't say good-bye to Mom, but she didn't seem to notice. She was staring down at Kasey.

"Tell you what," Mom said.

Kasey looked up, a glimmer of hope in her eyes.

"If you can promise me that you'll use your day planner and write down all of your assignments and let me know *in advance* when you need help, I'll help you out with this extra credit."

Kasey perked right up. "I promise!" she said. "I'll go get the questions!"

Mom's face fell. "Oh, Kasey," she said. "I didn't mean *tonight*. Sweetie, there's just no way I can do it tonight."

I had to turn away so I didn't see Kasey's expression.

"We need to work on our planning skills," Mom said. It was the kind of thing she would say to one of her underlings at work, but in the sad voice of the disappointed mother.

Mom shot Kasey a regretful look and then walked out. Her footsteps thumped up the stairs, and the bedroom door closed.

It was just my sister and me.

"Hey," I said. "I grew up in Surrey. Do I count?"

She looked up at me, her eyes heavy and dull.

"Why don't you go get your questions—"

"I can take care of myself," Kasey said, shoving her plate away and laying her head down on the table. A fat tear rolled down over her nose and landed on her sleeve.

Feeling stung, I stood up out of my chair and headed upstairs, trying to figure out why that sentence seemed to drill right into me.

Oh, yeah.

It was what I'd said to Carter in the clinic.

7

I WENT INTO MY ROOM and sat down on the bed, facing the door. I was restless. Part of me wanted to let my sister cry it out. I can't be Mother Teresa all the time, you know? She didn't want my help. Fine. Let her work through her issues on her own.

Right. So I wouldn't look for her.

I sat in silence for a minute.

Okay. I grabbed my camera. Here was the plan—I would go out and take a few pictures, and if I happened to find Kasey, I *might* talk to her, depending on how I felt at the time.

I slipped the camera strap around my neck and headed out into the hallway, making a lot of noise so she would know where I was.

The dining room was empty.

"Kasey?" I called quietly, stepping into the dark living room.

No answer.

I went back to check the kitchen—maybe she was sitting on the floor in the corner, eating ice cream out of the carton (it's been known to happen).

Nope. I opened the garage door. "Kase?"

I heard a thump below my feet.

The basement.

I'm no fraidy cat, mind you. I'm very open-minded about snakes, clowns, airplanes, and many other things that scare the bejeezus out of most people.

But I don't like the basement.

In fact, Mom doesn't like it either. It's the one thing we agree on. Going down there is highly discouraged on the basis of Mom's having found a nest of black widows two years earlier. The spiders were long gone, and the exterminators, who dutifully show up the third Thursday of every month, claim that they've never been back, but it's still off limits. I can't say I blame Mom. Knowing my luck, I'd find the one black widow strong enough to resist the chemicals. And I'd find it with my bare foot.

The basement door is right down the hall from the kitchen. I stood outside it for a long minute, staring at the doorknob. I really—and I mean *really*—had no desire to open it and go down those stairs.

But if that's where Kasey was . . .

I turned the knob and pushed the door open, waiting for an enormous, hairy arachnid to swing down and jump onto my face. Didn't happen. Maybe they'd all jumped onto Kasey, and the path was clear for me.

I took a step down, flipping the light on and closing the door behind me. There was a single lightbulb glowing pathetically over the stairs, and everything beyond that melted into a smudgy blackness, punctuated by shapes caught in the faint moonlight streaming through one tiny window.

The air was stale and stuffy. It made my head ache the same way a really humid day does. But I didn't see any spiderwebs in my path, so I kept going.

"Kasey?" I whispered. My voice sounded hoarse.

No answer.

The room was shaped like a U, with a center wall dividing the two sides.

I thought I heard something on the other side of the wall.

"Kasey, are you down here?"

Still no answer, but this time I heard a definite sound. I went around the U—as far as I could go and still be standing in a patch of light.

I'm not afraid of the dark, but I wouldn't say I *love* it. I was tempted to turn back. Even if my sister was down here, she clearly wasn't interested in company.

Besides, who's to say the noise was Kasey at all? It was probably gophers. Or huge rabid sewer rats.

I was a nanosecond away from making tracks back upstairs when I heard a muffled sniffle.

Even huge rabid sewer rats don't sniffle to attract their prey.

"Kasey," I said, trying to sound no-nonsense. "Where are you?"

"Down here," she said.

"Down where?"

"Under the card table."

Naturally.

"I have a flashlight," she said, and a weak yellow spot of light illuminated the cement floor ahead of me. I followed its path to the corner. Then Kasey shined the beam on her own face, which was puffy and wet with tears.

"Come on, Kase," I said. "Come back upstairs."

She shook her head furiously. "No," she said. "I'm never going back up there."

"Never?"

Her head bobbed in the darkness.

"Where are you going to go to the bathroom?"

She sighed. "I mean it, Lexi."

"So do I!"

"I'll use the guest bathroom."

"That's upstairs." I reached over and took the flashlight from her, shining it around the room. "Maybe there's a bucket around somewhere."

She sighed a sigh that was way too big for someone who hasn't even started high school yet.

I decided to give her a second to be alone with her thoughts, so I shined the flashlight around, looking for spiders. Just because we'd made it that far without being bitten didn't mean they weren't planning their attack strategy. I kept my eyes out for the shiny, blueberry-like body of a black widow.

I didn't find one. I didn't see any bugs at all.

I *did* find shelf after shelf of everyday items that should have been thrown away long ago. Mom will save anything. She'd even saved the boxes of other people's rubbish that were in the house when we moved here. Dad and I are much neater, but we know better than to try to toss any of Mom's precious garbage—excuse me, stuff.

"Lexi," Kasey whispered, "will you tell me a story?"

A story.

My thirteen-year-old sister wanted to hear a story.

I felt a sinking feeling in my stomach. I didn't know what to say.

She sensed my hesitation. "My brain is stuck. I need to change the channel."

Her hand grabbed my arm.

"Please," she whispered.

"A *story*," I repeated, hoping she would pick up from my tone of voice that it was a kind of a strange request. "Stories are for . . . little kids."

"I don't care. A short one. About anything."

"Um . . . there's a girl who lives on a farm in black-and-white, and then one day her house gets caught in a tornado and she wakes up surrounded by midgets and everything is in color."

"I've heard that one," she said. Her voice sounded tired and strained. "And you're not supposed to say *midget*. It's mean."

"Oh, Kasey . . ."

She started to cry again. "Please, Lexi, *please*."

Kasey had been normal once, had done normal kid things. She'd been bold and funny and stood up for herself. And now she was just . . . coming apart at the seams. Sitting under a card table in the basement. Talking to her dolls. Making a request a six-year-old would make.

Maybe I was an enabler. Instead of coddling her, I should tell her to make more friends at school, to do her own homework or take a failing grade. Not stand up for her anymore.

And definitely, one hundred percent, not tell her a story.

"Once upon a time," I began, surprising both of us, "there was a man and a woman who lived in a little shack in the country next to a river."

My voice was hard and shaky. I took a deep breath.

Kasey was silent. Afraid to say anything, probably, in case it would make me stop.

But I didn't want to stop. I felt more of the story welling up inside of me, like a breath that needed to be exhaled. "They were young and poor—so poor that, like, some nights they didn't have enough food to eat, but they loved each other so much that they didn't even notice."

Kasey drew in a quivering breath. I shined the flashlight around, making squares of light as I spoke. I moved the beam so fast that sharp glowing lines seemed to burn themselves into my brain.

"But the man worked really hard, and before long, they were doing well enough to build themselves a house." I stared at the basement ceiling—wood rafters, some that looked a hundred years old and some newer ones, and crisscrossing rows of metal pipes. "So he built the biggest house in the whole county, big enough to show their neighbors how rich they were. They had a huge oak tree in the front yard and they built a swing on it, and on nice nights they would sit outside and swing together, and when it was cold they lit a fire and stayed inside."

I could see it so clearly in my head; it was our house and our oak tree. And I could see the man and the woman, in their old-fashioned clothes, walking around, coming in through the front door, sitting in the back room with a fire in the fireplace.

"How did they meet?" Kasey asked.

"They met . . ." My eyes trailed the line of a thin pipe snaking around the edge of the room. "They met in college."

"How long ago is this supposed to be?" Kasey said. "Ladies in fairy tales don't go to college."

"This one did," I said. "They met in class and they fell in love."

He was sitting at the desk closest to the door when she walked into the classroom. She was all alone. After class he waited and spoke to her. He asked if she knew where the Remington Building was, and she did, because her father—

"Ummm . . . Lexi?"

I blinked. How long had I been lost in thought? And . . . more important, where was this coming from? I'd never so much as daydreamed any of this before, but as the words formed themselves, it felt like I was telling Kasey the plot of a movie I'd watched earlier that day. The details . . . everything was right there. I just knew all of it.

"They got married . . . ?" she prompted.

The words pushed out of my mouth before I had a chance to think. "So after they'd been married a while and built their house, they had a baby girl. And the mom stayed home to raise her, and the dad worked but spent all his free time playing with her and teaching her about

68

animals and music. And the other kids in the neighborhood were always around—"

"You said they were way out in the country," Kasey said, almost reluctantly.

"But the kids in town liked the daughter so much they walked miles just to be with her. And she made tons of friends and was everybody's favorite person to hang out with. She was like a little angel. She wore fancy dresses with bows and lace, and she had blond hair and a round face with cheeks that turned pink when she went out in the cold."

I could see the girl in my head as clearly as if I were looking at a photo of her. She ran down the upstairs hallway and into what was now Kasey's room, three little friends running after her. She loved to sit at the window and look out at the lane that led to town, waiting for her father to come home.

"What were their names?"

"Who?" Her question jolted the image out of my mind. The basement seemed to be getting warmer, and what had been the faint beginning of a headache was starting to pound.

"The man and woman."

"Well, her name was . . ." I gazed around the room, then it came to me. "Her name was Victoria. And the man's name was . . . Robert."

"And they all had beautiful exotic green eyes," Kasey said.

"Why does that matter?" I asked.

"Because I like green eyes, and they're running out. Soon all that will be left is brown eyes and blue ones."

"There's nothing wrong with brown eyes," I said. "Or blue ones like . . . ours." But the eyes that popped into my head were Carter's.

"I know," Kasey sighed. "But still."

In my head I saw the little girl dancing down the upstairs hallway. She stopped and turned to look at me.

She did have green eyes.

I didn't want to admit that Kasey was right. "So . . . where was I?"

"All the girls from town came out to play with me."

That word—*me*—swooped in at me, made me catch my breath.

I looked at her. "I never said the girl was *you*."

"Who else could it be?"

"I don't know," I said, looking up at the pipes again. Every time I looked, there seemed to be a new one winding around the room. "It wasn't you, though."

But as the picture of the girl faded back into my head, I could see a slight resemblance: the girl had the same soft caramel-color hair as Kasey, and the same sweet, soft eyes—although the girl's were green, and Kasey's were blue.

"It's *my* story," she said.

"Yeah, but it isn't you," I said.

"How do you know?"

Because I can see her when I close my eyes, that's how I know. "I just know, okay?"

"I *want* it to be me," Kasey said. She clenched her teeth, making her jawbone jut out near her ears. "You don't have to be a jerk about it."

I started to stand up.

"Forget it," she said. "Forget it. It's not me, okay?"

"All right." I took a deep breath. "So anyway, when she turned ten years old, the little girl got a beautiful doll for her birthday."

Kasey fell silent.

One pipe above our heads was covered in small red painted marks, a sloppy job. I couldn't even tell what the marks were supposed to be.

"And when she took it to school, all the other kids got jealous because they didn't have anything nice like that. But she loved her doll so much that she talked about it all the time. And eventually she started taking it everywhere, and acting like the doll was talking back to her. And the other kids were so freaked out that they stopped coming to see her. Gradually it got worse and worse.

They were mean to her at school and called her names and stuff."

The red-painted pipe was so old the surface was flaky, and the end I could see was open, not connected to anything. The other end . . . I followed the pipe with my eyes. It led deeper into the room, back toward the darkest corner.

She came home from school one day, gray and pale, and said she didn't want to go back. Her mother asked why, but the girl refused to tell. She was ashamed to say that the children in town were making fun of the whole family now—saying the mother was unfeminine for going to college, saying that they were vulgar show-offs for building such a big house for just three people.

"And the kids just got more and more suspicious," I said. "Pretty soon they started telling everyone in town that the little girl was crazy. That she thought her doll was alive."

The doll was her only friend. She sat in her bedroom staring at it, wishing it would wake up and speak to her.

"So one day when she wandered too near the school, all the town kids started teasing her. She ran away, but they chased her and grabbed her doll, and one of the girls took a pair of scissors and cut her hair off."

"The girl?"

"No, the doll."

Kasey breathed in sharply. A vicious doll-haircutting

was probably the worst fate she could imagine.

"So she tried to stay away from them, and she never took her doll with her anywhere. But the next time they saw her, they chased her home, and she was so scared that she climbed up the oak tree to get away from them."

"Wasn't her mom home?"

"No," I said.

"What happened?"

"The kids saw her in the tree—"

It was like the words were being planted in my brain all by themselves.

I could see it unfolding in my head—the girl climbing the tree, a pack of dusty, rowdy children shouting up at her, making fun of her, telling her she was going to tear her fancy dress.

"And they started . . . yelling . . ."

I forced myself to stop.

These were words Kasey didn't need to hear. It would just increase the crazy quotient in our house, which, frankly, didn't need any boosting.

I tore my eyes away from the pipes and spread my fingers flat on the ground. "Then the girl's mother came home, saw all the rude kids, and scared them away. But first she scared one of them so badly that she peed her pants and none of the other kids ever talked to her again."

It was a lie. Saying it made my throat hurt.

"Nice," Kasey said.

The knotted feeling in my chest grew looser.

"Yeah, well, that was . . . was the evil Megan Wiley," I said. The air in the basement was getting easier to breathe. As I went further from the story in my head, the words came out more smoothly. "And the girl came down, and she and her mom had tea, and it was cool. She went back to school and she was the most popular kid in her grade, because her mom made the evil Megan Wiley pee in her pants in front of everybody."

"And?"

"And what?" I stared into the corner, where all the pipes seemed to end.

"And then . . . ?"

I was done. My whole body was sore and tired, and I took that as a really good reason to get up and get ready for bed.

"And then nothing. She had all the bad town kids thrown in jail." I sighed. "Happily ever after. The end."

"Wait, Lexi . . ."

"What?"

"What about the doll?"

"Forget about the doll," I said. "Let's go upstairs, okay?"

Kasey's bright eyes still drilled into me. In the darkness they looked strangely blank.

I stared at her for a second, and the doll from my dream came out of my memory: *Your sister is crazy.*

She took a deep breath. "What?" she asked, even though I hadn't said anything.

"Forget it," I said. "Come on. I'll go first, make sure the coast is clear."

No point in both of us getting in trouble.

Kasey waited at the bottom of the stairs. I opened the basement door and crept out into the hall.

All clear.

I opened the door slightly. "It's fine, come up."

Then I went to the kitchen, so if Mom came downstairs, we'd look innocent.

I got myself a glass of water, sat at the table, and slowly sipped it.

Five minutes later I noticed with a start that the glass was empty and Kasey still hadn't appeared.

I went back to the basement door and opened it.

"Kase?" I asked.

No answer, just a rustling sound from the corner.

I took a slow step down, the blood in my veins suddenly electrified.

I went around the U with little chills running up my spine. A Kasey-size shadow was way back in the darkest corner of the room, near the long-abandoned tool bench, making clanking noises as it dug through piles of discarded junk. *Werewolf*, my brain said. *Zombie!* I snatched the flashlight off the card table and switched it on.

"What are you doing?" I asked.

My sister looked up at me, squinting into the beam of light. "Oh, hi."

"Answer me," I said. "What are you doing?"

"I heard something," she said, wiping her hands on her pants. "And then I . . . I thought I would see if I could find your ancestor report."

"Why would it be down here?"

She shook her head. "I thought you moved your old file cabinet down here when you got the new one."

"No. They're both in my closet," I said. "Now come upstairs."

She started slowly through the sea of junk, using her left hand to steady herself.

"Are you holding something?" I asked.

"What?" she said.

"In your right hand."

"No."

"Are you . . ." I sighed. "Forget it. I'm going upstairs."

The headachy, sleepy feeling was coming back. I wondered if maybe we had a toxic mold problem. As an afterthought I pointed the light at the pipes on the ceiling. Now that I was standing up, I was close enough to see the red marks for what they really were—

Skulls and crossbones. Dozens of them, stamped on sloppily.

Nice. So glad to know we'd been breathing poison air all night.

I climbed the stairs and went back to my spot at the kitchen table, drawing deep breaths to clear out my lungs.

Kasey followed me as far as the kitchen doorway. "Can you go get your ancestor report?" she asked.

"Why don't you go get it?" I asked. "Look in the cabinet on the left, top drawer—eighth-grade history, Miss Cardillo."

Kasey nodded, then looked sheepish. "Will you make me mac and cheese?" she asked sweetly, crinkling her nose. "Pleeeease? I'll do the dishes."

I shrugged. I was feeling a little better. "Sure."

She took a second, concentrating on something down to her right side, something hidden by the wall so I couldn't see it.

"What *is* that?" I demanded.

She froze and looked up. Caught.

"What's what?"

"Whatever's in your hand."

"I don't have anything in my hand, Lexi," she said.

I stared at her, and she gazed serenely back at me.

Just to be a little mean, I clicked the flashlight on and shined it at her face.

And maybe I was just tired or something, but—

Her eyes . . .

They were green.

Vivid green.

"I . . ." I couldn't think of anything to say. "Never mind."

"See you in a sec," she said, disappearing up the stairs.

8

A FEW MINUTES LATER Kasey came hippity-hopping into the kitchen with the report in hand, singing to herself. She gave me a kiss on the cheek and sat down.

She twirled a piece of her hair around a finger and flipped through the pages while I collected the dirty dinner dishes and put them in the dishwasher.

Somebody had to clean up. Mom would be content leaving them until the weekend. Dad might have done it when he got home, but it gave me something to do while Kasey read over my stuff and decided how much she could risk copying without getting caught.

"Mom's grandma was born in Surrey?" Kasey asked.

"Is that what it says?"

"Yeah," she said.

"Then . . . yes."

"Ooh," she said, unfolding a big sheet of newsprint. "Your family tree is pretty."

I glanced at it and remembered how the teacher was

so impressed that she hung it on the wall. That was back when teachers still liked me.

"I'd better make a new one," she said, pushing her chair back from the table and skipping toward the stairs.

Content with the clean kitchen, I took out a saucepan and filled it with water for the noodles. I set it on the stove and remembered that I hadn't wiped off the table.

I went back to the dining room with a dishrag, and when I looked out into the hallway I saw that the basement door was open, just a crack.

Kasey must not have latched it all the way.

I started toward it.

As I approached, the door slowly opened a few more inches.

"Kasey?" I asked. Maybe she was messing with me. I'd heard her thump up the stairs, but she could have sneaked back down.

In theory.

I could hardly force myself to take another halting half step.

A cool puff of air seemed to move across my legs, and a faint, bitter smell drifted into my nose.

"Kasey," I said in my best jokey voice, "present yourself."

"I'm right here."

I spun around to see Kasey looking at me from the kitchen doorway.

"What are you doing?" she asked.

I turned back to look at the basement door—

It was closed.

". . . Nothing," I said. "I guess."

"Come help me," she said.

I went back to the kitchen table and sat down. She'd brought a shoe box full of pens and markers and a giant piece of poster board. One nice thing about a mom who works in the office supply industry, you always have plenty of art supplies on hand.

"You do the trunk," she commanded, passing me a brown marker. I obeyed and found that drawing eased the fluttery, nervous feeling in my stomach.

"Sorry about what happened with Mom," I said.

Kasey shrugged.

"That's why I'm not ever having kids," I said. "It sucks to have to pick between your job and your family. Besides, I can live without drooling rug rats hanging off me."

She didn't even crack a smile.

"Mimi's mom stays home, right?" I asked. "And look how horrible Pepper turned out. So it's just as well."

Kasey sighed. "I don't care."

"So if you don't hang out with Mimi, who do you eat lunch with now? What about Devon?" I was really scraping the bottom of the barrel. Devon was best known as the kid who could name every *Star Trek* episode ever made—including all the spin-offs.

"I don't want to talk about it," Kasey said, looking away.

A thought nagged at me. "Kase," I said, trying to keep my voice light. "That day . . . did Mimi try to . . . do something to one of your dolls?"

My sister's eyebrows furrowed. *"I don't want to talk about it."*

Yeah, well, I did. And I'm the big sister.

Kasey's eyes lit up.

"Look, time to put the noodles in," she said, pointing to the pot on the stove.

The water bubbled enthusiastically in a roiling boil.

My hands immediately turned clammy and cold.

"Kasey," I said, "I didn't turn the burner on yet."

Her face went white.

"What's going on?" I asked.

Kasey stared at the stove, then leaped off the stool and grabbed the pot by its handle. I staggered backward, thinking for a moment that she was going to throw the hot water on me. Instead she poured it in the sink and dropped the pot in too.

She turned and stared at me, but it was as if she wasn't really looking at *me*. Like I was a stranger who looked vaguely familiar.

"I don't understand," I said.

Kasey's wide eyes got wider.

"Something really weird is happening," I said.

I thought about the story, the way it poured out of my mouth without permission. About the basement door swinging open. The cloud of cold air in the dining room.

With a start I remembered the lights we'd seen outside the night before.

"What could it be?" I whispered.

Kasey wrinkled her forehead. "Lexi, don't be mad, but . . . I think . . . maybe you're just tired," she said.

"No!" The burner! "The water was boiling and I—"

"Lexi," she said, putting her skinny arm around my shoulder, "*I* turned the burner on."

"But . . . when? Why didn't you say something?"

She swallowed. "When you were in the dining room a minute ago."

"Yeah, but . . ."

"You need to relax," she said. "You're getting yourself all worked up."

I glanced around the kitchen, which was lit warmly and smelled pleasantly of the spicy beef I'd just thrown away.

"Maybe you're right," I said.

"I know I am," she said. "Now, sit. Finish the tree."

I obeyed, feeling too bewildered to protest.

I don't think I'm a great artist, but Kasey seemed enthralled by the lines I drew. She leaned forward, her chin on her hands, and watched me.

"You're making me nervous," I told her.

"Sorry," she said, slumping back.

I concentrated on the silhouette of the tree trunk, plump and shapely, with gentle curves and little hollows. I drew a stub of a branch that had broken off, and another spot where a fresh layer of bark almost covered a gash in the side of the trunk.

I was vaguely aware of Kasey fidgeting across the table, making a click-click noise, and I could tell she was interested but trying not to show it.

Finally I sat up and looked at my drawing.

Wow.

Click-click.

It was totally different from anything I'd ever drawn. Usually I did well enough to get by in Pictionary— casual but effective line drawings.

There was nothing casual about this tree. It was covered in details. Even the drawing style was somehow different. The lines looked like they'd been drawn by someone else. . . .

Just like the story had been told by someone else.

Click-click.

And suddenly I felt sick.

Click-click.

I pushed my chair away from the table and looked up at Kasey.

"STOP!" I shouted, scaring both of us.

She paused midclick, and her eyes widened in distress when she realized what she'd been doing—

Opening and shutting the back cover of my camera.

Letting light spill in and expose the negatives.

"I'm sorry!" she squealed as I yanked the camera from her hands and snapped the cover shut. "Lexi, I didn't mean—"

"Don't talk to me, Kasey!" I said. "Or I will be forced to murder you!"

I rushed out of the kitchen and up the stairs.

Kasey followed me into the foyer but kept a safe distance away, staring up at me, her mouth an O, her eyes red and streaming tears.

"I can't believe you!" I called down to her, and then I went into my bedroom and slammed the door.

Mom's voice came faintly from behind her closed door.

"Girls, stop yelling. I'm trying to work!"

I let out an angry grunt and smacked my pillow.

A few minutes later I heard Kasey trudge by and

close her door. I felt kind of bad, but not bad enough to go comfort her.

Let her think about what she'd done.

Alone.

9

I DIDN'T SLEEP WELL. Can you blame me? I kept having those falling dreams, where you jolt yourself awake just before you hit the ground.

After waking up and checking the clock every half hour or so, at 5:30 a.m. I decided to get out of bed. I'd be sleep-deprived, but at least I'd have time to work in the darkroom.

Walking to the tiny guest bathroom at the end of the hall, I tried not to think about my ruined film, which left plenty of mental space to think about all the other strange things that had happened the previous night. The hairs on the back of my neck prickled as I passed Kasey's door, but when I reached the darkroom, a sense of calm washed over me. A sense of well-being.

As soon as I turned on the safelight (don't be too impressed—it's just a red lightbulb) and snapped the black curtain into place to keep light from leaking through the cracks around the bathroom door, all thoughts of boiling water and unstable sisters and absentee parents melted away.

A lot of people shoot digital pictures now, which is fine—it's just not for me. To me, taking digital pictures is like finding something. But working with film is like *making* something.

Besides, I cherish the time I get to spend in the darkroom—away from my family.

It's a pretty decent setup: an old enlarger (bought used from the junior college) and a table Dad and I built over the bathtub to hold trays of chemicals. Rolls of film and finished prints hang to dry on a clothesline behind the table.

What's funny is that when we moved in, the tub was already dotted with chemical stains, and we found darkroom supplies under the sink. So somebody else had had the same idea once upon a time. I guess a house like ours brings out people's creative tendencies. Maybe, in its own wacky way, Kasey's doll collection could be seen as an expression of creativity, not just a passive consumerist obsession (which is what I call it when I want to get a rise out of her).

I rolled the film into the coiled silver cage and filled the cylinder with film-developing chemicals. While that processed, I carefully took my camera apart and cleaned the lens.

When the timer dinged, I unrolled the film and clothespinned it to the cord hanging over the tub. I turned Mom's old hair dryer to COOL and spent a few minutes drying the film off. It had to be totally waterless—handling it when it was just mostly dry or a little tacky would ruin the images.

Next I cut the long strip of film into rows of five frames and made a contact sheet. That means you lay the film right onto the photo paper (so they're in "contact" with each other) and get a whole page of little tiny black-and-white photos. You use that to choose the pictures you want to make larger prints of. You can't just print everything or you'll waste a lot of photo paper, and photo paper is expensive. Not every picture is worth blowing up.

I hit the button and reached for the negative sleeve, then leaned down and held the negatives to the light—expecting to see a whole lot of nothing, after Kasey's disastrous actions last night.

A huge breath I didn't know I'd been holding escaped from my lungs.

They weren't ruined.

I got a piece of photo paper out from the triple-sealed black bag under the sink and set the page of negatives down directly on it, then hit the expose button. The light shined on them for a few seconds, then went off. I grabbed the paper and dropped it into the first tray of chemicals—the developer, which is where the images start to show up on the paper. I love watching this stage, seeing what comes out first.

I lifted the contact sheet out of the developer and put it in the next tray, the stop bath, which stops the emulsion from reacting to the developer chemicals. From there they go into the fixer, which gets rid of any extra light-sensitive materials left on the paper, and from there they go into a tray of cold water. Then they get inspected by me with my little magnifying glass.

I set them on the enlarger and turned the timer as far as it would go. I leaned in to look at the photos.

They were beautiful. You could see black sky, a big white moon, and the pinpricks of tiny stars. The house loomed in the foreground, glowing a kind of milky gray. The whole thing was slightly hazy—which I could assume was Kasey's fault. Never mind that it was kind of a cool effect . . . I was still totally annoyed.

Finally I got to the pictures I'd tried to take of the strange light. The image was slightly shaky, thanks to my inability to stand completely still, but there was definitely *something* there. And the motion blur even helped a little.

Hmm.

I leaned in for another look, and noticed a little white dot in the frame—a circle of light that seemed to be floating near the house.

I'd cleaned my lens right before I went outside, but a spot of dust could have snuck in.

Well, it was a good picture anyway, and I could fix that white dot if I enlarged it.

The last couple of photos, the ones close to the end of the reel, were actually ruined. One picture was half clear and half overexposed—you could just see the bay window in the study and part of Kasey's bedroom window before it faded to bright white. The mysterious glow near the tree was just barely distinguishable from the light leak. And of course, that was the only one where I'd managed to hold still enough that the picture wasn't blurred.

I studied the blob of light. In this particular frame I could see that it wasn't completely shapeless. It was oblong, and had stripes down the sides, and toward the top it got a little narrower and then rounded back out.

It actually kind of looked like a really vague silhouette of a person.

But that was impossible. Not only impossible, but silly too. If you stare at anything long enough, you can make yourself see whatever you want to see.

And there was a dust speck on this one too, but it looked even bigger. You could see it clearly—a little sphere of light, smack in the middle of the frame.

Well, you can't win 'em all.

At least I'd managed to get a few eerie portraits of the house. Not bad for a roll that should have gone to the great darkroom in the sky.

10

I WAS ON MY WAY back to my room when I heard a noise from downstairs.

Shuffle shuffle shuffle shuffle.

It stopped abruptly.

Gophers. The pipes. The house settling.

As I turned toward my door I glanced back at Kasey's room. For the first time I noticed a tiny bit of light shining through a crack. Her door was open. Only slightly, though. I craned my neck to see if I could see her outline under the covers. I couldn't tell, so I turned back around.

She was behind me.

I gave a little shriek and did that really embarrassing terrified hand-wringing thing.

Kasey just looked at me, completely calm.

It took me a second to catch my breath. "What are you doing?"

"Getting a drink of water."

"How did you get up the stairs without making any noise?"

She looked at me like I had a screw loose. "Socks," she said. She lifted her foot to show me. The underside was covered in a black coating of dirt, in the shape of a foot.

"Those are filthy," I said.

Something occurred to me.

"Did you just go outside?"

Kasey looked puzzled. "Why would you think that?"

"I just . . . heard—thought I heard . . ." I shrugged.

"Lexi, are you feeling okay?" She studied me intently.

"I'm fine," I said.

"Okay, because last night you got a little"—she considered carefully—"overexcited."

I couldn't keep my cool any longer. "Well, maybe if I hadn't had to follow you into the basement and then cook for you *and* do your homework *and* have you ruin my pictures—"

"Oh," she said. "Are they ruined?"

There was no regret in her voice, only mild curiosity.

"No," I replied. "Lucky for you."

"Sorry," she said, her eyes wandering up to the ceiling. "But you were acting really weird. It distracted me."

Was I acting weird?

The story, the tree, the basement door, the cold

air . . . all things that, in the light of early morning, seemed a lot more explainable than they had last night.

Maybe a *little* weird.

"See you later," Kasey said, padding away down the hall.

"Oh," I said. "Wait."

She stopped and turned around.

"Do you need any more help with your report?"

She shrugged. "It's cool. I finished it last night."

Oh. "Good for you," I said. "Can I see it?"

"Um, no . . . not right now," she said. "It's six thirty."

I nodded. "Right."

I hurried through my shower and getting dressed. For some reason I was highly disinterested in seeing my sister again that morning.

All this time I'd thought Kasey was kind of on the verge of something, and suddenly it hit me that what if, you know, it wasn't *her*? What if it was *me*? Can you go crazy without knowing you're crazy?

I mean, most crazy people do, right?

See, times like these make you really wish you had a best friend. Someone you could go to and be like, "Am I nuts, or . . . ?" and they would just tell you flat-out.

It was way too much to think about at seven fifteen, without even a Pop-Tart in my stomach.

Mom was in the kitchen already, watching her coffee

brew. She leaned against the counter, mesmerized.

She didn't look up when I came in, which was totally okay by me. I got a glass of juice, stuck my Pop-Tart in the toaster, and dropped a plate onto the counter with a clatter. Then I had to stop and wait, and the kitchen was quiet except for the electric buzz from the toaster and the soft, rhythmic bubbling of the coffee machine.

"Thanks for doing the dishes."

I looked up in surprise to see Mom staring at me.

"And helping Kasey with her schoolwork," she said.

I shrugged.

"I wasn't going to say anything, but I have a huge interview on Friday. For a vice presidency. But if I don't get the job . . ." She shook her head. "I'm so tired, Alexis. I want to be more involved with you girls."

My head swam. "Yeah, but . . . what would you do, quit?"

She stared at the coffeepot.

"Then how would we afford . . . ?" I let my voice trail off. Somehow it didn't seem to be the right thing to say. I laid my palm flat against the counter. "Does Dad know?"

"No," she said. "I guess I have to talk to him about it."

"Will you tell Kasey?"

"Tell me what?"

We both jumped at the sound of Kasey's voice. She stood in the doorway of the kitchen, clutching her report.

Mom took a deep breath. "Don't worry, Kase. Right now I think it should be between your father and I."

"And *me*."

"Yes, and you and Alexis too, and we'll talk about it as a family if it becomes an issue. I promise."

"No," Kasey said. "Your grammar is wrong. 'Between your father and *me*.'" She walked to the sink and filled a glass of water. After drinking the whole thing in one long series of glugs, she set the glass down on the counter and looked at Mom, who had frozen in place. "Just my opinion, but I don't think you'd make a great housewife." She glanced down at her watch. "I have to go. I'll walk."

She turned and left.

Mom stood speechlessly by the counter, staring at the spot where Kasey had been.

All of the temporary closeness between Mom and me escaped out the front door with Kasey, making everything suddenly seem wrong, embarrassing. I reached over and flipped the toaster switch up, grabbing my half-cooked Pop-Tart out of its slot. I dropped it on my plate and walked out without another word.

I WANTED TO FINISH UP AT MY LOCKER before Lydia arrived to pick another fight with the cheerleaders. After the past twelve hours, I couldn't handle any more drama.

So when a shadow fell over me as I searched for my copy of *Their Eyes Were Watching God*, I braced myself.

"Good morning," said Carter Blume.

My math textbook slipped out of my arm and landed on his foot with a painful-sounding thud.

The cheerleaders tittered.

Carter picked up the book and handed it back to me, an amused smile on his face.

"Sorry," I murmured.

"Eye for an eye, right?" he asked. "Foot for a forehead? No problem."

"Look," I said. "I just kind of want to be alone."

He nodded. "Okay, no problem." He took a step back and looked around.

I'd hurt his feelings. I had a chance to take it back, to tell him I didn't mean it.

But I didn't.

Instead I said, "Cool, thanks," and let him walk away. Then I turned back to my locker, trying to ignore the contemptuous stares of the cheerleaders. I slammed the door shut and walked past them.

In the courtyard I went right by the Doom Squad. No one even looked up. Not that I wanted to hang out with them, but it would have been nice if someone called me over. Whatever.

Somehow I ended up in the library. I thought I'd be safe there—it's always empty. Today was no different, except that right in my path, seated smack in the middle of one of the ancient, cracked, orange vinyl love seats was a single student—Carter. I sighed and walked over to him.

"Alexis Warren, you're *stalking* me," he said, his eyes wide.

"I swear, I had no idea you'd be in here," I said.

He smiled a twisted little smile. "No, I'm flattered." He looked around, kind of disoriented in (I hate to say) a very cute way. "But . . . I'll go."

All of a sudden he didn't seem like the worst company in the world. "You were here first."

He shrugged and reached for his bag.

"You can hang out if you want," I said. He was hoisting the bag over his shoulder.

I would have to come right out with it.

"Stay," I said, my heart beginning to pound.

Clear enough. He settled back against the worn sofa and smiled. "I described your house to my mother, and she's horrified. She's dying to see it."

I sat down on the love seat across from him. "That's just what we need. Architects making fun of our home."

He studied the leather-tasseled zipper pull on his bag. "Obviously you don't know anything about the art scene in Surrey. The worse something is, the more they like it."

I had to laugh. He sounded like some character out of a movie from the 1940s, always having a smart comeback. He could almost be cute, if he weren't such a Ken doll.

"Sorry I was rude before," I said.

"Which time?"

"Oh, ha-ha. I haven't been *that* bad." I didn't feel up to going into detail.

He looked at the ceiling and held up his hand like in *Hamlet*, when Hamlet holds the skull. "That is without a doubt the stupidest question ever asked in the history of humanity." He balled his hand into a fist as if he were crushing something.

"I didn't say it like that," I said.

He shrugged. "That's how I remember it. It's what I put in my blog, anyway."

I must have looked really horrified, because he burst out laughing.

"I'm just kidding," he said. "Really."

"You really *are* a politician," I said. Only it kind of didn't come out as jokey as I meant it. In fact, it came out so unjokey that it sucked all the fun right out of the conversation. Way to go, Alexis.

Carter was quiet for a minute, then gestured to my clothes. "At least you remembered your red and white for School Colors Day."

I looked down at the short-sleeved red T-shirt I'd layered over a long-sleeved white one. "Oh no," I said, laughing. "I swear I didn't do this on purpose."

"Your reputation is about to take a huge hit," he said. Carter, on the other hand, was proudly sporting an immaculate Surrey High sweatshirt.

"I think yours will be worse," I said, "if any of your friends see you with me."

He gave a little shrug. "I think you might be worth it."

Hearing that sent my brain spinning into confused blankness. I tried to show with my face that I didn't attach any importance to what he'd said, but I just succeeded in raising my left eyebrow really high.

He raised an eyebrow back and smiled. "I'm just remembering the first time I ever saw you."

"On the TV show," I said.

He shook his head. "No, before that. It was my first day at Surrey—I transferred two weeks into the school year, in the middle of September—and I was waiting in the office for my mom to sign some papers. I was listening to the secretaries, and they were all scandalized by some student who'd been caught putting bumper stickers that said 'Gas Guzzler' on every SUV in the parking lot."

Oh, yeah. My proactive environmentalist phase.

"And then you came in, and the principal came out to meet you, and you told her you'd skipped her car because you knew she was on the waiting list for a hybrid."

Yup. Strangely enough, that didn't really change Mrs. Ames's view of the situation.

He seemed to look off into the distance and smiled again. "That was the first time. The *second time* . . . How could I forget?"

He meant that stupid TV show. "I'd actually rather you forgot, if you don't mind," I said.

"What are you talking about? You were brilliant. Utterly amazing. You cut right through the drivel and made everyone else look stupid. And I'm not just saying that for the obvious reason." He smiled at me, his eyes squinting appraisingly. "I said to myself, 'Carter, there's a girl that you need to knock down in the hallway sometime.'"

Without thinking about it, I clammed up and sat back.

"What's wrong?" Carter asked.

"I just . . . I can't do this."

"What, take a compliment?"

"I can't be *me* and hang out with *you* being *you*." I tried to think of a way to say it. "I mean, you're nicer than I thought you would be, and it's cool about the architecture, but I . . ."

He leaned close to me and swallowed. "What?" he asked. His voice was low.

"I don't know," I said. "Just say something *real*. Everyone always just tries so hard, and it all comes out the same. I just want someone to say something real."

He broke his glance away from mine and looked at the carpet.

"Forget it," I said. "I'm sorry. That was rude, even for me. I'll go."

I grabbed my backpack.

"I tried to kill myself last year," Carter said.

My grip loosened and the bag fell back to the couch.

102

"And I had to transfer schools because my dad"—he laughed bitterly—"my dad is a psychiatrist, and if word got around, it would ruin his business."

I opened my mouth, then closed it again without saying anything.

"And nobody here knows," Carter said quietly, looking into my eyes without blinking. "Well, except you."

"I'm sorry," I said. Was that what you were supposed to say to someone who was suicidal?

"Don't be," he said. "It's funny . . . I'm serious about *Surrey Survey.* I know you didn't mean to, but you really helped me. It made things a lot easier. Overnight, I had friends and something to do with my time. It was . . . convenient."

I aim to please, after all.

"So what else do you do?" he asked. "Besides, you know, the TV appearances and the environmental terrorism."

"Nothing much," I said. We were back to the superficial stuff, but that was fine by me. One thing was certain—I'd think long and hard before I asked someone to get real with me in the future.

"Nothing? No sports? No arts and crafts?" He leaned toward me.

"Oh. Well, I really like photography."

He cocked his head to the side. "Really?"

I laughed. "Yeah, really. I take black-and-white pictures. I have a darkroom in my house."

"It's my civic duty to ask why you aren't on the yearbook staff," he said.

I recoiled. "Are you kidding?"

He stared at me very seriously for a few seconds, then laughed. "Yes, I'm kidding. I know people on the yearbook staff. They're not your type. And I don't think I could sleep at night knowing I'd unleashed you on them."

I exhaled. Carter knew how to keep a girl on her toes.

"So what do you photograph?" he asked.

"Oh, you know . . ." I said. I thought about explaining my current photographic mystery, but thought I should keep things light. "Lately I've been experimenting a lot with this German philosophy called gestalt. Not just taking a photo of a bowl of fruit, but of the table it's on, the room it's in. How it all adds up to make one image. Like, a house at night and the trees behind it and the moon and stars." *And a mystery glow in the tree.*

Carter's eyebrows went up.

"I'll stop now," I said, feeling more than a little dumb.

"No," he said softly, shaking his head. "It's fascinating. It's cool that you have this secret side."

"It's not a secret," I said. "And no offense, but why do you even care?"

"What do you mean?"

"I mean, haven't you heard about me? I'm rude. I'm always in trouble. I skip classes and none of the teachers like me. Why are we even doing this? Why do you care about *any* of it?"

He laughed again, a real, honest laugh. "Believe it or not, I care about it *because* of those things."

"Oh, right. Opposites attract." I looked around. "That's easy to say sitting alone in the library. Or in a car."

"What do you mean?"

Truth be told, I really didn't know what I meant. "I mean . . . we get along great when nobody else is around . . . but I just can't imagine hanging out in front of other people."

He shook his head. "Are you kidding? I'm not afraid to been seen with you public."

I widened my eyes and tried to sound solemn. "Well, maybe it's *the world* that isn't ready for our friendship."

He caught my mocking tone and sat back, shaking his head. Suddenly he brightened and leaned forward. "Then let's show *the world*," he said. It was like a challenge.

"I don't understand," I said.

His eyes flashed. "Come to the dance with me Friday."

The library floor could have dropped out from under my feet and I could not possibly have been more surprised than I was at that moment.

"That is . . . unless *you're* the one who's afraid to be seen with *me*," he said.

"I'm not afraid," I said.

"Then say yes. Come to the dance with me."

My brain was absolutely no help to me at this point. So my gut spoke instead. "Okay, fine." I shrugged. "If that will make you happy."

He looked straight into my eyes, and I noticed that our heads were so close I could smell his shampoo.

The bell rang.

Carter moved away quickly and glanced at his watch. "I'll walk you to class?" he asked.

I hesitated. We'd have to walk right past the Doom Squad.

"I don't want to cost you any friendships or anything," Carter said smoothly, but his cool voice sounded a little cooler than usual.

"No, it's fine," I said. I straightened my shoulders. What could they do, throw their leather bracelets at us? "I'll protect you if they attack."

He gave a wary smile.

We started across the courtyard. I was ready to face the hostile stares, but I wasn't prepared for what happened as soon as I stepped foot on the bricks. Lydia came tearing up to us, looking dismayed. I braced myself for an idiotic comment, but tried to put enough warning in my glare that she wouldn't bother.

She didn't notice.

"Alexis!" she said breathlessly. "Everyone's looking for you!"

My heart jumped to my throat.

"It's your dad," she said. "There was an accident."

I FELT LIKE TIME HAD HICCUPPED forward two seconds and left me behind. Carter grabbed my hand, and I vaguely noticed that he pulled me through the courtyard. Lydia was on the other side of me like a yappy dog nipping at my heels.

"Don't you know anything else?" he asked her, sounding irritated.

"They just told me to find Alexis!" she protested. "They kept paging her, but she didn't answer."

"The PA system in the library must be broken," Carter said. "We didn't hear."

In the front office, Mrs. Ames came forward to meet us. She did a double take when she saw Carter holding my hand, but then she put her hand on my shoulder.

"Your father is okay," she said. "He's at St. Margaret's hospital, and he's going to be all right."

Hearing that melted the steel rod that had been holding me up. I felt my legs go weak. If Carter hadn't chosen that exact moment to squeeze my hand, I might have passed out.

"Where's my mom?" I asked. "What about my little sister?"

"Your mother is at the hospital already, and your neighbor Mary Fuller is picking you and your sister up to drive you over there," Mrs. Ames said.

"I can drive her to the hospital," Carter offered.

"I'm afraid that's not permissible, Carter," she replied. "But thank you for offering. Alexis, come and sit down for a minute."

Sit down? Who could sit down at a time like this? I know this is weird, but I felt like if I stopped panicking or worrying for a second, something terrible would happen—and it would be my fault.

I looked up at Carter, my brain loading up another round of frantic questions.

"You really should sit down," he said.

I was outnumbered.

We followed Mrs. Ames into her office and I sank onto my usual spot on her sofa.

"What happened?" I asked. "Who called? Tell me what happened."

Mrs. Ames looked directly into my eyes. "Your mother called. Your father was in an automobile accident, and he's in the hospital, but he's okay. It's important that you go and be with your family, but it's not because this is a life-or-death situation, do you understand?"

So that meant I should act like a grown-up, right?

"You don't need to worry," she repeated in her principal voice. She sat down at her desk. Her brown hair fell to her shoulders in soft waves that began together but went in all directions as they brushed her Surrey Eagles sweatshirt. It was the hair of a woman with no time to blow-dry. Mom would cut off a toe before she left the house with hair like that.

"It's okay," Carter said. "Your dad will be fine."

I nodded. Nodding was easy. Things on the outside were easy. But inside I was a complete wreck. I didn't know what to feel. I mean, I didn't even really like my dad. But I didn't want him dead . . . or even hurt.

I felt something in me slide, slide, slide. Like I'd been standing on a hill watching all of this happening to someone else, and slowly the ground was coming out from underneath me. The air seemed stuffy and unbearably hot.

"Can we go outside?" I asked.

"Mrs. Fuller will need to come into the office and sign you out," Mrs. Ames said. "But we can wait for the car out front, if you want to."

"She does," Carter said, standing.

He did everything. He told Lydia, who'd been growing restless in the corner, to go back to class. He had the secretary bring me a glass of water. He carried my bag and made sure there were no ants on the bench where we sat down, and when we sat, he didn't say anything, just looked for the car.

I was so glad he was there.

A car finally pulled up. It was our busybody kindly-old-lady neighbor from across the street, Mary. She went inside with Mrs. Ames. Carter opened the door for me and handed me my bag. He leaned down and looked at Kasey, who was slouched against the back driver's side window, looking at us with wide eyes. Her arm was wrapped around her schoolbag as if it were a life preserver.

"Hi there," he said, and she raised her hand and waved weakly.

"Kase, this is Carter," I said. "Carter, this is Kasey, my little sister. She goes to Surrey Middle."

"Nice to meet you," he said. Kasey nodded, staring up at him a little dumbly. I hoped he didn't think she was slow or something. She was just in shock.

Mary came back out to the car, mercifully silent. She's usually one of those people who can talk until you want to toss yourself off a bridge.

"Thanks," I told Carter. "Thanks for—"

He shook his head. For a moment I thought he might kiss me, but he just touched my forehead with his hand. It was the softest gesture, like a feather brushing over my skin. "Call me," he said, scribbling his phone number on a torn-out page of his spiral notebook and thrusting it into my hand. "Especially if you need anything."

"Okay," I said, still reeling from his touch. Carter closed the door and the car pulled away.

"He's nice," Kasey said at last.

Neither of us said another word during the entire drive to the hospital.

Mom was inside, her purse slung heavily over her shoulder, chewing on her thumbnail and pacing back and forth across eight worn squares of linoleum. When she saw us, she came hurrying over and pulled us into a hug.

"Your father's fine," she said. "He needs medical treatment, but he'll be okay."

Kasey pulled away and looked at Mom with glassy eyes.

"What happened?" she asked.

Mom took a deep breath. "He was on his way to work, and something went wrong with the car. He veered off the side of the road and hit a tree, but he wasn't going very fast." She pushed her hair back off her face. "Luckily, he was going uphill."

"So he's okay?" Kasey asked.

"Yes, he's probably got a broken leg and some broken ribs and some other internal . . . problems." She patted Kasey's shoulder. "But yes, he's okay, thank God."

Mom went on about physical therapy and cuts and scratches and medical stuff. I sat down on a smooth plastic chair and wrapped my hands around the metal armrests. They felt cold and clean and solid on my skin.

I'd never been in an emergency room before. It was a lot like the ones on TV—the linoleum floor shone under the buzzing fluorescent lights. Everything looked polished and sterile. Even the smells were disinfected—sharp hints of alcohol and bleach.

As I sat there and watched the thick plastic hands of the clock tick forward, my thoughts turned pessimistic. So what, Dad was going to have to stay home from work? Who would take care of him? How would we pay our bills? Were we just supposed to sit here and stare at the sick people coming in and out all day? Did people really do that?

I felt nauseous and sticky and angry. I longed for the splintered cushions and exposed foam of the library sofa, the soft, sandy sound of Carter's voice. I remembered his fingers floating against my skin, and the thought made my throat feel tight.

The voices around us melted into a sickening murmur. I thought I might implode. But Kasey broke first.

"I have to go outside," she said, standing up.

"I'll go with you," I said. Mom nodded vaguely.

The sun made us both squint as we walked out through the double doors.

"Can we just go home?" she asked.

"I wish," I said. "We're supposed to be here for Dad."

Kasey stamped her foot on the sidewalk and let out a little grunt. "If one of us was in the hospital, *he* wouldn't come," she said.

"Yes he would," I said.

"I want to go home," she said.

"I know, Kase," I sighed.

"Don't you?"

"Sure. Whatever." I didn't have the energy to be reassuring.

Kasey crossed her arms in front of her. "I'll walk if Mom won't drive us," she said.

"Mom can't leave," I said.

"Then let's just go."

"Be realistic," I said. "We have to ask. Wait here, I'll be right back."

Mom was deep in conversation with Mary, so she just nodded and waved me away. Mary had started the story about her cousin who was killed in World War II. Anyone who's lived in our neighborhood more than three weeks has heard it like forty times. It takes roughly thirty-five minutes, start to finish, and she can modify it to fit any occasion—birthdays, Christmas, Halloween. . . .

"See you later," I said, and walked out before Mom could say no. I didn't want to be there any more than Kasey did.

13

THE WALK TO THE HOUSE WAS FAR—almost two miles, and it was hot. The bright sun had already baked off any of the morning's autumn coolness. Neither of us complained, though—we were too glad to be going home.

We were hit by a blast of cool air when we passed through the front door. Mom must have left the air conditioner on when she left for work, which is like the worst sin you can commit in the Warren household. There are starving children in Africa, and you have the nerve to leave the air conditioner running all day?

We turned all moony for a minute, dropped our bags in the front hall, held our arms out and spun in slow circles under the vents. Heavenly. Kasey shook her hair wildly.

I checked my watch. It was only ten thirty, and I felt like I'd lived at least a full day's worth of excitement.

"I think I'll take a nap or something," Kasey said. "I didn't sleep so great last night."

That made two of us.

She headed upstairs, and I flipped the air conditioner power switch to OFF, then went to the living room and sank into Dad's recliner. If I closed my eyes and concentrated, I could smell the lingering aroma of his aftershave. I thought about him, alone in his room at the hospital. Did he feel lonely and sorry, unloved? What if he died and that chair was the only thing we had left that smelled like him? I breathed in again but couldn't pick up the scent. Guilt flooded over me and left me feeling empty and scared and horribly selfish.

But as I reclined in the overstuffed chair, my relief was overwhelming. We would rest now and walk back to the hospital later, when it was cooler, and the sunlight wasn't harsh and colorless and raw. A light breeze would be blowing, and we could stop at the grocery store on the way and buy flowers.

Gradually, a dream floated in and took over.

The little girl in the fancy dress—the one from my story.

She's backed into a corner, crying. A crowd of kids has gathered around her, and I am one of the crowd. We have planned this for a week, now—since the day we saw her wandering through the graveyard with her doll, and Mildred told us that was a sure sign she was a witch.

We can't have a witch in our town.

We close in.

The girl pushes through the group and runs. We run after her, shouting war cries, down an empty road. Our feet pound against packed dirt, sending up clouds of dust. We run for a long time. Finally, a house comes into view.

My house.

But it's not my house in this dream.

The little girl is scrambling up the oak tree, desperately hauling herself from branch to branch, trying to reach the open window on the second story of the house.

I don't want to do this, but I can't stop myself. I reach down and scoop up a pebble from the ground. My hand reaches back, then sends it flying up at her.

"Cuckoo!" the girls are shouting. "Climb your tree, cuckoo bird! Fly away, cuckoo!"

The girl in the tree wails as she climbs higher and higher. Gradually, the constant stream of pebbles slows. The game isn't fun anymore.

But then the biggest girl says, "Scare away the cuckoo bird!" and drops one last pebble into my hand.

I take aim and throw it.

It hits the girl's hand just as she reaches for another branch.

And she falls—a long, long fall.

She hits the ground and lies horribly still, and time seems to grind to a halt.

No one says a word.

"Go, Patience," the big girl says. "Go wake her up."

I don't want to.

"You threw the last one!" someone says.

They are all urging me on now, scolding me and telling me it's my fault.

I take a step toward the body on the ground.

Surely she's only sleeping?

"Sarah," I say.

I go closer, and walk around her to see her eyes. They are wide open. A trickle of blood drips from the side of her gaping lips.

She is dead.

Next to her is the precious doll, whose hair is still clutched in Sarah's hand.

I step closer—

And suddenly the doll's eyes pop open, bright green and glowing.

I woke with a breathless cough and looked at the clock—twelve thirty.

I'd been asleep for two hours, and the air conditioner had been blasting the entire time. The house was so cold I could practically see my breath. I hurried to turn off the air conditioner, goose bumps erupting on my arms.

Problem: I'd turned it off two hours ago. Still groggy from my nap, I stood and stared at the thermostat, hoping something would happen.

Nothing did, of course.

Great. Now the air conditioner was wonky. Mom and Dad would assume that Kasey and I turned it on when we got home and somehow broke it.

I pried the plastic cover away. The little blue arm stood at seventy-five, but the thermometer read fifty-four degrees. So even if it wasn't off, it wasn't supposed to be running.

The cold was unbearable. I ran upstairs and peered through Kasey's bedroom door. She was asleep, little puffs of foggy breath escaping from her mouth. It was too cold for just a T-shirt.

The dolls seemed to stare in disapproval, and I knew if Kase woke up she'd probably flip out and spend the next six months paranoid that I was going to mess with her stuff when she wasn't looking. But the last thing we needed was for her to get a horrible flu from sleeping in the freezing cold. I went just as far as the closet, to get a blanket.

The shelves in my sister's closet (like the rest of her bedroom) were an absolute disaster. Books, jewelry, shoes, magazines, her old Snoopy phone that had turned yellow with age, all piled on top of one another. The pink blanket she used in the winter rested on the bottom shelf, with her backpack leaning up against it. As I pulled on the blanket, the backpack tipped over, spilling out a fan of multicolored folders.

I reached down to gather them, when I caught a glimpse of one of the covers.

MY ANCESTORS, it read. BY MIMI LAIRD.

I looked at the next one. MY ANCESTORS, BENJI BYERSON. MY ANCESTORS, JENNILYNN WOO. MY ANCESTORS, EVAN LITCHFIELD.

"What are you doing?"

The voice scared me so much that I dropped the stack of reports.

I just stared at her. "I came in to cover you up, but . . . why do you have everyone else's projects?"

She gave me a look that said pretty plainly that she didn't think it was my business.

"I'm a student grader," she said at last.

"A what?"

"It's new." Kasey yawned and scooted to the edge of the bed. "Don't bother with the blanket; I'm awake."

She followed my gaze to the papers on the floor.

"I'll get those later," she said.

I was kind of surprised she hadn't wigged out about me being so close to her dolls without supervision.

But she didn't look anywhere near freaking out. And if she wasn't going to freak out, I wasn't going to either.

"There's something wrong with the thermostat. Come help me check out the circuit breaker," I said.

Kasey followed me downstairs and into the garage.

The cold had seeped under the kitchen door and even the garage was chilly. If Mom showed up now we'd be grounded until college. How long would it take to warm up the house if we opened all the windows? Then Mom would never know . . . until the electric bill showed up.

Built into the wall behind the garage door was a metal cabinet. Opening it revealed about thirty chunky black switches. Kasey leaned in to look at them.

"What are those?"

"Fuses," I said.

"Which one is for the air conditioner?" Kasey asked.

I studied the little map at the top of the cabinet. Third down on the left, the little square was labeled "A/C."

"This one," I said, flipping the switch. "Go see if that worked."

Kasey ran inside. A second later she came huffing and puffing back. "Nope," she panted.

I stared at the rest of the circuits. "Okay," I said. "Stay here and flip this switch when I tell you to."

I went inside to the thermostat and looked at the little red light in the corner. "Flip it!" I called.

The red light went dark.

"Flip it back!" I called.

The light came back on. Then off, then on, then off, and on again. But none of that mattered, because the whole time, cold air never stopped blowing through the vent.

Kasey came in from the garage, shivering. "No luck?"

"No," I said, my teeth chattering. "We're going to get in sooo much trouble."

"So what else is new?" Kasey said. She approached the thermostat and grabbed the switch, moving it back and forth. I almost told her to stop because I was afraid the stupid thing would break off.

"I'm *freezing*," Kasey said under her breath. "Turn off, turn off."

Midflip, the air conditioner turned off. We stood in confused silence.

"Huh," I said. "Weird."

"I didn't do anything!" Kasey snapped.

"Did I *say* you did?" I asked, going back into the kitchen. "Jeez."

She stomped up the stairs, leaving me alone. I pulled a string cheese and a few pieces of sliced turkey out of the fridge and stood in the kitchen eating, just kind of looking around.

I looked at the garage door and then down at the floor. The light gray rag rug had dark smudges on it. Our footprints.

I lifted my foot and looked at the bottom of my sock.

It was covered in a fine dusting of grimy-looking dirt.

Just like the dirt I'd seen on Kasey's sock that morning.

So she'd been in the garage?

At six thirty in the morning?

. . . Why?

The contact sheet from my earlier darkroom session was completely dry. I counted down to the fifth row of negatives and over three, to the half-ruined, half-in-focus picture. I put the negative into a little frame, checked the focus, then set a piece of photo paper down and hit the timer.

After fifteen seconds I slipped the paper into the developer and stood back to watch the image emerge.

But there wasn't an image. Unless the whole paper immediately turning black counts as an image.

I pulled that page out and rinsed it clean before dropping it in the trash.

I set another piece of paper down and turned the timer on for five seconds, figuring it might be underexposed, but at least I would have a better idea of what time to use.

But no. This one turned black too.

A panicky feeling started to rise up inside me as I looked at the package of photo paper. There were two black plastic bags with fifty sheets each; only the top one should have been unsealed. But they were both open. And the stacks of paper weren't neat and even—they were irregular and off-center.

All of my paper had been exposed.

A package like this cost sixty dollars. With my current weekly allowance of twenty dollars, that meant three weeks of savings down the drain. And three weeks of more saving before I could even afford another package.

Three weeks without developing photos?

I started to feel kind of sick.

I'd told my sister a trillion times not to touch my stuff, not to even go into the darkroom, and she refused to listen.

Kasey was guilty. She had to be.

After a few deep breaths I went to confront my sister. My hands shook as I stalked down the hall and pounded on her door.

Stay calm, I told myself. *Be mature.*

She opened it, blue eyes wide.

"What?" she asked.

I took a long breath through my nose. "Just . . . tell me . . . why."

"Huh?"

My calm exterior shattered like a lightbulb dropped from a third-floor window. "Why did you do it, Kasey?

What did I do to you? I try *so hard* to be nice to you when nobody else even wants to be your friend, and you—"

Her hands flew up to her cheeks, which flushed pink. "Lexi!" she cried, dismayed.

I took a step back. "*Why*, Kasey?!"

"I didn't do anything," she said. "I swear I didn't. I don't even know what happened. I heard a noise and then all I remember is having the weirdest dream and then I was at school and they said come to the office because of Dad and I saw all the reports on Ms. Lewin's desk and later they were in my bag—"

"What?"

Her face fell slack, her jaw hanging slightly open, her breath ragged.

"What are you talking about, Kase?"

She shook her head and stared at the floor.

"I'm talking about my photo paper. Someone ruined it. All of it."

"It wasn't me," she said in a tiny voice.

"But wait—you *stole* those reports from school? I thought you said you were a student grader."

"No!" she wailed. "I told you, I didn't . . . I mean, I guess I took them, but I didn't mean to. I just looked in my bag and found them there."

"You're saying someone framed you?" I asked.

"I don't know. I guess so."

Knowing how spiteful kids could be, it was a serious possibility. "Did you see anyone near your bag?"

"I don't know!" she said.

My patience was paper-thin. "Kasey, either you did, or you didn't."

"Maybe!" she said. "I mean, I don't remember. But it had to be someone, right?"

Someone. More like Mimi Laird, or one of her snotty little friends. I didn't say it out loud, though, because Kasey seemed traumatized enough.

I sighed. "You're going to have to give them back."

"I can't!" she wailed. "I'll get expelled!"

"Teachers understand mean kids, Kase," I said. "You just have to do it soon so it doesn't look any weirder."

"Will you help me? I'm *tired*," she said pitifully. "I didn't sleep very much last night."

I didn't point out that she'd just taken a two-hour power nap.

A thought occurred to me. "Yeah, so . . . why were you in the garage this morning?"

Her nose wrinkled. "I wasn't in the garage."

"When I saw you in the hall, your socks were dirty—" I began.

"In the hall?" she asked. "I didn't see you in the hall this morning."

I stared at her.

"What are you talking about, Lexi? I don't understand."

I didn't understand either. But I did understand that all of these bizarre things were starting to add up and make me feel like I was going crazy. After all, what was that old saying? The common link between all your problems is *you*?

What if I was losing it?

"I'm going for a walk," I said, going into my room to get my house key.

"Can I come?"

"No!" I said. "I just want to be by myself for a while."

"No fair," she whined.

"You just stay here," I said. "And try to figure out how you're going to explain to your teacher that you stole everybody's reports."

"I *didn't!*" she yelled. "I didn't steal anything! Someone put them in my bag!"

Then she ran into her room and slammed the door.

At least she wasn't insisting on coming.

I went downstairs and out the front door, locking it as I left. Out of guilt, I glanced up at Kasey's windows to see if she was looking down at me.

She was.

I pulled my eyes away from her and glanced at the

oak tree, trying to forget its horrible role in my dream.

That's when I noticed the lines of the wood, the jagged edges of long-since-removed limbs, the soft overgrowth of bark on several of the scars left behind by pruning or broken branches.

The tree I'd drawn the night before—it was this tree. This exact tree, down to a tuft of grass growing out of a tiny hollow about six feet off the ground.

I had to get out of there. But I could think of only one place to go.

I hurried down the front walk, toward the street.

By the time I reached the school, most of the parking lot was empty. A few stragglers stood by their cars in small groups, talking. A crowd of kids waited miserably at the bus loop for their late bus. At the sight of the brick building, my body tensed, the way it does at 7:58 every weekday morning. But it was better than being surrounded by things that made me feel like I was coming completely undone.

One girl looked at me strangely. When I walked past her, she moved forward like she was going to say something, but her friend touched her arm and they both turned away.

As I passed the gym, a mob of cheerleaders emerged from the band room and went by me, chattering like first graders at a crosswalk. They weren't wearing uniforms, but their white-ribboned ponytails and packlike formation gave them away.

A couple of them looked at me and whispered, heads bowed together like horses nuzzling.

Megan Wiley was the last to exit. She carried a notebook and studied the papers inside it so intently that she almost walked right into me.

"Sorry," she muttered, and then looked up. When she saw me, she took an involuntary step backward.

I averted my eyes, waiting for her to make a quick retreat into the gym after her minions, but she didn't. Instead, when I glanced up, she was looking at me.

"How's your dad?" she said.

The question was beyond unexpected. "Um, all right."

"Lydia told everyone you fainted," she said. With a shudder, she added, "Then she said your dad was probably going to die."

I rolled my eyes and shook my head. For some reason my mouth felt like it was full of straw. "He's okay," I said. "Just broken bones, bruised organs. Limbs, ribs, that kind of thing."

The conversation could have ended there, but Megan swallowed hard. "I just . . . My mom died in a car accident when I was a baby," she said. "So I was really worried."

Wow.

"Wow," I said. What else could I say? The things you don't know about people. "I'm sorry."

"Well, I don't remember her, so . . ."

"Still," I said. Yikes.

"I live with my grandmother," she said, and then her eyes flickered longingly toward the door where all of her friends had gone.

"But thanks for asking," I said.

"I'm glad she's okay."

"No, it was . . . *he*. It was my dad," I said.

She blushed, her perfect cheeks turning a lovely rose color. "I mean—I knew that, sorry."

"Well," I said, wishing for a sinkhole or something to swallow me up.

We stood there, up to our ankles in awkwardness.

"Thanks," I said at last.

She smiled a tight-lipped smile and ducked into the gym.

Huh.

I stood there for a second. Then without warning the door opened, and Megan stuck her head out.

"If you're looking for Carter Blume, I saw him talking to Mr. Makely about five minutes ago," she said.

My expression was apparently so shocked that it was funny, because Megan laughed. It was a short, self-conscious laugh, but it wasn't mean or anything.

"See you," she said, and disappeared. This time I hurried away so she couldn't surprise me again.

Mr. Makely stood outside the library for twenty minutes after school ended every day. I'd probably have him for physics next year. He gave me a strange look as I entered the courtyard, and I got this weird, uncomfortable feeling that everyone thought my dad was dead. It made my heart beat funny for a second just to think about it. Carter wasn't there, so I headed toward the student parking lot.

When I got there, the first thing I saw was Carter in his car, studying his iPod. I stopped suddenly as it hit me—what was I doing? Why had I run straight to Carter? I hardly even knew him, and here I was, following him around after school like a lovesick loser.

The skin around my jaw and ears felt tight, and my eyes started to burn. I wondered how fast I could get someplace else. Just somewhere he wouldn't see me as he drove away. I scanned the parking lot and saw only low shrubs and a few cars that were all too far away to dash for.

I had no choice but to stand there and wait for him to notice me. He did a double take, then got out of the car and walked over.

"Hi," he said, his voice a question.

I looked at him, and the "wanting to crawl under a rock and die" feeling intensified.

"How's your dad?"

"He's okay."

Carter looked at me. "How are *you*?"

Amazing how suddenly there was no easy answer to that question.

"I'm fine," I said.

He just looked at me and shook his head. "No you're not."

That made me laugh, but laughing made tears spring to my eyes. "I know," I said.

He didn't say anything else. He held his hand out like I should take it.

"You don't understand," I said. "I think I'm losing my mind."

He looked at the sky and then at the ground. "I understand," he said.

And then I was engulfed in his arms and his smell, laundry detergent and shampoo and all that was clean. I closed my eyes and leaned against him and let everything go.

14

He twirled a twig between his finger and thumb.

"First of all," he said slowly, "I've known crazy people, and I don't think you're crazy." Then he sat up straighter. "I mean, your sister sounds like she's got some issues, but I just don't see it in you."

"Maybe I'm the secret kind of crazy," I said softly. "The kind where you keep it to yourself and then one day you just go off the deep end."

Carter took a deep breath. "I don't think you need to worry about that."

"What do you mean?"

He sighed and tossed the twig away. It landed in the water with a soft splash. We were sitting in the grass near the drainage canal at the park, which isn't as ugly as it sounds. It looks more like a little bubbling brook.

"You're . . . *strong*."

"Strong people can't be crazy?"

He smirked and ducked his head. "Strong people

don't just go off the deep end one day. That territory belongs to the weak."

Oh.

"I think you're being too hard on yourself," I said.

He shook his head but didn't look at me.

"Sometimes life really blows," I said.

"Yeah," Carter said. "Sometimes it does. For everybody, and most people can cope. But not . . ." He sucked in air through his teeth and stared into the sun. "Not me."

"But why beat yourself up? Who cares if you . . . ? I mean, who could possibly dislike someone just for going through something like . . ."

"You can say it, Alexis. It was a suicide attempt." He looked right into my eyes and then cocked his head to one side. "A botched one."

I turned back to the water and worked on braiding pine needles together, but finally my curiosity got the better of me. ". . . What'd you do?"

He lay back in the grass, keeping a wary eye on me, like a shy dog.

"Never mind," I said. "Sorry, not my business."

"Don't be sorry. I'm just not used to talking about it." He held his arm out to me. "Ever wonder why I only wear long sleeves?"

I took his forearm in my hands and pushed his sleeve

back, revealing a crisscrossed etching of scars.

"My mom came home early from a conference and found me," he said. "We had to redo the tile in the bathroom because the bloodstains wouldn't come out."

Without thinking about it, I hugged his arm close to me.

A second later I realized what I was doing and dropped it like a hot potato.

He laughed, a slow, easy laugh. The Carter laugh.

I just couldn't see how someone so graceful, so clever, could ever be so depressed.

I looked down at the ditch and sighed.

"How can you be so perfect all the time?" I said without thinking.

Carter looked at me in surprise and took a second to answer.

"Perfect?" he repeated. "Ha."

I didn't say anything. I was paralyzed by regretful shock over what I'd just said.

"Miss Vahrren," he said in a German psychiatrist accent, *"I'm ahfrait you ah delusional."*

"Delusional," I repeated. Sounded about right, given the events of the past day. But I pushed that out of my mind and concentrated on Carter. The fact that he hadn't laughed in my face made me bolder. "So then . . . what are your flaws?"

"What are my flaws? I have to *list* them?" He laughed ruefully and shook his head. "That's hardly fair. What are *your* flaws?"

"In case you haven't noticed, my whole existence is one big flaw," I said, lying back on the grass next to him and staring up at the sky. "I am a giant pimple on the face of humanity."

"That's kind of gross," he answered.

"At least I'm honest."

"That's not honest," he said. "That's paranoid and" —he thought for a second—"very pessimistic."

"Paranoid, pessimistic," I said, ticking them off on my fingers. "And gross. That's three. The tip of my flaw iceberg."

"I'm not calling you paranoid—"

"Just the things I say?"

He batted at my arm. "Maybe you *are* crazy," he said, but his tiny smile made my whole body tingle.

"Flaws," I said, all business. "Yours. List them."

"I'm a snob," he said easily.

"About what?"

"Oh, lots of things. Movies, books, school plays, people from the country."

"Which country?"

"*The* country. Like, farmers." He wrinkled his nose. "I don't even know why."

Oh, duh. Alexis's flaw number four: stupid. "What else?"

He hesitated. "I don't get along with my father," he said.

I could understand that one. I stared at a fluffy white cloud, waiting for a shape to pop out at me.

"I spend too much time thinking about myself. I blow things out of proportion. I've done very selfish things . . . and I'm not . . . brave." He squinted into the sunlight and gave me a wry smile.

"Stop." I turned my eyes away from what could have become a cloud alligator to look at Carter.

Somehow during our conversation we'd moved toward each other. Our arms were touching. My skin felt electric.

There was definitely more to Carter than his preppy exterior.

"I hope you don't really see yourself that way," I said.

He turned to look at me and narrowed his eyes. "How do you see me?" he said softly.

I gave him a gentle shove. "You don't want to know."

He waited.

"I think you're . . ." My voice went nearly silent. "Dangerous."

"Why?" he whispered.

"Because," I said, though I had no idea how to put it in words. ". . . You make me think too much."

Now he had turned his whole body to face me. "I've never met anyone like you."

I felt an urgent, almost magnetic pull between us. It made my throat feel dry and airy.

"This is so weird," I said, but it came out as a whisper.

He studied my face for a moment and then smiled.

Oh God, was it obvious that my heart was pounding? It was like those scenes in movies where the girl thinks the guy's going to kiss her, so she closes her eyes and puckers up. Except I wasn't just puckering my lips— I was puckering my whole soul.

"I can't help it, Alexis," he said. "I want to make you think too much . . . and then I want to hear the things you've been thinking . . . too much."

I was lying down, but that made me dizzy. This was *all* too much. I felt myself start to blush, so I raised my arm, intending to cover my face.

Carter grabbed my hand and held it.

Our eyes locked together. "You aren't the person you try to make people think you are," he said, sounding as though this had just dawned on him. "I feel . . . *safe* . . . when I talk to you."

My heart could have exploded.

"Lexi."

I grabbed my hand away and sat up as fast as I could. Carter sat up too, and raked his fingers through his hair.

Five feet away, still and wordless as a statue, was Kasey.

"Is something wrong with Dad?" I asked.

She shook her head. Then her gaze moved from me to Carter.

"What are you doing?" she asked.

"Kase . . . you remember Carter," I said. Carter stood up and held his hand out to me. He pulled me to my feet and didn't let go.

"It's getting late," Kasey said. She scowled, noticing our joined hands.

"Did Mom send you?"

"No."

Anger rose up in me like a tidal wave. "Go home, Kasey. I'll be there soon."

"I'm hungry," she said calmly.

"So cook something."

"You'd rather be with him than with me?" she said, her voice small and hurt. "I'm your sister."

Carter turned and touched my shoulder. "Go on," he said. "We can continue this another time."

I shook my head, more out of disbelief than protest. I could have strangled Kasey.

"Do you want me to drive you?" Carter asked.

"Thanks, but we'll walk," I said. I couldn't risk exposing the only good thing in my life to my sister. What if she started talking crazy in the car? Stories, dolls, stealing stuff from school . . . Oh, maybe she'd steal something from Carter. That would be just fantastic.

I turned to Carter and felt a smile fight its way onto my lips.

"Walk carefully," he said lightly. Then he bent down and kissed me on the cheek. "That's for the nice things you said."

"I didn't even—"

"Can we go?" Kasey interrupted. "Walking home is going to take forever."

I don't care if she's totally lost it, I thought. I'm going to murder her.

"Bye," I said. Kasey had started walking away.

"Good to see you again, Kasey," Carter called.

I looked at Kasey to see what she would do. She turned and glared at me, not even glancing at Carter.

Nice.

I ignored her the whole walk home. I was done trying to help her if she wasn't going to try to help herself.

After making a sandwich, I went straight upstairs and locked myself in my bedroom with the stereo turned way up.

A half hour later, I heard Mom's voice from the hall.

"Alexis?" she called. "Are you all right? Why is your music so loud?"

I went to the door and opened it, then went back and sat on my bed. She wandered in and sat next to me.

I switched off the music. "How's Dad?"

"He's fine," she said. "Maybe you can stop by after school tomorrow."

"I'll try."

"Are you feeling sick?" she asked, and put her wrist against my forehead. She drew back in surprise. "You have a goose egg."

"I know," I said. "Someone knocked me down at school yesterday." Seeing the concerned look on her face, I added, "Not on purpose. With a door."

Her brow wrinkled the way it does when she's worried. "They didn't call me."

"It wasn't that bad," I said, and thinking of Carter made me smile.

"Okay," Mom said, apparently not interested in the details. "Let me know if you want something for it. You don't have a fever."

"I think I'll lie down."

"All right, honey," she said. It sounded so alien to hear her say something momlike. She stood up and awkwardly touched my forehead. Then she looked around my room. "You're so tidy," she said approvingly. "You must have gotten it from your father. Certainly not from me."

True. She's pretty sloppy for a mom.

Her eyes stopped on the bookshelves. "What's wrong with your yearbooks?" she asked.

I looked at the shelf where all of my school yearbooks, from kindergarten up, are stored. The last one, my freshman yearbook, was missing, causing the whole row to lean at an annoying angle.

"One's gone," I said. Odd. My thoughts flashed to Kasey.

"It's not lost, is it?" I almost heard an accusation in Mom's voice—like I'd sold it for drug money or something.

"Well, technically," I said. "But I'm sure it'll turn up."

She sighed. "Those things cost a fortune."

Just as I was about to reply, a cell phone ring blared from across the hallway, and Mom sprang up off the bed.

"I'll be right back," she said.

I sighed and leaned back, hugging a pillow to my chest and closing my eyes.

A couple of minutes later Mom came out of her bedroom saying, "Okay . . . oh . . . thank you . . . yes . . . okay . . . yes, please do . . ."

She clapped the phone shut. Then she looked at me, but her eyes were unfocused.

"What?" I asked.

"That was a detective from the police department," she said, fluttering her hands in the air. "He said they have reason to suspect foul play . . . They looked at the car's brakes, and the wires had been . . . It looked as if they'd been *cut*."

I sat straight up. "Someone sabotaged Dad's car?"

"Yes, but . . ." She shook her head and lowered herself onto the mattress. "No, Alexis . . . not *his* car—*mine*. He was going to drop it off to get my oil changed."

I sat back against the headboard and looked at Mom, who was just staring down at the carpet.

"Oh my goodness," she said, her voice shaky. "Listen, don't tell Kasey about this. It would be too much for her."

"Yeah," I said. "Sure."

Mom touched my forehead gently before standing up and making her way out into the hall, dazed.

Thinking about Kasey made me think about the reports in her backpack.

Was it possible that the same kids who did that somehow came to my house and did this? Decided to pull a prank on our parents? If Mimi was mad enough about her arm, maybe she put part of the blame on Mom. . . .

But that would be, like, *attempted murder*. Even the most obnoxious eighth grader wouldn't try to kill someone else's mother.

Unless . . .

Unless she thought Kasey would be in the car.

A half hour later, the doorbell rang. Thinking it might be the police, I rushed to the top of the stairs and watched Mom open the door. But it was just a pizza delivery guy.

Mom looked up at me. "Are you hungry?"

I shook my head.

Mom looked tired. Her face was pale and her hair was tugged back into a sloppy bun.

"Can you get your sister, then?"

I swallowed hard, just as Kasey bumped into me from behind. It was enough of an impact to make me grab on to the wall, feeling a split-second panic that I was going to fall down the stairs.

"Oops," she said.

Mom took the pizza into the kitchen, and Kasey took the steps at half her usual speed. Halfway down, she stopped and turned to look at me.

"What's *your* problem?" she asked.

Your friends are trying to kill you, I thought, but I forced my shoulders back and kept my voice strong. "I don't have a problem. . . . Listen, do you think we should talk to Mom about those reports in your backpack?"

Her hand squeezed the railing so tightly that the muscles in her neck seemed to tense up.

"No," she said. "We oughtn't."

"We *what?*"

She glared at me. "I said *no*. It's done. Resolved. I already took them back to school."

"You *did?*"

She made an irritated noise. "I'm not *completely* helpless, you know."

She took the rest of the stairs two at a time and slipped into the kitchen.

I stared after her while my thoughts rattled around in my head.

Nope. I didn't believe her.

I crept down the hall to Kasey's room. Inside, the only light was a faint slant of yellow spilling in from the hall, illuminating a little display of threadbare rag dolls on the other side of the room. When my eyes had adjusted and the lumps of blackness had taken on furniture shapes, I looked around for Kasey's book bag.

I found it on the floor between the bed and the doll shelves on the far wall, and as I crouched on the carpet I felt as if dozens of pairs of eyes were watching me, angry at my trespass.

The bag was unzipped.

And empty.

It had basic school stuff—pens, a couple of empty notebooks, the last two issues of *Doll Fancy* (no wonder

she had no friends left, if she read that stuff at school)—
but no reports.

I stood up and surveyed the semidarkness, trying to
figure out where she would have stashed them. I even
remotely considered the possibility that she was telling
the truth.

And that's when I saw my freshman yearbook lying
open at the foot of the bed.

It was open to a page of last year's seniors, and Kasey
had made a red mark on one girl's portrait. Why would
she do that?

I turned the book so I could see it better in the light
from the hall.

And then the light grew narrower.

Under my gaze, the door jerked a little, almost as if
I'd woken it up.

And then slowly, an inch at a time, it began to close.

I grabbed the yearbook, and the door slammed shut
in front of me, closing me in the dark.

Fear pulsed through me like flashes of light. I was
paralyzed by shock, too frightened even to move,
although some distant part of my brain was yelling at me,
Get out!

And then came the worst part by far.

For a split second I thought it was my imagination,
but I knew—I just *knew* it wasn't.

A puff of cold, wet air on my neck. The smell of rotten eggs.

I yanked the door open, practically throwing myself at the wall across the hallway. I hardly had time to look back at Kasey's door before it slammed shut again.

I ran into my room, switched on my light, and locked myself in.

After a few minutes I caught my breath and sat down on the floor near the wall opposite the door. I wanted a clear view.

What *was* that?

After a couple of minutes I convinced myself that I'd overreacted. The cold air could have been caused by an open window, which would also explain the breeze that slammed the door in my face. The smell was just musty old dolls.

I set the yearbook down on the floor and flipped through it. All in all, I saw probably eight girls whose pictures had red marks, just a little check mark in the corner of the photo. . . . Some of them I didn't know, but a few I knew all too well . . . Pepper Laird . . . Megan Wiley—

But Megan's was different.

There was a big, red X drawn through her picture.

In all fairness, it would make sense if you thought I drew the X myself, but I didn't. My obsessive neatness pervades every aspect of my life; I was the kid who hung

Barbie's clothes on their little hangers at the end of every play session, and parked her pink Corvette in its space under the dresser. No happy-face stickers ever stuck to any of my bedroom furniture. And my yearbooks, though they represent some of the most miserable hours of my life, are pristine.

It was Kasey, obviously. But why would she do that to Megan's picture?

I mean, how would she even know who Megan was?

And then I remembered the tacked-on ending to my story from the basement.

It wasn't late, but I felt completely drained. The previous two nights' meager sleep hadn't been enough to keep me going, especially not when faced with a little sister dabbling in vandalism and parents being targeted for assassination.

After I brushed my teeth, washed my face, and put on my pajamas, I went downstairs to check the dead bolt on the front door. It was locked.

I checked the back door too, and then went through the kitchen to check the door that led from the side yard into the garage. This is where someone would have had to come in, to mess with one of the cars.

Dad's car was parked in its usual spot.

As I neared the door, I stopped short.

There was a chain lock.

No way could someone have come in through this door.

That meant that whoever had come inside had been *through* the house. Or . . .

A strong chill went through me, making my hands shake, as I recalled Kasey's dirty socks.

Had my sister, in a last-ditch effort for popularity, actually joined in on some twisted scheme to sabotage our mother's car?

Had she come out here and opened the chain lock, to let someone in?

It didn't make sense. She insisted that she hadn't been in the garage—

But then, she insisted that she hadn't been in the hallway that morning, either.

I trudged upstairs and closed my bedroom door behind me, hesitating for a split second.

"Shhhh . . ."

I opened my eyes to see Kasey sitting on the edge of my bed, luminous in the blue moonlight.

"Shhh . . ." she repeated.

"Kasey," I said, "what . . . ?" Behind her, the door gaped open into the dim hallway.

"Hello, Alexis," Kasey whispered. "I saw you in the dark."

"What are you talking about?"

In the low light, everything seemed drained of color, like it was happening in black-and-white. Even Kasey's eyes shone bright black with flecks of white.

But she didn't answer.

Now I was wide awake. "What do you want, Kasey?"

But her attention had wandered away from me. I followed her gaze to my desk, where the yearbook lay open.

"Why did you draw in my yearbook?" I asked.

She ignored the question. "Come play with me, Alexis," she said, and her eyes burned even brighter. "Come outside and play with me."

"Are you crazy?" I kept my eyes on her monochromatic face and reached my hand out toward the lamp on the nightstand. "I don't *want* to go outside."

I switched the light on.

She ducked her head away, but I swear, for the split second I saw them—her eyes were green.

"GET AWAY FROM ME!" I ordered.

She stayed hunched over, facing the door for a few seconds, and then she turned around and looked at me through blank eyes—*blue* eyes.

"What *is* that?" I asked. "Some stupid contact lens thing?"

She seemed puzzled. "No, Lexi . . . I have twenty-twenty vision."

"Go to bed, Kase."

"Why did you want me to come in here?" she asked, looking around.

Was she kidding?

"What are you talking about? I didn't *want* you in here . . . It's the middle of the night!"

She slumped and leaned away. Her hand brushed the hair back away from her face. It was a gesture of elegance, practiced and casual.

Then she reached out to my arm. Her fingers brushed my skin. *"We can be friends,"* she whispered.

I felt a sharp burn and looked down to find four red marks across my skin, where she'd touched me.

"You know what?" I said. "I'm sick of this. Get out of here."

Kasey stood up suddenly, and grabbing the yearbook from my nightstand, threw it at the wall as hard as she could.

"What—?"

Then, with hard eyes, she backed away and hit herself in the face.

It took me a moment to process what I was seeing—my sister with an angry red mark on her jaw—and by the time I realized what she'd done, she was huddled on the floor screaming at the top of her lungs.

A second later Mom came running in, bleary-eyed. She looked at my sister crying on the floor, and then up at me, and the look in her eyes sent a chill through my body. I sat in a ball on the far corner of the bed. I couldn't find any words to explain.

Mom reached down and touched Kasey on the shoulder.

Kasey looked up at her, the red mark on her jaw getting brighter by the second.

Mom and I both gasped at the sight.

"Kasey . . ." Mom whispered, kneeling down to get a closer look.

My sister huddled down tighter and shied away from Mom's hand.

"Mommy," Kasey sobbed.

"What, baby? What happened?" Mom cooed, putting her hand on Kasey's back.

"Mom—" I said urgently.

Mom held up her hand, and I knew there was no use. There would be no "baby" for Alexis tonight.

"Lexi hit me," my sister said between choking sobs.

Mom took a moment to study the mark on Kasey's face, then looked up at me.

"She's lying," I said. "She did that to herself."

"To herself?" Mom repeated. "That doesn't make any sense!"

"And she threw that book at me," Kasey added.

Mom glanced over at the yearbook, which of course had fallen open to Megan Wiley's page, displaying the scribbled red X over her picture-perfect smile.

"Mom, can we talk about this?" I asked. "Alone?"

Mom looked up at me incredulously.

"You don't understand . . ." I said, even though I knew it was useless. She didn't believe me. Not in the slightest.

"You're right, Alexis," she said. "I don't understand."

"Don't be mad, Mommy," Kasey said. "Lexi knows she oughtn't hit people. She's just sad."

"Do you know what kind of *day* I've had?" Mom exclaimed. "Alexis, I know you're angry, but you don't have to take it out on your little sister!"

I didn't say a word. Kasey and Mom stood, and Kasey linked her arm through Mom's.

"Can I sleep in your room tonight, Mommy?" she asked in a pitiful voice.

Mom's shoulders slumped. She sniffled and nodded. I felt a pang in my chest.

"She's lying," I said as they walked out.

Mom didn't turn around, but Kasey did, and her green eyes flashed at me as she closed the door behind herself.

I sat down on my bed and pulled my left sleeve up to look at the marks on my arm. They looked like a really bad sunburn, and they were tender to the touch.

Could a person really snap as suddenly as it seemed Kasey had? One day, be a nice, normal girl, and the next be a total maniac?

Unless Pepper Laird had been telling the truth.

And Kasey had actually broken Mimi's arm on purpose.

Maybe she hadn't snapped all at once; maybe she'd been getting worse all the time. And then somehow it had come to a peak in the past day—breaking down after dinner, stealing the reports from school, exposing all my photo paper. . . .

And having something to do with what happened to Dad?

The numbers on my digital clock glowed blue. 2:41. It was the middle of the night. I had to spend four more hours in darkness with a crazy sister in the house.

I lay awake, staring at the ceiling, listening for any sound that might mean Mom was in trouble or that Kasey was coming back. But I didn't hear anything, and eventually I faded into an uneasy sleep.

15

THE NEXT MORNING I heard Kasey bumping around in her bedroom, humming, but she never came out. I'd grabbed a cold Pop-Tart and a Coke, and I was almost out the front door when Mom appeared at the top of the stairs.

How great would it have been if she'd said, "Let's clear the air, Alexis. We'll sit down in the dining room and you can tell me your side of the story."

But of course that didn't happen. She stared down at me.

"You don't believe her, do you?" I asked.

"I don't know what to think," she said. "I only know what I saw. And I know that your sister is terrified of you, Alexis."

"Kasey's not terrified," I said. "She's just a really excellent liar."

Then I saw my sister. She appeared behind Mom, moving silently, catlike, and glowering at me, arms folded.

"Maybe we just need to have a talk about it," Mom sighed.

"Forget it," I said. "Maybe later."

"No," Mom said. "I don't want to forget it. I want to resolve it."

From where I stood, it felt pretty darn resolved already. She'd made up her mind. I scooped my schoolbag off the ground and opened the door.

"Don't you dare walk out of this house, young lady!" Mom yelled after me.

But I did, and she only followed me as far as the foyer. I'm sure she spied out the window as I started down the street, but I didn't want to look back and check.

My early departure got me to school super early, so I sat on a stone bench in a deserted corner of the courtyard. Carter's car wasn't in the parking lot yet, and I didn't feel like talking to the Doom Squad, who were monopolizing the picnic tables with their usual lively discussions about manga and local bands, everyone trying to hog the spotlight from everyone else.

I wondered if anyone would notice if I just sat there alone, on that bench, in that corner—for the rest of high school. But eventually I got up and headed toward homeroom.

When the bell rang, I was starting to think I might

get through at least a class or two without incident. And then the classroom door opened.

Kasey waltzed right in as if she did this every day. A couple of people who knew she was my sister glanced at me.

Mr. O'Brien, the teacher, looked at her curiously, but just then the morning announcements began over the loudspeaker. Kasey stood perfectly still, not even seeming to breathe, watching me.

The teacher looked at Kasey expectantly. Probably thinking she was a freshman with a message from the office or another teacher.

But my sister didn't move. She just stood there.

I stood up and went to Mr. O'Brien's desk, positioning my body so that Kasey couldn't see my face.

"That's my sister," I said.

"What does she want?" he asked, craning his neck to look at her. I moved to block his view. "She should probably get to class."

"Um," I said. "She's not a student here."

He looked at me, puzzled.

I searched my head for an explanation but couldn't find one. "I'll be back in a minute," I said finally.

I grabbed the hall pass from the chalkboard ledge and walked past Kasey into the hall. She followed, and I heard my classmates buzz as the door swung closed.

I kept walking until I got to the parking lot. Then I spun on her, my arms folded.

"*What*, Kasey?"

"Mother made you an appointment with a psycho . . . psycho—"

"Psychologist?" I said. "*Mother?* You mean Mom?"

"Yes," she said, not even blinking. "I am not supposed to say anything."

I am not, I repeated to myself. *Oughtn't. Mother.* What was with the strange speech?

Of course, that was pretty much the least of my worries.

She was so calm—that was the weirdest thing. My neurotic, scaredy-cat little sister, standing there, watching me with eyes as smooth and untroubled as a fresh blanket of snow.

"So Mom thinks I'm a criminal. That's not news."

Kasey glanced down at my arm, squinting a little in the sun. The marks from the previous night were hidden under my sleeve. "That's not the only thing," she said, smoothing her shirt and looking away into the distance. She watched me from the corner of her eye.

"What do you mean by that?" I asked, wanting to reach out and shake the coolness out of her.

"I mean, she's going to find something tonight," Kasey said.

I didn't answer.

"Something that will make you look very bad."

"Like what?" I had no idea what she was hinting at.

Suddenly I caught a glimpse of the school security guard making his rounds in the distance.

I put my hand on Kasey's shoulder and steered her away, toward the gym. She didn't resist or even look up at me, just walked beside me as if we were taking a nice sisterly stroll.

I looked down at her again as we rounded a corner that hid us from the security guard.

"What are you trying to say?"

"You don't want to get arrested, do you?" Kasey asked, her lips working hard to keep from smiling.

"If you're trying to scare me, you're going to have to be more specific," I said.

"I'm just saying," she said, shrugging. "Just don't be surprised if the police show up."

"The police? Is this because of what happened to Dad?" She smirked.

"Do you know who's responsible for that, Kasey?" She shrugged.

"Was it someone you know?"

Her smirk twisted into an ugly smile.

"If you know anything about that, you need to say something," I said.

"Oh, don't worry about *me*," she said.

I stared at her.

"Kasey," I said slowly, "what exactly is Mom going to find tonight?"

The security guard appeared.

"You young ladies need to get to class," he said. "Especially you, Alexis."

Yeah, yeah. I put my hand on Kasey's shoulder and began walking again.

"But you can prevent it," she said.

"Prevent what?"

"The attempted murder charge," she said.

I took a staggering step away from her.

"Just start minding your own business, Alexis," she said. "That is all I ask of you."

We'd stopped near a set of double doors, the entrance to the gymnasium. I glanced back toward the halls of classrooms, but Kasey headed inside.

The banquet trappings were gone; instead we found a silent shipyard of floats for the next day's parade. We drifted through the rows, Kasey studying each float.

She finally stopped in front of one that was draped in white plastic sheeting with giant red cardboard shooting stars all over it. A long wooden bench was built on either side, so the sponsor club could sit and wave at the bystanders. Running through the middle, between the benches, was a small forest of artificial Christmas trees, some still with bits of leftover tinsel on them. Kasey stared, entranced.

"What are you doing?" I hissed at her.

"Pardon?" a voice asked, and Megan Wiley came around the front of the float.

Oh, perfect.

"Is this your float?" Kasey asked, her voice flat.

Megan glanced at me, and then smiled down at Kasey. Ever the diplomat.

"Yeah, it is. Well, it's the cheerleaders'. Are you going to watch the parade?"

Kasey shrugged, then wandered away for a second, staring at the decorations on the side of the trailer. Megan and I were left alone. But I was too busy watching my sister to look at Megan.

Finally, Kasey came meandering back to us.

"Well, have a good day," Megan said, and through her pristine politeness I could tell she was ready to be done with the conversation. She turned to look at the float.

"I will keep a special lookout for *you*, Megan," Kasey said, her eyes locked on Megan's profile.

Suddenly an image popped into my head. The yearbook photo with a giant red X through it.

"Oh good, thanks," Megan answered, turning to Kasey

with a cheery, I'm-nice-to-dumb-kids smile on her face.

Then, almost as if she'd seen a monster standing there instead of my little sister, Megan's smile vanished, and she took a shaky step backward.

Kasey's innocent gaze never faltered.

Megan touched her hair self-consciously and shot me a bewildered, questioning glance—almost like I'd said something out loud. A moment wobbled between us, and then I shook it off.

"Come on, Kasey," I said, grabbing her arm. "I'm sure Megan has more important things to worry about."

"I have to go," Megan said abruptly, and disappeared around the other side of the float.

As soon as we were out of the gym, I turned to my sister.

"Don't you dare," I said. "Whatever you're planning with the police. Who put you up to this? Mimi?"

Kasey smiled brightly. "I must go," she said, and turned around and started walking away.

I followed her.

"Kasey!" I said.

She stopped, but didn't turn around. I had to circle around in front of her to see her face.

"I mean it," I said.

"See you after school," she said, resting her hand on mine for a split second before I backed away. Then she stepped to the side and walked off past me. I didn't turn around. I didn't want to watch her go.

Something moved next to the gym and caught my attention. I looked up to see Megan Wiley hovering, almost hidden, around the far corner. Watching me. No—watching Kasey.

I turned and found myself face-to-face with the security guard. His name was Hal. I knew him too well. I'm sure he felt the same about me.

"Hey, you're bleeding," Hal said.

I looked down at my hand, where Kasey had touched me.

It was a mess of shallow cuts.

"Oh that," I said. "I have to get back to homeroom." And I walked away.

My mind ablaze with these latest horrors, I did what any high school student does in the face of a major crisis: I went to class.

First, second, and third period were fine, apart from my aching hand, the nagging fear of what would be waiting for me when I got home, and the feeling that everyone was staring at me. Pretty much the usual. I tried to pay attention to the class work to keep my mind off of prison and the idea that Kasey might be planning to, you know, frame me and get me thrown in jail.

No way could I talk to Mom about it. I debated going to Mrs. Ames, but I didn't think she'd believe me either.

No one would believe me. It was unbelievable. That was my problem.

But when I got to fourth period, who should be standing in the doorway but Megan herself. I saw her from all the way down the hall, searching the crowded corridor. I tried to mentally will her not to be looking for me, but she stepped into my path before I could get by.

"We need to talk," she said.

"No thanks," I said, trying to go around her.

"I mean it, Alexis," she said, her voice low.

She grabbed my elbow and pushed me away from the classroom. I followed her into the girls' bathroom, where she spun on me.

"Something is wrong with your sister," she said.

Somehow I'd suspected this was coming, and at the same time I felt like she'd poured a glass of ice water on my head.

"She's acting weird, right?"

I looked at Megan. She really looked like the popular kid straight out of a Hollywood movie. Even her teeth were sparkling white.

"Not really," I lied.

She narrowed her eyes. "We've never been friends—"

"Yeah, and I'm sure it breaks your heart," I said,

which was what a person like me was supposed to say to a person like her (in the movie version, at least).

"But right now I'm telling you that something is definitely off with her. What's her name? Kayli?"

"Her name is Kasey." My stomach turned.

I expected her to say, *"Pepper Laird is right and your sister is a psycho, and oh, by the way, she seems to be planning to kill me for some reason, as demonstrated by her strange behavior in the gym, oh, and has she by any chance scribbled over my picture in your yearbook?"*

Instead she said, "Please don't think I'm crazy."

"Why would I think you're crazy?" I'd been there when Kasey went all *Children of the Corn* on her.

I saw a spark in her brown eyes that seemed to be a glimmer of hope. "Alexis, I have a sense for this stuff, okay? All my life I could tell when something was—"

Suddenly I had a mental image of Pepper and Megan plotting against Kasey. I mean, so what if Pepper was right? Maybe Kasey *was* crazy. That was still no reason to release the cheerleaders on her. Maybe Mimi and Pepper and Megan were working together, and the whole thing was one giant conspiracy.

"I'm sorry," I said. "I don't really think it's your business that my little sister is eccentric."

"Eccentric?" Megan said. She looked genuinely surprised. "Alexis . . . your little sister is *possessed*."

I had to put my hand on the sink to keep from toppling over onto the grimy tile floor.

"Like ghost, demon, dark side, Voldemort," Megan went on. "Has there been anything strange going on at your house lately?"

I shook my head.

"Like weird noises, or sounds, or smells, or pockets of cold or hot air—"

"No! Stop!" I cried, although of course there'd been noises, sounds, smells, cold air. All of those things.

"Has Kasey had any blackouts? Has she—" Megan went pale. "Did she have something to do with your father's accident?"

"What my sister does at home is private!" I said.

But I couldn't get up the energy to say anything else.

"I felt it," Megan said. "Like, in my body. When your little sister was in the gym."

To be honest, she was freaking me out a little. Maybe . . . maybe if she really was serious, she could help somehow. Maybe she knew how to fix Kasey.

Or maybe she would tell the cheerleaders that she'd played a huge trick on me and I fell for it, and I would be a total laughingstock.

"How nice for you. I'm going to class," I said, heading out of the bathroom.

Megan matched my pace.

"You can't pretend you didn't see it," she said.

Ha. Shows what she knew. I could be a very good pretender.

We got to the classroom, and I reached for the door. She placed the flat of her hand on the door and held it shut.

"It could get bad," she said.

She looked at me with her lips pressed together, her eyes wide and solemn. No trace of perkiness on her face.

"It's my problem," I said. "Not yours."

"But I want to help."

"You don't have to worry. I'll stop her. I won't let her hurt you."

Megan drew back, her eyes wide. "Hurt *me?*"

Whoops.

"Why would she—"

The door swung open. Megan had to jump back to keep from getting hit.

"Were you two thinking of possibly joining us?" the teacher asked.

Megan and I slipped through the aisles to our desks, but I glanced up and saw her watching me, and I knew our discussion wasn't over.

After class I slinked into the library to avoid running into Megan. The librarian was engrossed in a romance novel, but as I walked past her desk, she looked pointedly at the NO SLEEPING ON THE COUCHES sign and then went back to her book.

It wasn't that I believed Megan, but . . . I just had to see for myself.

I went to the bank of computers with Internet access and did a search on possession. The screen went bright blue with a block of white text that said, "RESULTS RESTRICTED." "Exorcism," "ghost," and "poltergeist" produced the same answer.

Then I wandered through the shelves, completely unable to find any books that had anything to do with evil sisters.

Finally I went to the librarian's desk and asked her straight-out where I should look for books about demonic possession. The look on her face clearly said it was just what she'd expect from someone like me.

"We don't stock those books anymore," she said. "Ever heard of the CPA? Concerned Parents Association? They deemed those subjects inappropriate for children."

"So you threw them all away?"

"No, we didn't *throw* them away," she said, sounding exasperated.

"Then can you tell me where they are?"

"No."

I guess she expected me to give up, so when I stood

there and waited for an explanation, she sighed.

"Look, I don't want the CPA breathing down my neck again. They sent a mole in here last year begging to look at a book about witchcraft. Ten minutes later I'm in the principal's office. . . . Why don't you try *Harry Potter*?"

"Please," I said. "I'm a special needs case."

"You think so?" she asked, sounding kind of amused. She set her romance novel down and looked at me. So I was more interesting than a book called *Home Is Where the Heart Is: A Darcy Sloane Mystery*.

I knew she'd never believe me, and that, coupled with a mixture of exhaustion and exasperation, made me bold. I pulled up my sleeve to reveal the burn marks on my arm. "My little sister came into my locked bedroom last night and did this to me. And she showed up here this morning and did this." I showed her the back of my hand, the crisscross of razor-fine cuts, amazed at how matter-of-fact my voice sounded. "I personally think she's just crazy, but Megan Wiley? The cheerleader? *She* thinks Kasey's possessed by the devil. Or possibly just a demon."

The librarian sighed and opened her desk drawer and pulled out a book, plopping it on the counter. "How about this one?"

I looked at the title: *Cutting Through the Pain: Helping Teens Who Harm Themselves*.

"I'm sure this is a very good book for someone who

has different problems than I do," I said, pushing it back to her. Then I left the library.

When the bell rang and kids began streaming through the courtyard, I looked around for Carter. I felt a flutter in my stomach thinking about yesterday at the park. The heart is an amazing thing. Even on the verge of my entire life completely falling apart, I couldn't make myself stop thinking about how blue Carter's eyes were, how blond his hair was, how much he knew about architecture. . . .

After a minute or so, I gave up and started down the hallway toward my locker to pick up my Spanish book.

Megan Wiley was waiting for me.

And not ten feet away was a whole horde of cheer-leaders.

Great. Where were the police when you needed them? I would have handcuffed myself and jumped into the cruiser.

I slowed down, hoping they would move on, but Megan just stood there. I decided that I'd rather brave Señora Gregory's fury by showing up without my book than talk to Megan in the middle of the hallway.

But when Megan realized I wasn't planning to stop, she walked over to block my path. She even put her hand on my arm.

"What did you mean when you said you won't let her hurt me?" she asked.

"Megan, with all due respect, butt out."

"You're fooling yourself if you think things aren't going to get worse," she said.

I glanced at the cheermongers, who were practically drooling as they strained to hear what she was saying.

"Why are you so desperate to interfere with my life?" I asked.

But the thing was . . . secretly, I kind of knew I owed Megan an explanation. If she was in danger, didn't she deserve to know what was going on? But I was like a freight train barreling toward the end of the tracks—no turning back.

And everything she said scared me more.

"I'm only trying to help you," she said. She was indignant, not angry.

"Let me be clear. I don't want your help," I said.

Our audience had grown. The between-class crowds had stopped to eavesdrop.

"If you would just talk to me for a minute—"

"Talk to you?" I repeated. "Oh yeah, because we have such a wonderful, open relationship. I should pour my heart out to you."

Anyone else would have walked away.

But Megan didn't. She gritted her teeth and seemed to brace herself. "Okay, Alexis. I'm sorry we're not better friends, but that doesn't mean I don't understand what you're going through."

"Understand?" I asked.

I heard a murmur pass over the crowd, and I knew that this was a confrontation that some people in the school had been hoping to see for a long time.

I barreled ahead. "Sorry, this is a little more complex than spelling out words with your arms or getting your nails done. I somehow doubt that you comprehend the problems *real* people have."

For the first time Megan noticed the gathered crowd. She lowered her voice even further and sounded genuinely confused. "Why won't you talk to me?"

The thing was, just like with Carter and the architecture thing, I really did want to hear what she had to say. I just didn't want to hear it from *her*.

Alexis's universe, Megan's universe. One is over here, and the other one is waaaaaay over there. Completely separate. And that's how I liked them. But now Megan was stirring the pot.

I'd seen firsthand the damage her clique could do. No way was I going to let them loose on Kasey.

Crazy or not.

"You guys already messed with my best friend," I said. "Now you're coming after my little sister?"

And then I thought of the perfect thing to say, the

thing that would put Megan in her place, hopefully make her go away. For good.

I took a deep breath. "I don't want to be your next victim. I know you think because your mom is dead that you have the right to say whatever you want. But please. Leave me out of this. Leave my family out of this."

Boom.

Silence.

Megan stepped backward and knocked into one of the kids who'd been watching us.

"Leave her alone," someone said, and I assumed they were talking to me.

A tall, lanky guy, the star of the basketball team and arguably the single most popular boy in the entire school, took a step toward Megan. "Lay off her, Wiley." He looked at all of the cheerleaders and shook his head, disgusted. "What's *wrong* with you? Could you guys just try to be human for once?"

Megan looked at him in disbelief. Then she looked at me.

I hated myself.

She still didn't look angry—just hurt and confused, which only made me hate myself more.

"I just wanted . . . to help. . . ." she said.

Then she walked off, a line of girls trailing after her in defeat.

The basketball player patted me on the back.

"Take it easy, Pink," he said, and walked away. The crowd in the hall hovered for a moment, taking everything in, and then dispersed.

I stood alone in the hallway as the bell rang, feeling totally numb. Then I felt a hand on my shoulder.

Mrs. Ames.

She looked down at me, a deep frown on her face.

"I need to see you in my office."

16

Mrs. ames ushered me back to her office.

"You have a telephone call," she said, waving me to her desk chair. The receiver sat off the cradle.

My father is dead. My mother is dead. Kasey is dead.

"Hello?" I said, surprised that I could formulate a proper word.

"Alexis, it's Mom."

"What happened?" I braced myself for the worst.

"What? Nothing. What do you mean?"

"Dad's okay?"

"Oh . . . yes, sorry," she said, sounding only a fraction as apologetic as she should have, for giving me such a scare.

I sighed out the huge breath I'd been holding.

"I talked to the police," she said. "They made a mistake. The brakes weren't tampered with."

"They *weren't?*"

"Yes, they went over the car just now—"

"They're positive?"

"Yes, they're definitely sure," she said. She drew in a slow breath. "Alexis, I'm sorry about . . . the way it looked last night. . . ."

I had two options: one, tell her what Kasey did and try to explain the whole sordid mess, with Mrs. Ames breathing down my neck; or two, let it slide for now and explain later.

I went with Option Two. "You know last night wasn't what it looked like."

She sighed. "I have a brother, Alexis. I know that siblings can be a little too rough sometimes."

I couldn't believe she had somehow rationalized it to herself that way. That she had convinced herself I was capable of hitting my sister in the face.

"It's a long story," I said, and I felt Option One bubbling up inside me, dying to get out.

"You can tell me when I get home from work," Mom said. "We have a few things to talk about, actually."

Like shipping me off to a psychologist?

"And don't think I see Kasey as blameless. She's been kind of high maintenance lately, hasn't she?"

I shrugged, not that she could see it.

"Are you still there?"

"Um, yeah. But I have to get to class."

"I'm so sorry, Alexis."

"Yeah, well," I said. "I'm glad about the brakes."

"Me too. Okay, Lex. I'll let you get going."

"Hey, wait—"

"What?"

"Did Kasey go to school today?"

Mom paused. "I think so. Was she sick? No, I'm sure she went. She keeps talking about this research she's doing. It's all she can think about."

Research?

"But she said she'd try to go by the hospital this afternoon and see your father." Mom sighed. "I made her promise to take a break from her project—"

"What kind of project?" I asked.

"I don't really know," Mom said. "Something with genealogy, maybe? Did you have to do one of those?"

". . . Yeah."

"I've never seen her so intense about schoolwork. Maybe you two can go to the hospital together. Will you remind her?"

My mind was already swimming with thoughts of Kasey and what this newest information meant.

"Okay, if I see her," I said. "I'd better go. Bye."

"Bye," she said.

I hung up before she had a chance to say anything else.

Mrs. Ames sat quietly on the far side of the sofa,

looking around the room curiously. A new perspective for her, I guess.

"Good news?" she asked.

"Great," I answered. I couldn't force myself to sound cheerful.

She stood up, giving me the look that means she knows I'm not a bad person, no matter what anybody else thinks. "Off to class, then," she said gently.

"Sure thing," I said, scooping up my bag and walking out the door.

When the final bell rang at the end of sixth period, dread washed over me. I sat at my desk for an extra ten minutes, pretending to be organizing my notes, but finally the teacher stood up and grabbed her purse.

Where was I supposed to go now? My first priority was, of course, to avoid Megan. My second was to avoid having to go home and face my mother or sister. My third (and this might win for second if the circumstances were right) was to find Carter.

Megan wasn't waiting by my locker, thank God, but someone else was.

Pepper Laird.

I waited for her to say something about Mimi—or Megan—and I racked my brain, trying to figure out what I could say to shut her down.

But she spoke before I had a chance to.

"Did you know that Carter and I have been sort of on the verge of seeing each other for a while?" she asked in a loud, clear voice.

Um, no. And to be honest, I didn't really care. The idea of them together wasn't upsetting to me—because it seemed so completely impossible.

"Good for you," I said.

Pepper twisted her sweet sixteen ring around and around her finger as we spoke.

"Nothing too serious," she said. "But I thought for a while he might ask me to the dance."

"Maybe he will," I said.

"Noooooo," she said. She was being altogether too calm for my taste, talking in a really smooth voice, like we were business associates or something. "No, you couldn't possibly think that, because he's taking *you*."

"Not your business," I said, slamming my locker shut and starting to walk away.

Her voice got louder. "I just thought you cared about him," she called.

I turned around.

"You know, whether he has friends or not. Whether he fits in." She stared straight into my eyes. "Whether he's happy."

I shook my head. "I have no idea what you're—"

"My cousin was a senior at All Saints when Carter was there," she said, her voice hardly louder than a whisper. "She told me what happened."

I felt like a balloon that someone had let the air out of. "What are you . . . ?" I took a step closer to her. "You know nobody here knows about that. You wouldn't say anything—"

To Pepper's credit, she looked truly shocked at the idea. "No!" she cried. "Hello, I have *morals*."

Right. I fought the urge to roll my eyes. "Then why are you saying this to me like you have something hanging over Carter's head?"

"Because *you're* the one with something hanging over his head," she said, her lips in an almost sneer. "And since you're clearly too blind to see it, I thought I'd point it out. What do you think his life would be like if he started hanging out with you and your grotesque friends?"

I tried to imagine Carter interacting with the Doom Squad, but just couldn't form the mental picture. Then I thought of how nice it had been at the park, just the two of us. And then I pictured an endless string of days sitting at the park—just the two of us.

It seemed a little monotonous, to be honest.

"Do you think they'd be nice to him? Wouldn't it be embarrassing, watching him try to fit in? And then, if you ever break up, do you think his old friends will take him back?" She frowned and leaned closer to me. "Do you think he could handle being as completely alone as you are?"

Up close, Pepper's skin was a blanket of freckles, her eyes shallow hazel pools that seemed to let light pass right through. Her eyelashes were so pale you could hardly see them.

"I know how meaningless this must sound to someone like you. But I actually do care about Carter." She stepped back and arranged her bag over her shoulder. "Do you?"

Was it possible that I'd become so much of a loner that I'd never be able to have a boyfriend without feeling smothered? What if I got in over my head—and then discovered that I'd dragged Carter in over his head too? But by then it'd be too late. I'd be over him. And I'd be trapped.

I watched Pepper walk all the way to the end of the hall and through the double doors.

Of all the many thoughts that sprang into my head about her, this was the one that got my attention: She was right.

It was one of those perfect fall afternoons where people can't stop telling each other what a beautiful day it is.

"Beautiful day," the crossing guard said helpfully.

The sky stretched huge and dark blue and seemed to press down on the edges of the earth. It was warm in the sunlight, but a cool hint of breeze shook the leaves on the trees. They shimmied and quaked and reminded me of that dance move called "jazz hands," where you stretch out your hands and wiggle your fingers.

I forced myself to stop thinking about Carter and focused on Kasey instead.

Possessed.

That had to be, like, the stupidest thing I'd ever heard.

I mean, how ridiculous was it to assume that just because Kasey was acting a little crazy, doing a few weird things, that she was actually possessed?

And anyway, Dad's brake wires hadn't been cut. That was big, because it proved that Kasey didn't do it. And that was really important because "not trying to kill someone" ranked a lot lower on the psycho scale than "trying to kill someone." And that meant that Kasey was maybe only slightly nutso instead of downright padded-room-worthy.

I slowly made my way toward Whitley Street, excuses for my sister's behavior knitting together in my head. By the time I reached the house I practically had it all rationalized as a figment of my imagination.

But I still felt a spike of dread in my spine as I put my key in the dead bolt.

The front hall was quiet. The whole place was quiet. Surrey Middle didn't let out until 3:15 p.m., and it was only 3:00. So, according to my fresh, optimistic outlook, I wouldn't see my sister for a half hour or so.

Which gave me time to snoop around her bedroom. Kasey did still steal those reports. That was worth looking into, right?

First I went to the kitchen, pulled out the phone book, and called the main office of Surrey Middle School. When the secretary answered, I put on my best "adult" voice.

"Hello," I said. "I'd like to see if one of your students was absent today."

"I'm sorry," the woman replied. "We only release that information to family."

"Oh," I said, in my normal voice. "Well, it's my sister."

"What's the name?"

"Kasey Warren."

A pause, the clicking of keys on a keyboard. "Your sister is listed as 'present.'"

"Great, thanks."

I hung up and climbed the stairs, feeling even better.

I set my stuff down outside my door and hovered for a moment outside Kasey's bedroom.

"Stop being a wimp," I said out loud.

The sound of my voice gave me a burst of courage. I

put my hand on the knob and turned, pushing the door open and stepping inside in one motion.

Kasey was sitting on her bed, looking out the window.

Fear flooded over me when I saw her, and I was about to say something in my own defense, when I suddenly realized she hadn't even turned around.

I stood very still and watched her. Her eyes were wide open and she sat with her legs crossed, her long hair pulled back with barrettes, her fuzzy peach sweater glowing in the sun.

She didn't seem to see or hear me at all.

I cleared my throat.

Nothing.

"Kase," I whispered.

She didn't move.

Fear seized me so fiercely that tears sprang into my eyes. I took a step backward toward the hall.

"Why are you leaving?" Her voice was flat, cold.

I stopped. My fists curled so tightly that my fingernails dug into my palm.

"I just wanted to see if you were home," I said.

"But the secretary told you I was in school, didn't she?"

Tell me about it.

"I thought I heard something," I said.

"You're lying."

"Kasey . . ." I said. "What exactly are you doing?"

She still didn't look at me. "I'm thinking," she answered.

"About what?"

"About something someone offered me."

"Who?"

She didn't answer.

"Do you mean drugs?" I found myself hoping it was that easy, but with every silent second that passed as I waited for an answer, my highly precarious sunny outlook grew cloudier.

"You don't have any friends," Kasey said, as if the thought had just occurred to her.

"I have a few."

"I didn't have any friends either."

She turned away from the window, and her eyes searched the shelves of dolls.

"I do now, though, Lexi," she said. "I have a new friend. She says I'm . . . special."

I moved a halting step closer to the bed. "I've always been your friend, Kasey." I moved forward and put my hand on her shoulder, but she yanked her body away as if I'd burned her.

"Don't touch me!" she cried.

I didn't want her to see my trembling hands, so I stuffed them into my pockets.

"Who is she, Kasey?" I asked. "Where did you meet her?"

She looked at me for the first time, her face in shadow. All I could see of her eyes was the light glinting off them from the window.

Did I even want to know what color they were?

Suddenly my sister was off the bed and right in front of me, holding on to my forearm so tightly that the skin around her fingers was turning white.

"I don't know what to do," she said. Her voice was small and scared.

"I'll help you," I said. "Kasey, maybe your new friend isn't . . . nice. Maybe it's not a good idea to take . . . whatever she's offering."

"But you don't understand," she said. "When I do what she tells me to, it's like magic. Nothing is scary. Even if people are mean to me, I don't care. And everyone does what I say."

Magic. My heart sank back in my chest.

"What do you mean . . . they do what you say?"

My baby sister was possessed.

She seemed to have forgotten that she was holding my arm. The pressure slowly increased as she spoke. "I mean I can tell people things, and they just want to listen to me. They believe me. Like the attendance lady at school. I called, Lexi, and I told her to mark me as present. And she did."

"Who . . . who else have you done that to?"

"Officer Dunbar," she said.

Oh no.

"I went to talk to him this morning about the car," she said. "I told him he was wrong, what he wrote on that form about the brakes—so he changed it."

"Oh . . . Kasey," I said.

She let go of my arm and went back to the window. There were no cuts or burns this time.

"I did it for you, Alexis. They were going to arrest you."

"So it was true—the brakes . . . ?" The "attempted murder" threat this morning—she was going to somehow pin the whole thing on me.

Kasey ducked her head and turned away.

"No, oh no, Kasey, *please*," I said.

"It wasn't *me*, Alexis," she said. "I didn't cut the brake wires."

"But you know who did?"

She raised her hand to her mouth and started nibbling on her fingernails, then shrugged.

"Kasey, Dad could have been killed."

"I know!" she said. "But that was an accident. It was just supposed to be a joke."

"But you didn't do it?"

She shook her head emphatically.

"Then . . . who did?"

"My friend."

None of this made sense. I felt like I was talking to the Cheshire cat.

"Kase, who is this person?"

My sister's voice went squeaky, and she covered her face with her hands as if she was embarrassed. "She's just someone I met."

"Can I . . . meet her?"

Her fingers fell away from her face. "Maybe." A puzzled frown pressed her lips into a pout. "I mean . . . maybe you already have."

"I don't understand," I said.

But I was beginning to.

In the hallway the other day, with the dirty socks.

"Kasey," I said, "do you remember coming into my room last night?"

She flushed pink. "Yeah," she said in a tiny voice.

"How'd you get that bruise on your face?"

Now her eyes flashed and she raised her chin defiantly. "You threw a book at me."

"No," I said. "That's not what happened."

She started chewing on her fingernails again.

"You don't remember," I said. "Because it was your friend in my room. And it was your friend in the hallway with the dirty socks. And stealing the reports from school, right?"

"I guess," Kasey said slowly.

"Listen to me!" I said. "You got that bruise because you hit yourself in the face."

"You're lying!" she cried.

"I never take off my rings," I said, holding up my hand so she could see them. "If I had hit you, you would have scratches on your face."

She touched her face, and her fingers traced the smooth skin of the bruise.

"Kase, *there is no friend.*" A thought dawned on me. "You have, like, multiple personalities. You just need to see a doctor and get some pills or something."

She walked over to the window and put the palms of her hands flat against the glass.

"I know you're lonely," I said. "But *I'll* be your friend."

Not that schizophrenia was so great, but at least it was a medical condition. It had symptoms and a diagnosis and treatments.

She rested her head against the glass, then backed away from the window and turned to me.

"You fool," she said. Her voice was low and hard and angry. "You cannot chase me away. *I like it here.*"

Then she dashed toward me, lifted her hand and gave me a shove that sent me flying across the room. I crashed into Kasey's dresser and fell to the floor, the air completely knocked out of my lungs.

Her strength wasn't the strength of an angry thirteen-year-old.

It wasn't . . . human.

But that was impossible.

"Kasey—" I croaked.

"You are just jealous," she snapped. Her voice grew thin and rasping.

I looked up into her burning green eyes.

"I want to talk to Kasey," I said, trying to remember something, *anything* from the TV movies I'd seen about people with split personalities. "I want to talk to my sister. I know she's still here."

"You do not know *anything*." But she turned away and rubbed her eyes with her balled-up hands. Her shoulders slumped, and her face relaxed into its usual pout.

Kasey was back. "Lexi . . . why are you down there?"

I stared up at her, unable to stop my body from shying closer to the floor. "You *pushed* me."

"No I didn't."

Was it possible that she really didn't remember? ". . . Your *friend* pushed me."

She looked around the room, like I'd been talking about a real person. Then her eyes got a faraway look. "Oh," she said.

"Who is she?" I asked. "*What* is she?"

Kasey hugged herself tightly and turned away.

"Please," I begged. "Make her leave us alone."

I saw the muscles in Kasey's jaw clench up, then relax, then clench up again.

"Just tell her to go away," I said. "She's your friend, right? She'll do what you want?"

She thought about it for a few seconds. Then she lifted a hand and studied her fingernails. "I like it, Lexi," she said.

She *liked* it? Liked messing with brake wires and stealing things from school and pushing people so hard they flew across the room?

"But . . ." My voice wavered. "I'm still your sister, right?"

She shrugged. "Yeah."

"So we can . . . we can . . ." We can what? I didn't know. If only there had been a poster in the clinic: HOW TO TELL IF YOUR SIBLING IS POSSESSED BY THE DEVIL OR JUST COMPLETELY MENTAL!

I was scared out of my mind and trying to keep her talking, keep her with me.

"Don't worry, Lexi, I haven't made up my mind yet. I have until midnight tomorrow."

"Kasey, I promise I will be your best friend, I will do whatever you want—"

"That's not friendship," she said, her mouth pulled into a tight frown. "Friendship isn't just about doing what the other person says."

Oh, sure, *now* she finds a backbone. "But isn't she telling you what to do?"

She shook her head vigorously. "Not all the time. Sometimes she listens to my ideas."

I really didn't want to know, but I had to ask. "The thing with the car . . . whose idea was that?"

Her blue eyes narrowed and there was a hard glint in them. "I told you, she cut the brakes . . . but it was my idea to talk to the police."

That was a good sign, right? That meant Kasey still cared, on some level.

"Lexi, I'm not asking for your permission. I'm not even asking for your opinion."

Clearly not.

"I just thought you deserved an explanation."

"Kase, what if we talked to Mom about this?"

"Don't."

"But Mom and Dad probably wouldn't want you to—"

"*No.*"

Tears splashed onto my cheeks. "What am I supposed to do?"

She cocked her head to the side. "Live your life, Alexis." Her eyes suddenly flashed from blue to green, a vivid emerald that seemed to burn right into me. "Your pathetic, lonely life."

Then she grabbed her schoolbag and walked out, leaving me alone on the floor.

The front door slammed shut, and I collapsed, laying my head down on the carpet, crying tears of rage and fear and helplessness.

After a few minutes of intense self-pity, I forced myself to stand. I grabbed my sweatshirt and my house key and stumbled down the stairs, ignoring the sharp ache where my shoulder blade had made contact with the edge of Kasey's dresser.

The afternoon sun was blinding after the muted light of our dark house. I stepped out onto the front porch and looked around for my sister.

Midnight tomorrow . . .

As my eyes adjusted and the world faded into view again, my heart sank.

She was long gone.

There was only one option left.

I had to find Megan.

THE FOOTBALL FIELD WAS EMPTY when I arrived back at the school, and something inside of me deflated. All my courage had been used up during my confrontation with Kasey, and now I was alone.

And scared.

I sat down on the lowest bleacher and stared at my hands. *Keep going*, said the voice in my head. *Go to her house. Find her.*

But I just couldn't. The longer I sat there, the more powerless I felt. Possessed or not, Kasey had almost killed our dad. With every passing minute she fell deeper under the power of whatever it was that was controlling her.

I heard chattering female voices and knew it was my last chance to get out of there before I was in it for real. I would have to face Megan, take whatever she dished out, and then grovel for her help—possibly in front of the entire Surrey High School cheer squad.

Did I have a choice? I could go home, break into the emergency cash jar, put some clothes in a backpack, and hit the road. Run away and leave the whole mess behind me. There would be plenty of room on the open road for new, smaller messes.

But it was too late to run away.

"What's *she* doing here?" I recognized Pepper Laird's voice, and the talking stopped short.

I looked up.

There they stood, toned, tanned, and all set to do high kicks and catchy chants. One thing was wrong with the picture, and I was it. If looks could kill, I would have been a charred pile of ex-Alexis on the bleacher seat.

Like a swan gliding through lily pads, Megan sailed to the front of the pack and stared down at me. Her eyes were cool, emotionless. They had none of the passion that I'd seen in them earlier when she'd offered her help. I'd waited too long.

"Don't worry, Megan, we'll get rid of her," Pepper said.

"I'm calling security!" someone else said. Four cell phones flipped open.

But Megan simply looked at me. And I looked at her.

Five seconds passed. Ten. No one said a word.

Finally Megan took a deep breath.

"Pepper," she said, "please start the warm-up without me."

Pepper stared in confusion for a moment and then obediently clapped her hands together three times. "All right!" she called. "Two laps, let's go!"

And the cheerleaders, Pepper included, took off in two neat lines down the track.

Megan stayed. She crossed her arms in front of her chest and watched me.

It sounds silly to say, but seeing her standing there, I completely understood why she was so popular. There was something about her that was regal, composed. She was one of those people who never let you see them sweat. I had a vision of throwing myself at her feet, begging her forgiveness.

That was probably what it would take.

I stood up.

"I told you it would get bad," she said.

Fair enough. "Megan, I'm sorry—"

"No, Alexis. Don't apologize."

I closed my mouth.

"I get why you hate us. What they did to Beth Goldberg sucked, okay? But if we're going to do this together, you have to trust me."

I shook my head in confusion, but Megan mistook it for a rejection.

"I never said anything, because it sounds like I'm making excuses. But I was in Ireland with my grandmother when they put that presentation together. I wouldn't have let them do it." She swallowed hard. "I swear, Alexis, on my mom's grave."

I did *not* want to talk about graves and mothers.

"You don't have to forgive me, but you have to believe me. That I'm not messing with you." She had her arms folded in front of her, hands gripping her elbows.

It was the first time I'd ever seen her look . . . not perfect. Not in control.

I believed her.

"Something horrible is going on with my sister," I said. "And I'm not a hundred percent sure, but there's a chance . . . you're right. Or she might just be completely psycho."

"Pyscho how?"

"Like hearing voices," I said. "Multiple personalities. Doing crazy stuff. Only . . ."

She waited for me to finish.

"Only . . . superstrength isn't really a symptom of a mental disorder, is it?"

Megan shook her head. "Sorry to disappoint you, but no."

My head started to ache. "And, like . . . amazing powers of persuasion . . ."

She reached out and put her hand on my arm. "Trust your instinct, Alexis."

I swallowed hard, looking at her perfectly polished red fingernails.

Her voice was gentle. "What do you really think?"

What did I think? "I think . . . she's possessed."

"I'll help you," Megan said immediately.

She grabbed my arm and started toward the parking lot.

"I want to know everything that's happened," she said. "And we need to go to your house. Whatever it is, it's probably there."

I looked up at the squad, almost done with their first lap. "Don't you have to tell someone you're leaving?"

"They're smart girls," she said, not stopping. "They'll figure it out."

A sarcastic reply made it all the way to the tip of my tongue, but I swallowed it right before it slipped out. I grabbed my sweatshirt and hurried to catch up.

"So what happened?" Megan asked.

"She cut the brake wires in my mom's car," I said. Might as well lay all the cards on the table. "She was going to frame me for it, but somehow she convinced the police it was an accident. And she has some weird plan. She said something about midnight tomorrow."

Megan led me to an ivory VW New Beetle. She was the only sophomore I knew who had her own car.

I glanced back at the entrance to the school. The double door began to open.

Carter walked out.

"Hold on," I said.

Carter saw us, did a double take, then waved and headed straight over. "Where've you been?" he asked.

In spite of everything, I couldn't keep a tiny smile off my lips.

Carter glanced at Megan questioningly, but didn't ask. Instead he lowered his voice and looked right into my eyes. "Is everything okay?"

I shook my head.

"I'm sorry," he said, touching my wrist lightly. The brush of his fingers against my arm would have made me melt in my shoes if Megan hadn't been staring at us impatiently.

"You guys are going to have to do this later," she said, flipping her cell phone open to check the time. "Alexis and I have things to do."

Carter looked bewildered. "Where are you going? I'll come."

"No, you can't," I said, pulling my wrist away from him.

"You really can't," Megan said, turning toward the car. "Sorry. Come on, Alexis, let's go."

There wasn't time to explain the whole situation. My

heart ached—I longed to be wrapped in his arms again, pour out my troubles, make everything feel okay, even if it wasn't.

"Call me," Carter said, reluctantly taking a half step back.

"I will," I said. "I'm sorry."

"Get in," Megan ordered from the driver's seat. I sat down in the passenger seat and let my bag slip to the floor as Carter walked away.

I guess I sighed kind of melodramatically or something, because Megan gave me a sideways eye roll as she backed out of the parking space. I noticed how delicately her slender hands moved the gearshift, the way her fingers grasped the steering wheel, and I felt like a clumsy, galumphing oaf. As we drove away from the school, I glanced back to see Carter's car pull out of the parking lot and turn in the other direction.

"How long have you two been . . . ?" Megan said.

"What? We're not. Nothing's going on."

"The way he was looking at you . . . that's definitely something."

"I guess Pepper thinks so too," I couldn't help saying.

"Pepper? She likes him, but he doesn't seem to be into her."

"She came to my locker and had a talk with me."

"What did she say?"

I recalled the dejected look on Carter's face, and Pepper's words came back to me. Already I was bringing him down, hurting his feelings, leaving him on his own. "Nothing."

"Right," Megan said. "Because Pepper's famous for saying nothing."

I didn't respond.

"Now tell me everything," she said. "How long has the weird stuff been happening?"

"Since Tuesday night," I said.

"And is it just your sister?"

Interesting question. Dad was safely tucked away in the hospital—well, perhaps "safely" wasn't the right word. And Mom? Sure, she was distant and detached, but that was just Mom being Mom.

"Yeah, just Kasey," I said.

"Now skip to the part about me."

I'll spare you the gory details, but it wasn't long into my little story that Megan had to pull the car over to the side of the road so she could devote all of her attention to staring at me in indignant disbelief.

When I reached the part about Kasey showing up at school that morning, I hesitated. Megan was glaring at me so fiercely that I couldn't concentrate.

"If I'd known this was going to happen, I never would have—"

She raised a finger in the air and closed her eyes. I took it as a very clear way of saying, *Leave me alone for a minute or I will push you out of my car.*

A few seconds and some deep breaths later, she spoke. "Okay, Alexis," she began, "I'm not going to pretend I'm happy about being cast as an evil villain in your stupid little fairy tale."

"Megan, I didn't know—"

"Quiet," she said. "Let's just put the past behind us and not worry about it." She exhaled. "For *now*."

She put the car in drive and pulled back onto the road, shaking her head.

"Well . . . it's convenient," I said at last.

"What is?"

"If it had been about somebody who didn't believe in ghosts . . ." I said, but I didn't know how to finish. A sour, empty ache growled to life in my stomach. My arms felt weak, and I closed my eyes.

"So . . . what changed your mind? Why did you suddenly decide you needed my help?"

"Oh God," I said. I hadn't even talked about what had happened at the house, Kasey's evil hoodoo.

So I told her. As the story went on, I felt more and more ridiculous. My thirteen-year-old sister cops an attitude and I run for cover.

I waited to hear what Megan would say.

"Tomorrow at midnight . . . What's Friday? Is it an important date—her birthday or something?"

"No."

She drummed her fingers on the steering wheel. "It's cool that you kept her talking. You never know what she might have done otherwise."

I hadn't thought about it that way. The weak place in me felt a little stronger.

For the first time since we'd gotten in the car, I wondered where we were going. We were driving past the new developments where houses as big as museums were being constructed on lots so small that they hardly had space for a front or backyard. (Dad makes faces and calls them McMansions. Mom keeps quiet, which I assume means she wouldn't mind living in one someday.)

"We're going to my house," Megan said. "I need to change out of my cheerleading clothes."

"Okay," I said.

"Listen. My grandmother might be home. If you say even a single word about this to her, I'll be grounded until college."

"All right," I said, instantly certain that I would somehow slip up and ruin everything. *Hi, nice to meet you! Your granddaughter and I are just going to mess with the Dark Side for a while. I love those flowers, are they violets?* "She doesn't believe in . . . it?"

"That's the problem," Megan said. "She does believe. Very much. So she tries to keep me away from it."

"But she knows you're interested, right?"

"Yeah."

"How did you start believing in the first place?" Interest in the paranormal wasn't really the "in" thing at Surrey High. It's not the kind of thing you'd chat about during lunch.

Megan turned down the radio. "Do you believe in angels?"

Uh.

"I'm not sure," I said. "Does anyone?"

"Um, yeah, a *lot* of people do. And once you believe in good things, it's not that hard to believe in . . . bad things."

"So you believe in angels?"

"Yeah." She shrugged. "I mean, not the harps and feathers kind. But I know *something* happens to good people when they die." Her cheery tone thinned. "People like my mom."

I was desperate to turn the conversation away from Megan's mother, so I said, "How long have you lived with your grandmother?"

Which, as a changing-the-subject tactic, was a complete failure. It was just another way of calling attention to the fact that Megan's mom was dead. Way to go, Alexis.

"Since I was two years old." She glanced at me. "It's okay, I can talk about her. My dad was never even in the picture. Somewhere out there is a man who has no idea he has a daughter. Although, from what Grandma says about him . . . he probably has more than one."

And I thought *my* dad was absentee.

"I don't even remember my mom," she said. "Not really. Every once in a while I feel like I do, but then I think it's probably just a *Sesame Street* flashback."

"Do you have aunts and uncles?" I asked.

"Nope," Megan said, shaking her head slowly. "Just me and Grandma."

"I didn't even know that," I said, trying to figure out how you could be in school with someone for so long and not know such a huge thing about them.

"Well, it's not like you ever tried to get to know me."

Ouch. The sting of truth.

"So, bottom line. If she suspects that I'm trying to have anything to do with ghosts or spirits, she'll ship me off to boarding school and I'll end up in a convent."

"If she's so strict about it, why are you doing it?"

"I'm sorry, Alexis," she said. "I didn't realize you were the only person on the planet allowed to think for yourself." Then she shrugged again and cocked her head to one side. "Besides that your little sister seems to be fixated on me? I have my reasons."

WE RODE IN SILENCE until we reached a large beige house with lots of clean white trim. Megan pulled into the driveway next to an enormous silver BMW.

"She's home . . ." Megan said, staring at the front door the way a gladiator might watch the gate the lions come running out of. "You'll have to distract her while I get some things from my room."

Inside, Megan led me down a hallway that spilled out into a huge, sunny living room. To our left was a spacious kitchen, where a woman in her sixties stood at the counter, leafing through a pile of mail.

"Megan," the woman said, looking up at us in surprise. "What are you doing home? Don't you have practice?" Her gaze lingered on my hair, but she didn't say anything.

"Yes," Megan said, which wasn't *technically* a lie. "Just changing and grabbing a few things for the float. Grandma, this is Alexis. Alexis, this is my grandmother, Mrs. Wiley."

Mrs. Wiley, indeed. This was not the grandmother I'd been preparing myself for. Instead of a sweet, frumpy housedress, she wore a sleek burgundy suit that I instinctively knew was more expensive than about five of my mother's suits put together.

"I'll be right back," Megan said, giving me a pointed look and dashing up the stairs.

Mrs. Wiley gave me the once-over.

"Are you on the squad?" she asked. She reminded me of the stepmother in Cinderella, except not mean—just cool, reserved. I could see where Megan got it.

"Um, no," I said.

Ergh, *lie*! Lie, you idiot.

Mrs. Wiley waited for an explanation, her salon-groomed eyebrows pressing closer together. I felt like a piece of art being studied at a museum—or more likely, in Mrs. Wiley's case, a small company about to be gobbled up by a huge corporation.

I groped in the back of my mind for something to say. "I'm doing a photo shoot for the school newspaper."

"Ah, a photographer," she said. I waited for a suspicious reaction, but she didn't seem interested in providing one. I could have died of relief.

"I dabble," I said, mentally willing her not to ask me about the school paper. I didn't even know if they *had* photographers. When I looked at her to see how she would reply to this, her eyes weren't on me. They were fixed on the window over the sink—or rather, somewhere in the distance.

"Megan's mother was a photographer," she said. "A good one. She used to win contests." Then a tremor seemed to move through her body, and she looked down at the mail on the counter.

"I didn't know that," I said. It was the only thing I could think of to say.

"Do you want to study photojournalism in college?"

Back to the photography. "Not really," I said. "My stuff is more . . . artistic. But not pretentious," I added quickly.

"I do dislike pretension," Mrs. Wiley mused, tearing open an envelope. "I wish Megan would take up an interest in something like photography."

"She's a really good cheerleader; she could probably even get a scholarship."

Grandma tut-tutted under her breath. "And spend college funneling beer and dating football players. It's not the scholarship . . . I just wish she would use her mind instead of her muscles."

I was surprised to feel the urge to defend Megan spring up inside me. I didn't even know what I would say, except that I'd seen her countless times walking around school with her eyes glued to her black cheerleading notebook. As much as I disliked the whole idea of shaking pom-poms and hopping around in short skirts, it didn't seem fair to say that Megan wasn't good, or that she didn't work hard at it. That thought took a second to settle in, and I brushed it away before I had time to feel like a huge hypocrite for everything I'd ever thought or said about Megan.

The kitchen was mercifully quiet for a minute or two. I gazed around the room, trying to look mesmerized by the iron candelabra on the counter, but just when I was feeling confident that the hard part of my job was over, Mrs. Wiley spoke again.

"Are you going to the dance Friday night?" she asked.

"Yeah," I said, immediately regretting it. If I had just given her a simple "no" and acted dejected, she would have left the subject alone.

"Do you have a date?"

"I guess that's kind of what it is," I answered.

"What does your dress look like?"

My dress?

I tried to picture a dress in my head, but all I could think of was the pastel Easter dresses Kasey and I had worn as little girls. Somehow, baby blue with puffy sleeves and chicks embroidered on the front didn't seem to cut it for Homecoming.

"I guess I don't have one yet," I said.

"It's getting late," Mrs. Wiley said, sounding a little concerned. Then she perked up. "You should borrow something of Megan's."

"I don't think her clothes would fit me."

"Yes they would," she said, giving me a decisive up-and-down glance. "You're the same size. You're taller than she is, but that shouldn't matter."

She smiled kindly and went back to the mail. I felt a slow flush spread up the sides of my face. No way could she think someone like me would even be friends with Megan, much less fit into her clothes. I was so . . . so different. Megan was perfect, and I was . . . not perfect. Megan was skinny and fit, and I was . . . well, I was plenty skinny, but since I didn't work for it, it didn't seem possible that we could wear the same size anything.

"What could be keeping Megan?" she asked. "Why don't you run up to her room? First door on the right at the top of the stairs."

"Okay," I said, hoping my relief wasn't too apparent. Mrs. Wiley was nice, but if she pressed for any more information—a simple question about earrings or footwear—I would blow the whole operation.

I bolted up the stairs and knocked on the first door on the right.

Megan opened it and looked at me in surprise.

"What about my grandmother?" she asked.

"It was her idea," I whispered.

I slid through the door and Megan eased it shut again behind me. Then she walked over to the bed and got down on her hands and knees, digging around behind the dust ruffle.

"Do you need help?" I asked.

"No," she said, her voice muffled. "I'm almost done."

I leaned against the door, part of me still shocked that I was standing in Megan Wiley's bedroom. I can't say what I was expecting, but her bedroom didn't look like a stereotypical cheerleader's room. There was some evidence that a pom-pom pusher lived there, but it was minimal—mostly confined to one shelf of the bookcase.

The rest of her stuff was just an eclectic mix of books and knickknacks. It was kind of cluttered, but not in the way that drives me crazy, like Kasey's room—it was clutter with a purpose, like one of those expensive designer furniture stores in the mall. It made me think of a professor's study, only instead of maps and journals, there were embroidered pillows and polished stone sculptures.

I noticed a black-and-white photo in a silver frame hanging on the wall near the closet. It was of a very young Megan and younger Mrs. Wiley sitting on a flat rock in front of a lake. "Did your mom take that?" I asked.

Megan pulled her head out from underneath the bed and stared at me. "What are you talking about?"

I pointed to the picture. "That photograph."

Megan stared at the photo for a moment. "Why—? I doubt it. It's just something I've always had." She took a step toward it, looking at the image—her own tiny face staring seriously at the camera, and Mrs. Wiley, smiling and elegant in her picnic dress.

It was almost like Megan had never really looked at it before.

"I like it," I said. "It's really good."

"But . . . why would you ask that?" she said, looking back at me. "If my mother took it?"

"Because your . . ." I didn't know what to say. "Because your grandmother said your mom was a photographer."

The corners of Megan's eyes crinkled. "She told you that?"

I nodded cautiously. Maybe Megan considered these little pieces of information private, secret.

But she didn't seem angry, just puzzled. "She told you something about my mother. Something she never told me." Her voice was calm, but kind of *too* calm—the way a person talks when they're in shock. She pulled the frame off the wall, then placed it upside down on the bed and pried the metal clips off. Lifting the backing away, she gently picked up the photo by its edges.

I stayed where I was. I'd done plenty already.

She breathed out softly. "Come look," she said, wonder in her voice.

I went to her side, and she pointed to a corner of the photo that had been hidden by the mat. Someone had signed it faintly in pencil, with a first initial and their last name.

"Shara Wiley," Megan said.

"Is that . . . ?" I studied the next word.

"Mom," Megan said. She shook her head and kind of sank onto the bed.

"Wow," I said.

Megan set the photo down carefully on the frame and turned to me. "My grandmother adopted me after the accident. She never talks about my mom. Never." She glanced back at the photo. "They didn't get along well, and they weren't speaking when Mom died. I guess it was horrible for her."

"I'm sorry . . ." I said. I couldn't finish the thought.

I leaned in closer to look at the image. It was really a nice shot, not too posed or phony, the way a lot of people's family portraits look. And Megan was a cute kid, with one eyebrow raised skeptically.

"Hey," I said, noticing the bracelet hanging off her chubby toddler arm. It was one of those hearts that looks like it's been cut in half. "I have a charm like that."

Megan reached to her neck and pulled a gold chain out from under the sweatshirt she'd put on, revealing the dangling charm. "I still wear it," she said. "I think these things were pretty popular."

"It's really cool that your mom took this," I said, marveling that I'd never even thought to take a picture of my family.

"Thanks," Megan said, delicately replacing the photo in the frame. I could tell by the tightness in her voice how meaningful this was for her. "I guess there's time for this later. Right now we have more pressing issues."

"I'm really sorry," I repeated.

Megan ignored my apology. "Grandma said she was a photographer?"

I nodded. "A good one. Award-winning, your grandma said."

"Wow," Megan said. And then her eyes lost their focus and she stared off in the distance. She hung the picture back in its corner and looked at it one last time. Then she glanced at me. "You're into photography, right? Maybe sometime you could show me . . ."

Her voice trailed off.

"Are you kidding?" I said. "Of course."

And I meant it. I mean, I totally owed it to her, but more than that . . . I just got this subtle vibe from Megan that I didn't get from anybody else. That if I showed her my photos, she would understand. She would get them. The idea of having an intelligent conversation about photography was as oddly irresistible as the thought of listening to Carter insult my house with all his fancy architectural terms.

Megan sighed. "I guess we're ready to go," she said.

"Oh," I said. "Your grandmother told me to ask you about dresses, so if she asks, just say we talked about it."

"What about dresses?"

I hesitated. "She said I should borrow one from you for the dance."

"You don't have a dress?"

I shrugged. "It doesn't matter."

"You should take one," she said. "Then she won't ask any questions." She went to her closet and pushed the doors open.

I felt extraordinarily silly. "Megan, I don't think any of your clothes . . ."

"Chill," she said, scanning the racks of clothes. "It's just for show. You don't have to actually wear it, but you might as well."

"If I'm even alive for the dance," I said, only half joking.

She turned and looked at me solemnly. "You will be, Alexis," she said. "I promise we'll find a way to fix what's happening."

I sighed. The fact that she took it seriously made it seem so much harder. Half of me wanted someone to convince me that it was all in my head. Then I could pop a magic pill and go back to my normal life.

Except, what was my normal life? Could I go back to hanging out with the Doom Squad? Could I go back to hating Megan?

"What are you going to do with your hair?" she asked, reaching toward the back of the rack. "Have you thought about wearing it up?"

"No," I said truthfully, because I hadn't thought about my hair at all.

"Okay, don't hate me for this," Megan said, and turned around, holding out a dress . . . a *pink* dress.

When I say pink, I mean Pepto-Bismol pink. Easy-Bake Oven pink. Beauty-pageant pink. I took an involuntary step back, as if she were holding a snake. "Uh-uh. No way."

"Come on, it would be adorable. You'd look like a punk-rock Barbie doll."

"No," I said. "Megan, no. People would think—"

"I thought you didn't care what people thought about you."

Crud. "I would look like a *strawberry*."

"Not even," she said. "I'm telling you, it would be the cutest thing ever."

I looked at the dress. It was kind of 1960s looking, with a neckline that went in a straight line from the top of one shoulder to the other, and no sleeves. It flared a couple inches under the bust into a puffy skirt that went down to about knee-high. The fabric was kind of stiff, so it stuck out.

"Take it. You're taking it. You have to," she said. "Everyone will die."

"Oh, great," I said. "Just what I need."

"What, for people to think you're cute and have good fashion sense? That would be devastating. Oh, oh— I know what's missing." Her eyes swept over the room, searching for something. "Where's my tiara?"

I couldn't take it anymore. "Fine!" I said. "I'll take the dress, but nothing else. No accessories."

I'd only meant to make us safe from her grandmother, and now I was being talked into wearing a pink princess dress. I hadn't worn pink clothing since fourth grade. We had to leave before she found the tiara.

"Yay," Megan crowed, and she draped it over my arm. She took one last look around the room.

"Are you going Friday night?" The question kind of slipped out.

"Yeah. Kind of have to. School spirit, rah rah rah."

"Who are you going with?" I asked.

She shrugged. "Myself."

"You don't have a date?"

"Who needs a date?" she asked. "He'd just try to dance and look stupid anyway."

Who's punk-rock now?

We didn't even pause as we walked by the kitchen. Megan picked up her schoolbag from the front hall and shouted over her shoulder, "Bye, Grandma!"

"God keep you," Mrs. Wiley called back as we walked out the door.

"Why did she say that?" I asked. Was she on to us?

Megan shrugged. "That's what she always says."

19

THE AFTERNOON LIGHT HAD BEGUN to fade from pale white to gold, and the wind had picked up, sending whirlwinds of fallen leaves tumbling across the street. When we paused at stop signs, the leaves blew against the car and made faint scraping noises.

"We'll go inside and look around a little," Megan said, drumming along to the song on the radio, "and then maybe we'll have something to work with."

"Megan," I said, hesitating.

She turned the radio down. "Yeah?"

"I don't want this to sound weird, because you obviously know more about these things than I do, but my sister is seriously unpredictable right now. I don't think we should mess with her."

She drove on, not looking at me, not saying a word.

"It's just that it could get . . . risky. I don't want you to get hurt."

"I'm here of my own free will," she said. "Stop making up reasons to feel bad."

She went on tapping lightly on the steering wheel, and I stared out the front window of the car, trying to ignore the fear that hovered over my thoughts like an approaching storm. Megan and I had reached a delicate balance—and I didn't want to upset that balance by second-guessing her.

Neither of us said a word as she turned onto Whitley Street.

We parked across the street from my house. After turning the engine off, Megan gazed silently out the window, not moving, not even to take off her seat belt. The air in the car seemed to settle, and the only sounds were our breathing and the scratching and skittering of the leaves outside.

I glanced at her out of the corner of my eye. She sat straight up, her body rigid with stillness, like a tiger crouching in the grass. The sudden change in her behavior frightened me.

"Are you okay?" I asked.

I didn't even notice her hand move, but her seat belt clicked and went flying in violent release, scaring me out of my skin. I gave a shriek, which seemed to wake her up. Her lips pulled tight in a grim little line, revealing tension she didn't want me to see. It was suddenly as if the house, and whatever was inside of it, were more than she'd bargained for.

But if she wasn't going to admit it, I wasn't going to challenge her. "Ready?"

She gulped in a breath of air and nodded resolutely. "Let's go."

The car doors unlocked with a soft click, and we stepped out onto the road. The wind hurried by us, moaning softly. The perfect fall day was cooling into a chilly twilight, and the sky seemed to glow soft brown. I shivered involuntarily.

Megan grabbed her bag from the trunk and faced the house.

"The dress?" I asked.

She shook her head. "Leave it for now."

I closed the trunk. The noise seemed to get lost in the wind.

We must have looked like a solemn little procession, staring up at the house as we crossed the street and went up the front walk. I volunteered for the front position, and Megan followed a few steps behind me.

The front door was unlocked. I pushed it open and hesitated for half a second before going inside.

"Is she here?" Megan whispered.

"I don't know."

"Wow," Megan said. I turned to see what she was looking at, but she was just studying the foyer. I tried to see it the way she was, the high ceiling plastered with cherubs and angels, the leaded-glass window over the front door, the sweeping staircase opening up in front of us, the ornate handrail with its carved roses and vines. . . .

"Let's go upstairs," she said.

As I reached the top of the steps and listened for sounds from Kasey's room, I began to relax; although, as I learned earlier, it didn't have to *sound* like she was home to mean she was. The door was open. I edged closer and sighed with relief; the room was empty. Even if Kasey *was* home, she definitely wasn't in her bedroom.

Megan came more slowly up the stairs, looking back at the foyer and peering down the hall.

"I feel like I've seen this place before," she said.

"There's one in every scary movie," I said, trying to lighten the mood. "Do you want to see my sister's room?"

I went alone into Kasey's room while Megan hovered a few feet behind me. The longer we were in the house, the quieter and more withdrawn she seemed to get.

Nothing struck me as out of the ordinary. I turned around to leave, but Megan wasn't there. She'd wandered down the hall and stood just at the top of the stairs, studying the wallpaper, dragging her fingertips across it.

"Hey," I said. "Maybe we should go outside for a minute."

She turned to look at me, but instead of answering, she went ghostly white and seemed to freeze in place, staring over my shoulder down the hallway.

Not a good sign.

"Megan?"

She didn't answer. Didn't even move.

I took a step toward her.

"Wait," she said.

An order.

I obeyed. Too afraid even to move my head and follow her gaze behind me, I stared at her, trying to read her expression.

Nothing. Her face was blank.

"Sarah," she said. "Sarah."

". . . Megan?"

"Sarah, Sarah, Sarah—"

"Megan, what are you saying?"

After a moment she seemed to wake up. Her eyes went wide and she shook her head furiously, but the name wouldn't stop coming out of her mouth. Her whole body was stiff, her muscles so tense that the tendons showed in her arms.

"Sarah, Sarah, Sarah, Sarah—"

"Megan!" I cried. "Quit it!"

But she couldn't. It was like me, in the basement, with the story.

I grabbed her by the shoulders and shook her hard. "Megan! *Stop it!*"

She stopped, blinking a few times. Finally her gaze settled on me, and her glazed eyes seemed to clear.

"What happened here?" Megan gasped.

"Why do you keep saying that name?"

"In this house," Megan said. "Something happened in this house."

She collapsed.

Down the hall, Kasey's door slammed shut all by itself.

Megan had fallen gracefully into a little heap in the corner. I knelt at her side and felt her wrist for a pulse. It was there—weak, but there.

"Come on," I said, shaking her shoulder gently. "Wake up."

Megan stirred; her eyelids fluttered open and then slid shut as if they were weighted. Her lips moved in an attempt to speak.

"Megan, come on, wake up. We have to get out of here."

I grabbed her by both shoulders and pulled her up to a sitting position.

She blinked. "Let's go," she whispered, color flooding her pale cheeks.

I helped her to her feet, and as we went down the

steps, her hand gripped the banister as if it were a life preserver.

"What just happened?" she asked, her voice shaking.

"I'll tell you outside," I said, holding her by the arm as we crossed the foyer and hurried out of the house.

While Megan rested against the side of her car, my eyes searched the house, looking for any strange light or movement—Kasey's face in a window. . . . But there was nothing.

After a minute, Megan raised her head and looked at me.

"I'm okay," she said, trying the words out.

I didn't ask if she was sure, but our eyes met, and hers darted away.

"I *am*," she insisted. I waited for her to climb into the driver's seat before I walked around to the passenger side.

Once we were safely in the car, she gripped the steering wheel in her hands and tightened her fists until the skin over her knuckles was white. She took a long, deep breath in and held it.

"Who's Sarah?" I asked. The name seemed vaguely familiar to me, but I couldn't place it.

"What?"

"*Sarah.* You just kept saying that name . . . Don't you remember?"

"No," she said. "I really don't. All I remember is feeling something evil."

She leaned back against the seat, staring intently at the steering wheel.

"You know how I keep saying I'm doing this for me . . . ?" She hugged herself tightly. "Ever since I was a little girl, whenever I was around people—fortune-tellers, psychics—they're all afraid of me."

"Afraid how?"

"I just walk by their tents, and they come out and start yelling at me. Not the fake ones, but the real ones— the ones who aren't just making stuff up."

I didn't want to ask what they yelled.

"They tell me *Sarah is here* and *Sarah is angry* and *Sarah hates you*. And they're so scared; they just want me to go away. They get so upset."

"Who's Sarah?" I asked her.

"That's what I want to know."

I looked up at the house. It looked so serene from the outside.

"Whatever I felt in there," Megan said, "it's totally evil. Like *bad* evil, Alexis."

She exhaled and started the car. As we drove down Whitley Street, away from the house, her face seemed to at least soften a little bit.

Where could we possibly go after that?

"We're going to the library," she said.

I nodded and leaned back in my seat. But as we neared the stop sign on the corner, something caught my eye. In the rearview mirror I could see our neighbor Mary guiding her gigantic grandma car into her driveway.

"Stop here," I said, undoing my seat belt. "Park right around the corner and wait for me." Before Megan could even ask where I was going, I was already out the door and cutting across the neighbors' yards to Mary's house.

I reached her as she was hoisting her trunk open. I gave her a bit of a scare, which made me nervous because she's so old.

"Good heavens," she said, looking at me. "Alexis, are you all right?"

"Yes, fine," I lied.

"It's not your father, is it?" she asked.

"No, no, nothing like that."

I glanced at her trunkful of grocery bags.

"Do you want some help with these?" I asked, nodding toward them.

"Well, no . . . you're all out of breath," she protested, but I knew she didn't mean it. I scooped three bags into my arms. Mary grabbed the small brown sack with the eggs in it and started up the front walk. How on earth did she ever manage to get all of her own groceries inside? She must have had to make a separate trip for every single bag.

Up until a couple of years ago, I went to her house a few times a week and had lemonade and cookies while she asked me all about school and friends and life. She never ate any of the cookies, but she always had plenty around. They must have just been for me, and for Kasey, when I dragged her along. When was the last time I'd been there? I thought of a whole package of cookies going stale waiting for us to come visit.

It took two trips to get all the groceries inside.

Mary pulled a chair out from the kitchen table for me. "Would you like some lemonade?" she asked, making a move for the refrigerator.

"Actually, I can't stay long," I said. "I just have a question."

"Oh, that's too bad," she said. She let the fridge door slip shut and turned to me. "What's your question?"

"You've lived here a long time, haven't you?" I asked, even though I knew she had.

"Elvin and I moved here in 1972," she said. Elvin was her husband. He died before we moved in, but I'd heard plenty about him over the years.

"Did you ever hear about anything weird happening in my house?"

Mary froze.

Aha.

Then she shook her head. "Maybe you'd better run along," she said, suddenly very interested in the contents of one of the grocery bags.

"What was it, Mary?"

Now she looked right at me. "Perhaps when you're a little older," she said. "But I don't feel right telling you now. Not when your father—not when you've got so much stress already."

I wasn't leaving that kitchen without names, dates, details. Everything she knew, I was going to know. I crossed my arms and looked back up at her. "I won't tell my parents you told me, if that's what you're worried about."

She stared at the floor. I kept my eyes on her. The sunshine coming through the window silhouetted her puff of silvery curls.

"I need to know," I said simply.

She turned away, but I knew I was breaking her down. "Who's Sarah?"

"Sarah?" she asked, spinning back, her eyebrows forming a deep V on her forehead. "I don't know anything about a Sarah. Do you mean—"

She abruptly cut herself off.

"Mary, please, it's *so* important."

"No, Alexis, I just don't . . . Oh, for heaven's sake.

Let's see . . . They moved in at the end of the summer, 1995."

"Who?"

Mary paced and fidgeted for a moment, wiggled her fingers, stared out the window. "I . . . I don't remember."

A lie. We both sighed at the same time.

"Can't you just give me a *hint?*"

"No. I can't. I can't say any more."

"Just tell me, did someone get hurt?"

"I guess so . . ." She stared helplessly at the ceiling, gripping the cross that hung from a chain around her neck. "I don't know if I would say *hurt*, but she did . . . die."

I fell limply against the back of the chair. "In the house?"

"Goodness," she said. "This was a mistake."

"No, wait—someone died in *my* house?"

She sighed like she knew it was too late to stop now. "Yes, in your house."

"From natural causes?"

"No, dear," she said.

"What year?"

"Let's see, it was 1996. October. The middle of October."

"So . . . okay, wait—nobody lived there until we moved in?"

"No, an older couple moved in for a year, but they

moved out very quickly. They didn't seem to like the neighborhood."

"What was their name?"

"Oh, good heavens, I'm terrible with names. . . ." She frowned in concentration, the corners of her eyes and lips turning downward. "Sawamura. Walter and Joan, they were Japanese. Not very outgoing."

"And then it was vacant until my family moved in?"

"Vacant, yes," she repeated.

Holy cow. I leaned back in my chair.

"Are you sure I can't get you some lemonade?" she asked.

Then I remembered that Megan was waiting for me.

"October 1996," I said, jumping out of my seat.

"Oh, Alexis, I hope you won't think about it too much. It was just so awful, we hate to talk about it."

Well, obviously.

"Thanks, Mary," I said. "You've been a big help."

She nodded vaguely. "Just try to relax and get some rest. I know you're worried about your father—"

"I'll come by soon for some lemonade," I told her, my hand on the doorknob.

Mary stood and sighed, then nodded. She looked tired. "You do that, dear," she said, and then I was gone.

20

"I KNEW IT," MEGAN SAID, for like the tenth time. "I *knew* it. If it wasn't natural causes, that means it was *murder*—no wonder the house is so . . ." We were walking across the public library's parking lot, and she was all worked up. She'd been talking nonstop since I got back in the car.

"Let's find out some more details," I said. "She could be wrong."

"That's not the kind of thing you just forget," Megan said. "I'm surprised you haven't heard about it until now."

"Most of our neighbors have moved," I said.

"I don't blame them."

"But what about what happened to you? What about the story? And my dream?"

She stopped just short of the stairs outside. "Maybe those were just a manifestation. Like how if you have a stressful day it gives you weird dreams. The ghost's anger could be coming out as this bizarre fairy tale."

"How do you know all this stuff?"

She shrugged. "I read a lot."

"I don't know," I said. "It felt so real."

She held the door open for me. The smell washed over me—cold air, old books, floor wax—the scents of my childhood afternoons.

The head librarian, Miss Oliver, shot us a stern look over the top of her pearly pink reading glasses.

"Where do we start?" Megan asked in a low whisper. "The paranormal books are in special collections, behind the checkout desk."

"I think we need to check the newspaper archives," I whispered back.

"The online archives only go back to 1999," Megan said. "We have to use the microfish."

"The what . . . ? Oh," I said. The microfiche. It's pronounced "micro-feesh," but I can see why she would say it that way.

She pointed. "They're in the back corner."

We found the ancient machines gathering dust behind the biographies. I switched one on, and its screen lit up with a lazy yawn. Next to the machines were row after row of shoe box–size metal drawers, which held the slides of information. Megan grabbed a three-ring binder labeled "MICROFICHE LOG" from the top of the cabinet and started flipping through it.

"Drawer 5E," she announced.

I pulled open the drawer to see hundreds, maybe thousands, of sheets of celluloid film, each containing a six-by-ten grid of articles no bigger than a fingernail. Four dividers broke the drawer into sections. The second one said SURREY-DENNISON SENTINEL, OCT. 1996.

Megan flipped to the center of the October sheets and pulled one out.

"It doesn't get any more specific than this," she said. "I've been looking for articles that mention my mom's accident for about two years."

"And you haven't found anything?"

She wrinkled her nose. "Grandma won't talk about it, and Mom's headstone only says the year. So I had to start in January and go from there." She sighed. "I'm up to April, and I haven't found a thing."

I thought of my own mother and felt a nervous shudder run through me. I also couldn't help but be impressed by how well adjusted Megan was about the whole thing. And then I couldn't help but wonder if I'd have cut her a little more slack all this time if I'd known she'd had such a hard life.

Megan pointed at the screen. "Start looking."

I set the slide in the little metal tray and slid the whole thing into the slot on the side of the machine. A newspaper article showed up on the screen in negative— yellow-white print on a black background. I tried to move to the next article, but the images spun by dizzy-ingly. Finally I found one with a date on it: October 4.

"Wrong date," I said. "We're looking for the middle of the month."

Megan switched the slides. The date on the new one was October 18.

I began scrolling through the articles one at a time. Megan leaned in to look at the first few, but the screen was really only big enough for one person. She backed away and continued flipping through the drawer.

My eyes were already tired of searching the tiny print. I was approaching the last square on the page and starting to doubt that we'd ever find anything.

Then I saw the headline.

YOUNG MOTHER'S DEATH RULED SUICIDE.

Local residents were shocked by the October 15 death of Surrey resident Shara Wiley. Now they have even more reason to be dismayed as the coroner's report categorizes the death as a suicide and possible murder attempt on Wiley's two-year-old daughter, who, after presumably escaping out the back door of the house, was found wandering on Whitley Street by neighbors.

Shara Wiley.
Megan's mom.

I leaned in again, my heart beating so hard I could barely sit still enough to read the tiny print.

Wiley was found deceased in her home at 989 Whitley Street after neighbors called police to report having found the two-year-old, but not being able to reach her mother. All doors and windows had been sealed off, and a gas pipe in the house had been disconnected. Wiley died of asphyxiation and exposure to toxic fumes.

Police initially considered the possibility of foul play, but after continuing investigations, the death has been ruled a suicide. Wiley, 27, bought the historic house in 1995 and lived there with her daughter. She worked part-time as a grocery clerk, but had recently begun pursuing professional photography following years of award-winning amateur work, including the grand prize in *Western Enchantment* magazine's annual photography contest. A 1987 graduate of Surrey High, Wiley returned to her hometown following a seven-year residence in San Francisco.

The coroner declared Wiley dead at the scene. She was unmarried. Her daughter was turned over to the custody of relatives, who refuse to speak to reporters. As of press time, police investigations continue.

"Alexis."

I jerked to attention and looked at Megan.

"What is it?" she asked, trying to edge around behind me. I blocked her path with my chair.

"Wait," I said. "Maybe we should . . . We can print it out. Do you have a quarter? I don't think I do." My clammy hands groped in my pockets for change, but they were empty.

I could tell that Megan wanted to push me out of the way and read what was on the screen. But then our eyes met.

She nodded slowly and fished a quarter out of her bag, then stuck it in the coin slot. My fingers fumbled as I pressed the big green PRINT button.

The ancient gears inside whined and groaned and then a page shot out the side with the article printed on it in shiny black ink.

We both reached for it, but Megan was faster.

She started scanning the words.

I tried to think of something to say that might soften the blow.

But of course there was nothing.

"Huh," she said, and kept reading. I couldn't look away from her. It felt like my duty, my responsibility. Soon I heard her breath catch in her throat. She pulled the page into her chest, crinkling it against her heart.

She looked at me, eyes intense and searching, like a hurt, confused animal.

I took a step toward her, but she held her arm out to keep me away. She leaned up against the row of metal cabinets and finished reading the article. Then her fingers released it, and it floated to the floor.

"My mother . . . tried to kill me," she whispered. Her eyes were unfocused, like she was seeing a progression of possibilities, answers.

"Megan . . ."

"All those psychics—they weren't saying *Sarah*. They were saying *Shara*. I'm so stupid. All these years I've just been hearing it wrong," she said, tears brimming in her eyes. "Grandma told me she died in a car accident. . . . Why didn't she tell me the truth?"

"I don't know," I said. "I'm sorry."

"We have to go back to your house." Her whole face seemed to harden. "I want to talk to her. I want to ask her why."

A second passed. My heart thumped so hard it hurt.

"It's dangerous," I said. "Megan, remember what you said in the car?"

It's evil.

"If my sister is possessed," I continued, "if there's something in the house that wants you dead, and Kasey was home when we got there . . ."

Megan lifted her chin and leveled her gaze on me. My body seemed to vibrate with a striking new fear—that Megan would do something stupid and get herself killed.

"I don't care," she said. "I'm not afraid."

"She could . . . she could really kill you." Was that what all of this was about? Megan's mother's ghost trying to finish what she started?

She made a noise of protest, more of a whimper than an actual word, but I knew exactly what she couldn't say. She had to at least *try*. Wouldn't anyone feel that way? Wouldn't I?

I would.

But still.

"You can't go back until we know more," I said, trying to steady my shaking voice.

"Maybe she's changed," Megan said. "Maybe she's angry because she's stuck in the house and she wants to talk to me."

"No," I said.

She shook her head like she hadn't heard me right. *"No?"*

"No. Not today. Maybe tomorrow."

"What," she said, her voice edged with hurt, "like you're going to stop me?"

"I will if I have to," I said.

"Alexis," she said. "I thought we were . . ."

"We *are* friends," I said. "That's why I can't let you

do this. Just give it one day. We'll keep researching, keep looking for ways to—"

"Ways to do what, to destroy her? She needs *help*, not—" She shook her head, looking for a word.

I could imagine how much it would mean to her to know her mother. I felt her pain and loneliness as if they were my own, and my whole body ached with sadness for her.

That's how I knew we were friends.

I shook my head.

"You can't stop me." Her voice was low.

"I'll call your grandmother," I said. "Or I'll call the police and have you arrested for trespassing."

She was silent.

"I'm not saying *never*," I said. "Just not tonight, not until we know more."

"We know plenty," she said. I could feel her anger, as hot and raw as the tears streaming down from the corners of her eyes. "Don't you *dare* call my grandmother."

I didn't even blink. "I will," I said.

She knew it. Her shoulders slumped and her head dropped, her hair falling forward in front of her face. As she turned to leave, I heard a ragged sob escape from her mouth.

"Megan," I said, but she had started weaving through the bookshelves toward the front door. As I followed her, a million thoughts raced through my mind. I shouldn't

have told her. I should have kept it hidden. She was in terrible danger.

She was already climbing into her car when I caught up to her. I grabbed the door before she could slam it.

"Go straight home. Or go to Pepper's. Don't go to my house." I felt a desperate surge of fear. "Megan, *please*, you can't."

She was sobbing silently, her shoulders trembling, her face soaked with tears. "I know," she said, leaning forward and resting on her steering wheel.

"I'm sorry," I said. "I'm so sorry."

She turned to look up at me. Her eyes shone in the fading sunlight, and a quivering breath shook her whole body.

"*Why?*" she cried. "Why does she have to be *bad?*"

I put my hand on her shoulder.

"I can't help you anymore, Alexis. I have to go now," she said, shrugging my hand away. I jumped back as she slammed the door.

The car screeched out of the parking space and sped out to the road.

Megan wouldn't go to my house, I knew it.

She was safe.

But I was on my own.

21

I WALKED BACK INSIDE, feeling like I might shatter into a hundred pieces.

Miss Oliver looked up as I passed the checkout desk.

I felt myself swing over to her, almost as if I'd been drawn there by a magnet.

"Excuse me," I said. "Is there any way I can get back to special collections?"

She glowered and beckoned me closer. "If you aren't eighteen, you need to be accompanied by a parent or guardian." She looked me up and down with an expression that said she knew I wasn't eighteen.

I nodded and tried to hide my disappointment. I didn't have the energy to persist.

"All right," I said. "Thanks. Never mind."

Back at the microfiche, I decided to check out articles from the days following the deaths. I pulled another few sheets from drawer 5-E. Sheet after sheet of slides turned up absolutely nothing.

I felt totally lost, aimless, without Megan. But I had no choice other than to keep going.

I was rereading the printout of the first article when Miss Oliver appeared. Her eyes widened at the sight of the mess I'd made, but she seemed grimly gratified that someone was actually doing research.

"Find what you were looking for?" she asked.

I shrugged. "I guess so."

"I wouldn't normally say this," she said, peering down at me, "but you seem so committed to your project that I hate to deny you access to research materials."

I stared up at her, not understanding.

"The library closes in thirty minutes," she said, speaking a little more slowly. "If you need to look at any . . . *special* books, I'll let you."

"Oh . . ." Then I got it. "*Oh!* Thanks, I'll be right there."

I had one more stack of slides left to look at. I considered skimming them, but I wanted as much time with the special collections as possible. So instead I slipped the whole pile into my bag and made my way up to the front desk.

The library was deserted except for a few die-hard academics. The clock hands pointed to eight thirty.

Miss Oliver beckoned me around the back of her desk to a door I'd never even noticed before. She unlocked it, reached inside and flipped on a light switch.

"I'll come get you"—she checked her watch—"in twenty-five minutes."

I nodded and slipped past her through the doorway. The door closed with the sharp bark of wood against wood, and I was alone.

The only light was the dim green glow of a dying pair of fluorescent bulbs. It took my eyes a moment to adjust. And then I saw the shelves.

They took my breath away.

Seven feet tall, overflowing with books of every shape and size, all colors and ages and thicknesses. They completely encircled the L-shaped room, with a few lined up in the middle of the floor as well. On closer inspection, most of the special collections didn't seem all that unusual—just a bunch of dusty old books. I crossed my fingers that I wouldn't have any trouble finding the section I was looking for.

I didn't have to worry.

The paranormal books filled an entire giant bookshelf of their own. And unlike the rest of the books in the room, they seemed almost to hum. They really *were* special.

Thinking I should be methodical, I started at the bottom. But pulling out each book, opening it, and then carefully returning it to the overcrowded shelf was too slow.

New strategy: I grabbed a book randomly from one of the middle shelves and looked at the cover. It was a paperback called *Interpreting and Healing the Aura*, and the cover was an eighties-style man with a feathered haircut looking serenely up at a rainbow. A halo of pale gold glowed from his head. Close, but not quite right.

I pulled more books out, one by one, and glanced at the titles. Most were completely irrelevant. I know what they say about judging books by their covers and all, but I was running out of time, so I decided to ignore the newer books and focus on the ones with dark leather covers—the old ones.

I pushed a white paperback out of the way to get to a black leather spine with gold writing on it. *The Origins of Pagan Holidays.* Forget it. I pushed another white paperback out of the way to get to a half-disintegrated blue cloth book *Supernatural Case Studies in Northern Ireland 1952–1966*. Then I saw a black spine peeking out from behind a white paperback and reached up to push the white book out of the way.

What was with all the white paperbacks?

And then I realized.

There was only one white paperback on the shelf— and I couldn't seem to stop picking it up.

When I touched it, a tiny lightning bolt of electricity jumped from the book to my fingers. I yanked my hand away and took a closer look at the cover.

Unlike the cheery rainbows and seagulls on the other paperbacks, this one had a rough charcoal illustration of a woman whose face was distorted in a scream, her eyes rolling back in pain, or fear, or something.

The title was *Dealing With Hostile Spirits: A Definitive Guide.* I flipped it over to inspect the back cover and saw a picture of the author—an Asian man in his fifties. "Walter Sawamura is an internationally renowned expert on the subject of . . ."

Sawamura . . . ?

The Sawamuras, Walter and Joan.

The people who lived in our house after Megan and her mom.

So an expert on ghosts—not just ghosts, but hostile ones—moved into our house after a mysterious suicide. And moved out as soon as he could manage.

Suddenly the thin white paperback seemed to weigh a hundred pounds.

Then I snapped out of it. I had to be ready to leave before Miss Oliver came back for me. I stuffed the book in my bag and started for the door, which flew open just as I was reaching for the doorknob.

I shrieked and jumped backward.

Miss Oliver looked at me like I was out of my mind. "A little jumpy, are we?"

I didn't feel like making small talk. "I'm fine." I turned sideways to squeeze past her.

We were the last two people in the library. As I neared the exit I saw the security sensors set up on either side of the door and stopped short. The bar code on the book in my bag would set off the alarm, and then she would catch me—or I would have to run.

I took a deep breath. If I bolted, would she chase me? Did she know my name?

"Wait a second," Miss Oliver called from behind the counter.

"We'll walk out together," she said, reaching beneath her desk and flipping a few switches. All of the library lights switched off, and the red power light on the security sensors faded.

No alarm sounded as we walked through in silence, and I waited as Miss Oliver locked the front door and lowered the gate and locked that too. I had no idea that libraries were having such security issues. Maybe because of people like me, who steal rare books and microfiche slides.

"Is someone coming for you?" Miss Oliver asked, looking around.

"Um, no," I said. "But it's okay. I'll just walk."

"Walk?" she asked doubtfully. "That isn't safe. Where do you live?"

"Whitley Street," I said.

She looked at me like I was a stray cat who'd taken up residence on her porch. "I'll drive you," she said at last, unlocking the door of the only car in the lot, an old square Buick with dulling paint.

We rode in silence. When we reached Whitley Street, I pointed to my house. She slowed the car.

"*This* house?" she asked.

How many times had my friends' parents asked me that question, in that tone of voice? It was so clear to me now—they really meant, "*This* awful house, with the horrible, violent past? You live, eat, sleep, brush your teeth in this terrible place?"

"Yep, this one," I said. It was the same thing I'd always said.

22

I CLOSED THE DOOR QUIETLY BEHIND ME.

"Alexis, is that you?" Mom's voice called out.

I dropped my bags on the stairs and crossed the hall to the kitchen, where Mom stood in front of the open freezer door, studying the stacks of TV dinners.

"Sorry I didn't call," I said, steeling myself for a lecture.

"That's all right," she said. "I just got home myself. Kasey told me where you were."

I glanced at the staircase. "She did?"

"Doing research at the library, right?"

"Um . . . yeah."

"Your sister's been working too. She's totally wrapped up in some project for school." Mom spoke quietly, like we were gossiping. "It's not like her. I've never seen her so dedicated."

"Hmm," was all I could manage.

"I'm microwaving taquitos for Kasey. Did you eat yet?"

"No, but I'm not hungry," I said, and then I grabbed my bag and climbed the stairs.

As I neared my bedroom door, Kasey's door opened and she took a half step out into the hallway.

She stared at me with cold eyes, her arms crossed in front of her chest. "Long night at the library?" she asked.

I didn't answer, just walked into my room, holding my head as high as I could manage. When the door was safely locked behind me, I set my stuff down and took a few long, deep breaths.

I changed out of my jeans into a pair of sweatpants, and sat on the floor at the foot of the bed with my bag in front of me, ready to do more research.

Speaking of research, what was this mysterious project of my sister's? Stealing the reports from school, reading up on all those families . . . What could any of it have to do with Shara?

After a minute, Mom's voice called up the stairs announcing dinner, and I heard Kasey thump briskly by, leaving her room unwatched.

But for how long?

I peered out into the hall. Voices drifted up from the kitchen—Mom's tired chatter and Kasey's emotionless staccato—and I figured, if this was going to happen, it had to happen now.

I stayed close to the wall for the ten feet I had to pass

to get to Kasey's door; then I ducked inside and looked around to make sure there were no ghosts playing rent-a-cop for her.

Coast clear.

I tried to forget the feeling that had come over me when I'd been in there the previous night—the feeling that I now suspected meant I wasn't alone. But the air seemed dry, and held only the faint aroma of dolls—a mixture of dust, plastic hair, and something like old books.

So I was alone. For now.

The room looked like a tornado had hit it, as usual. Kasey's desk was a mess of books and loose papers. She'd been busy, all right—but why?

I went closer to the desk and saw a stack of photo-copies and other papers. I grabbed the stack and flipped through it. The photocopies were pages from public records—mostly birth and death announcements.

The other pages were hand-drawn or computer drawn family trees. There were five of them, and at the top of each was a name and a page number. They'd been torn from her classmates' ancestor reports.

So I guess the whole thing about returning them was a lie.

I stopped on one that culminated in MELISSA MARGARET LAIRD—Mimi. The tree went all the way back through several generations, and Kasey had either highlighted or crossed out several of the names on the page.

Same for the rest of the reports.

Finally I set them down and tugged the red notebook out from the pile on the desk.

I opened it and skipped through pages of Kasey's school notes. There were about ten new pages at the end, and the first few were filled in Kasey's messy chicken scratch—not just words, but interlocking circles, a ragged tree, random chaotic doodles. . . .

The effect was mesmerizing, and I found myself staring for several moments before I suddenly realized I didn't know how long I'd been standing there. I had a feeling Kasey wouldn't just leave her precious work unprotected for long. I was about to make a run for my room when I noticed the last page.

It was covered in lists, written in the smallest scrawl imaginable. The page was so full that if you blurred your eyes, it looked gray.

And she'd written everything backward, like that movie where the kid writes *REDRUM* all over the place.

I picked one list to try to focus on. It took forever to get my brain adjusted to reading backward.

IVY COLEMAN (RIDGE) (died 1974)—
3 children

1. *SON*: ??? *Ridge*
   DAUGHTER??
2. *DAUGHTER*: *Rhonda Ridge (Hutchins)*
   (died 1983) (1 daughter)
   DAUGHTER: *MIRI HUTCHINS*
3. *SON*: *John Ridge (died 1990)*
   (2 daughters)
   DAUGHTER: *Eve Ridge (Hamilton)*
   DAUGHTER: *Delores Ridge (Oliver)*

Delores Oliver?

Librarian Delores Oliver?

I didn't recognize any of the other names.

I needed more time with the list, but Kasey was still working on it. She'd notice right away if it was gone.

I listened out in the hallway but couldn't hear anything but TV noises from downstairs. Maybe Kasey had decided to take a load off for a while and watch some game shows.

I had an idea.

Clutching the notebook close, I darted down the hall and through the study to the darkroom.

The paper was thick, but she'd written with dark ink, so maybe it would work—if I set the exposure long enough.

Except I was out of photo paper.

Then I remembered my extra-fancy matte paper, the

stuff Dad got me last Christmas. It cost, like, two dollars a page, and to make sure I didn't accidentally use it for regular stuff, I kept it wrapped in a towel at the bottom of one of the bathroom drawers. Kasey didn't even know it existed, so maybe . . .

I opened the drawer.

There it was.

I put a page down under the enlarger and then set Kasey's list, print side down, right on top of it. I cranked the timer and let it run for ten seconds, twenty, forty-five. Finally, after a minute, the light clicked off.

This was taking way too long. I dropped the paper in the developer and ran back out to the hallway with the original.

Footsteps were thumping up the stairs.

I dashed into Kasey's room, nearly tripped over a shoe on the way to her desk, and slammed the page back onto her notebook.

But there was no time to get out.

I hurled myself into the closet.

It was practically impossible to keep my breathing quiet, especially when Kasey came sauntering in and looked around. I watched through the slat as she stretched her arms like a cat and then sat on the foot of the bed, looking around the room.

She didn't seem to know I was there.

Come on, come on.

The print was *cooking* in the developer right now. I'd be lucky if it wasn't just a solid square of black.

But I had more immediate problems.

Kasey pressed her hands to her temples and shook her head like she was trying to shake something off. She squinted her eyes shut and pinched the bridge of her nose.

Then her whole body jerked, and just like that, the struggle was over.

Her movements became fluid, deliberate. She smoothed her hair down and looked around the room.

I felt nauseated.

It wasn't Kasey anymore.

She froze, and her hazy eyes focused, hardened with the effort of listening.

Don't look in the closet, don't look in the closet—

She stood up, tilting her head to one side.

I held my breath.

She took a half-step toward me

The bedroom door opened.

Kasey drew back and blinked as she looked toward the hallway.

"Kasey, honey, I need you to get your clothes out of the dryer."

"What?" Kasey asked. Her hands fidgeted and tugged at a belt loop on her jeans.

"Your *laundry*," Mom said. "The laundry you were supposed to fold?"

Kasey sighed, took a last wary look around, and left. As soon as I heard her feet on the stairs, I ran back to the darkroom, yanked the page out of the developer, and slipped it into the stop bath.

It was dark, but legible. And, as an added bonus, the words that had been backward on Kasey's page were now normal—lists and lists of names in unsteady handwriting.

There would be time to read them later. I did a rushed version of my usual cleanup, stowed the photo paper back in the drawer in case I needed it again, and went back to my room with the print hidden under my shirt.

I sat on my bed, trying in vain to make a connection between the names on Kasey's paper. Finally I set the list aside and moved on, pulling the library book and microfiche slides out of my bag. I held one slide to the light but couldn't make out any detail—just little blocks of text and teensy black squares.

A series of quick taps on the door made me jump and drop the slide.

"Alexis?" Mom called.

"Hold on," I said. "It's locked."

I opened the door to see her standing in the hallway

with her jacket on and briefcase in hand.

"So listen," Mom said. "I have to go back to the office for a while and try to make up some work from yesterday. Just an hour or so. The new senior VP is coming Friday, and I really want to be prepared. . . ."

I could hear the excitement in her voice.

Suddenly I felt bad for Mom, really bad. Imagine working for something for years, watching people get hired below you and then promoted to be your boss. Imagine your family never saying thank you, or even telling you they're sorry you work so hard and nobody acknowledges it.

What was this, Challenge Alexis's Long-Held Assumptions Day?

"Can you hold down the fort for a while?"

"Um . . . sure."

Alone with Kasey. I tried not to think about it.

Mom shifted her briefcase to her other hand.

"Mom," I said.

"Hm?"

"I know you really want to get promoted, but . . ." Uh. "Even if you don't, you know, you're still . . ." Hmmm. Running out of words here. "I mean, thanks for working so hard."

She smiled. "That means a lot to me." Then she touched my shoulder and left.

I settled onto my bed and stared at the bookshelves across the room. I couldn't bring myself to put the vandalized yearbook back in its place, so I'd stuffed it into the bottom drawer of my desk.

No sound came from Kasey's room, but I could imagine what she was doing: sitting hunched over her desk, making lists and more lists and randomly copying names down into her notebook.

I fell back against the pillows and closed my eyes, too weary to sit up. I tried to clear my thoughts, but I kept remembering Megan's face as she read the article and learned the horrible truth about her mother. Then I thought of innocent toddler Megan, in the photo at the lake with her grandmother, oblivious to the fact that the woman with the camera was soon going to try to kill her.

How long had Shara planned before she got up the nerve to actually go through with it? When she looked through the lens that day, had she looked at Megan with hatred?

But how could you take such a photo, hating your subject? How could you wait until the light shined perfectly on the water behind her, catching the windswept flyaways of her baby curls, the deep thoughtfulness of her tiny eyes? There was *love* in that picture.

I thought of the charm bracelet Megan had worn

that day, the one she still wore every day, hiding her past beneath her expensive sweaters and cheerleading uniform.

Then I realized with a start: my charm. It wasn't just *any* charm: if Megan had actually lived here, that meant mine was probably the other half of hers.

Our house before this one had been tiny and cramped—so the Gothic expanses of the new one towered over me. I was seven years old. (It took me two years to figure out that we didn't actually live in a mansion.)

That first night, after Mom tucked me in and gave me a kiss, I lay staring up at the ceiling.

And that's when I heard it:

The whispering.

At first I thought it was coming from the hallway, but when I peeked out, nobody was there. I dove back under the covers, and the whispers seemed to get louder. Even with my hands over my ears, I could hear the voice slithering and hissing like a nest of snakes in my head, until finally I could make out two words:

Come play.

It must be Kasey, I decided. But it was too late to play.

Thanks to Kasey's daylong series of screeching temper tantrums, the whole family was drained. Our parents were Exhausted with a capital "E" and any little girl caught sneaking out of her bedroom would be in Trouble with a capital "T."

Come play, the whispers begged.

I folded the pillow over the sides of my head to block out the sound, but it didn't work.

I was determined not to go to my sister's room, but I felt myself drawn to the window and figured *that* wasn't breaking any rules. I gave in to the urge and went to the cushioned window seat, pressing my hands flat against the panes of glass. Then I reached down and unlatched the window, pushing it up and letting in the cold night air.

Come play.

Something rose up inside me, a burst of bravery, and for some reason I decided that I must climb out the window. I must climb the giant tree. I had to do it to prove to myself that I wasn't afraid of the new house.

As I knelt and began to stick one foot out the window, the whispers grew louder and more excited, and I grew more confident that what I was doing was absolutely the right thing. Think how proud Mom and Dad would be the next day. Think how impressed Kasey would be.

I set one foot lightly on the roof and shifted a bit of my weight to it, but my foot slipped a little on the loose shingles, and I thrust a hand toward the wall behind the curtain to steady myself.

I got my balance back, but as my hand pressed

against the wall, panic surged up inside of me. The whispers became slower, angrier, as I stared down at the twenty-foot drop off the edge of the roof.

Suddenly I didn't *want* to come play.

It was wrong. It was dangerous. My parents wouldn't be proud—they'd be horrified.

My hand felt along the wall for something to grab on to, to get the strength to pull myself back inside. I was distracted by the swirling roar of whispers in my head, scolding me and beseeching me to *Come play*, *Come play*, *Come play.* . . .

What my hand found was a small piece of metal, tied with a loop of ribbon, hanging off a tiny nail in the wall.

I grabbed the metal, and the whispers went silent.

With a burst of strength I hauled myself back inside and shut the window, locking it, and climbed back into bed. In the moonlight I stared at the object in my hand—a flat silver heart, cut in half with a smoothed over zigzag edge. There were letters on it, *S*, *H*, and half an *A*, and below them, *M*, *E*, and the round back of what could have been a *Q* or an *O* . . .

Or a *G*.

When I woke up the next morning I would have thought the whole thing was a dream, except for the presence of the charm and ribbon, which I'd wrapped around and around my little hand and held on to like a talisman.

For years I slept with that heart under my pillow. I never really stopped to wonder where it came from or who it had belonged to. I liked it, on some deep level, and I thought, on the same deep level, that it liked me back. It was my lucky charm.

The whispers never bothered me again.

After eighth grade, when Beth and her mom moved away, I gave up on the concept of luck. If there was any such thing, I figured, I was getting the bad end of it. Better to reject the whole idea outright than to keep inviting bad luck to kick me around.

So I packed the charm in my treasure box of knick-knacks and forgot it existed.

To put it simply, our attic is an abomination.

Box after box of old clothes, worn-out bed linens, and faded, ripped towels. My childhood toys, passed on to Kasey and then hidden away and forgotten. A few pieces of furniture covered in white sheets that glowed in the moonlight like phantoms.

It's like a graveyard for household goods. It's intimidating even in daylight.

As I stepped off the ladder onto the creaking floorboards, I took a deep breath, flicked on the dim overhead light, and looked around.

Just had to find my treasure box.

Which was in the attic . . . somewhere.

It was clearly hopeless. In the two years since I'd stored it, approximately eight million more pieces of junk had been shoved in front of it.

I plowed all the way to the back wall and found nothing. I moved Kasey's old pink clock radio out of the way and reached for a box behind it.

The radio turned on all by itself. I nearly jumped out of my skin until I realized where the music was coming from. Then I saw that the clock was on—red numbers and everything—and the radio was playing, and all the while I could see the cord neatly coiled up around it. Not plugged in.

I spun around to see if someone was in the room with me, but I was alone.

The tinny twang of a pop-country singer poured out of the speakers, occasionally fading out under a wave of static, and without thinking, I kept my hands held out in front of me, as if the clock was going to fly at me and I was going to block it.

"And though we may be apart, you're always in my heart, so baby please come home. . . ."

I stared down at the radio, afraid to touch it. What if I got a shock?

"Because home is where the heart is. . . ."

The radio switched off.

I stepped back. *Home is where the heart is.*

All week that phrase kept popping up. Carter had said it to me in the car. It was in my fortune cookie. It was the title of the school librarian's book. It was almost like someone was trying to tell me something.

Well . . . I *was* looking for a heart.

Home is where the heart is.

Home.

I looked around.

My eyes stopped on the old dollhouse, wedged between a bed frame and a stack of old boxes.

It was just a guess, a dumb hunch. I was embarrassed and a little irritated at myself for even considering it. But I walked over to the dollhouse anyway, and peered in the window.

My treasure box.

Home is where the heart is.

I knelt on the floor, the box lit up by a shaft of moonlight, and carefully lifted out each item until I came to a little velveteen coin purse. I loosened the smooth braided rope and held it upside down over my hand. The heart charm and its ribbon tumbled out and landed in my palm.

I went back down to my room and spent the next hour and a half staring at what had once been my most prized possession, trying to figure out how something I'd trusted so much as a little girl could be connected to someone who turned out to be so evil.

Mom's car pulled into the garage at 11:50 p.m. When I heard her come up the stairs, I followed her into her room and closed the door.

I had a plan.

"Oh, Alexis," she said, yawning, "what are you still doing up?"

"Can I sleep in here tonight?"

"Well . . . of course you can. Is everything all right?"

"Yep," I lied. "I just need to turn off my bedroom light."

I closed the door behind me and went back to my room. The heart charm was right where I'd left it, on the dresser. I debated for a few seconds, then tucked it into my pocket, switched off the lamp, and went back into the hall.

I almost ran smack into my sister. She stood in the middle of the hall, her body angled toward Mom and Dad's bedroom, eyes fixed on the doorknob.

I froze.

Slowly, slowly, she turned to face me.

"Hey, sis," she said, her voice soft and casual.

"Kase . . . is it you?"

Her face looked angelic in the soft gold of the hall light. "Of course it's me, Lexi."

"What are you doing?"

She looked around, then shrugged. "Nothing, I guess."

"Well . . . maybe you should go back to bed," I said.

Her lips pressed together in a pout. "See?" she hissed. "This is why I had to find a better friend than you. My *other* friend never bosses me around."

We stared into each other's eyes.

"I just don't want anyone else to get hurt," I said at last.

"Then you should be more careful whose bedroom you snoop around in," she said, turning on her heel and stalking back into her room.

The door closed behind her, all by itself.

23

A SUDDEN SHOCK OF BRIGHT LIGHT hit my eyelids, jerking me out of my sleep. For a moment I wondered where I was, and then I saw the pale blue floral of the bedspread and remembered.

Mom stood at the window, dressed and made up, her dirty-blond bob neatly turned under.

"Sorry," she said. "That was brighter than I thought it would be."

I looked at the clock—7:12.

"I'm going in early today," she said. "You'll be all right getting to school?"

"I'll manage," I said, sitting up and swinging my feet to the floor.

She kissed me on the top of my head and hurried out. I heard her knock on Kasey's door and then call a good-bye from the hallway.

I waited until I felt the rumble of the garage door closing after her and went back to my own room. I grabbed a pair of jeans and a T-shirt (careful not to wear school colors again), then took the world's fastest shower and ran down to the kitchen and swigged a cup of orange juice.

"Where's the fire?" Kasey said darkly from the kitchen doorway.

I didn't answer. For now she just seemed to be regular grumpy morning Kasey. I stuck my hand in my pocket and felt the smooth edge of the heart charm, suddenly wondering if it had been wise to bring it downstairs with me. If Kasey got too close to it, would she— would *Shara*—gain some evil power from it? Would she recognize it and demand it back?

What if it reminded her of Megan?

I let go and brought my hand out of my pocket.

"I have to run," I said, rinsing out my cup and setting it on the counter. I grabbed my backpack from the bottom of the stairs and left.

I walked toward the school as far as the stop sign on the corner, then went all the way around the block and came back to my house from the other direction. I crept across the side yard and stood behind the overgrown bushes while I waited for Kasey to make her appearance. Surrey Middle started at 8:30, so she should have been out of the house at 8:15, but she came sauntering out at 7:54 and started down the street in the opposite direction from the middle school.

She held a stack of notebooks in her arms as she strode down the sidewalk, oblivious to anything around her.

Including me, as I followed a half block behind. I tried to stay out of her eye line, but I didn't have to worry. She was hell-bound for her destination and didn't even look behind her once.

I followed her the five blocks to the quaint little downtown shopping district, where moms with strollers and men and women in suits seemed to dominate the sidewalks. No one noticed my sister as she trudged up the stairs of town hall. I went in after her and just caught a glimpse of the back of her sweatshirt as it disappeared down a hallway.

"Pardon me, miss," said a man sitting next to a metal detector. "Can I help you?"

"That's my sister," I said. "I have to ask her something."

"She was here all day yesterday too," he said. He waved me through the metal detector, and I darted through the crowds to see where Kasey had gone.

I found the long hallway and went all the way to the end, where there was a single door. The metal sign on it read HALL OF RECORDS.

By the time I got to school, first period was half over. I

figured I might as well go to the office and get my late slip before Mrs. Anderson sent me. But when I told the secretary I'd been over seeing my dad at St. Margaret's Hospital (for lack of a better story), she wrote me a pass without marking it in the book.

"You take care, now, dear," she said, handing it over with a sad smile.

Between classes I stopped by my locker and felt a dozen pair of eyes on me. The cheerleaders were all staring warily from their row of lockers. They were clustered so tightly that I couldn't see Megan.

But really, it didn't matter. What could I possibly say to her?

I arrived at fourth period and sat in my usual desk at the back of the room. I was flipping through my textbook when I caught a flash of red and white out the corner of my eye.

"Hey," someone said.

I glanced up to see Megan standing next to me.

"Oh, hi," I said.

"Um . . . will you sit next to me?" she asked, playing with the hem of her satin cheerleading uniform.

I hesitated for a millisecond, wondering if the people around us were paying attention. It was long enough that Megan's eyes flickered away self-consciously.

"Yeah, of course," I said, picking up my bag off the floor.

I followed her across the room; she gestured to an empty desk.

"It's okay," she said. "Chloe sits there. She'll move."

I set my stuff down and got settled. Another girl in a cheerleading uniform, Chloe, came wandering over and exchanged whispers with Megan. Then she went across the room to my usual seat.

I looked expectantly at Megan, thinking she had a question or something.

She wrinkled her nose and gave a sad little tip of her head. "No real reason," she said. "I just wanted to be around someone who understands."

"I'm really sorry," I said.

"It's okay," she said. "I'm trying to figure out how to stop thinking about—"

"What? This sucks!" I looked up to see Lydia standing a few aisles over, glaring down at Chloe.

"It's cool, Lyd," I said. I tried to wave her over so I could explain, but she didn't budge.

"No, *not* cool," she said. "They took your chair."

Everyone in the classroom, including the teacher, seemed to be enjoying the conversation.

"No," I said. "They didn't. Don't worry about it."

"I'm not worried," she said. She drew up to her full

271

five-foot-nothing. "I'm *pissed*. On your behalf."

"Lydia," I said loudly, because loudness is the only thing that gets her attention. "I'm fine. Go sit down. Leave it alone."

"But I—"

"I *want* to sit here," I said, and the whole class fell silent and stared at me. I figured, what the hell, and added, "Next to Megan."

Lydia sputtered and sniffed and plunked down in her own seat.

I turned to Megan and rolled my eyes.

"Sit with me at lunch?" she asked.

This time I nodded right away, not stopping to look around and worry about who was watching or what they were thinking.

And as class progressed, I found myself actually looking forward to lunch. Not just because it was something new, but because I felt a connection with Megan. More than all the haunted house stuff. More than my crushing sadness over the circumstances of her mother's death, and the circumstances of her discovering those circumstances.

No, it was something like the old Beth feeling. A kindred spirit kind of thing.

As the bell rang, Megan stood up with her bag slung over her shoulder and waited for me to gather my things.

We made our way down the hall side by side, and I felt like some old rusty door was opening up inside of me, releasing something that had been bottled up for years.

She chewed silently, looking blankly ahead. I swallowed the last bite of my rice pilaf and reached down to my pocket for the heart charm.

"So . . . I realized," I said, hesitating. "Yesterday? At your house? When I said I had the same kind of necklace as you . . ."

I set it gently on the table.

"It's the other half of yours, isn't it?"

She reached into her collar and pulled the chain out. Hers had the letters *RA* and *GAN*.

SHARA. MEGAN.

"Yeah," she said.

"Do you . . . want this one too?"

She stared at it for a long minute, then shook her head. "Nah. You keep it."

"Seriously?"

"Seriously," she said, swirling her bottled water. "How's your sister?"

"Weird."

"Did she hurt you again?"

"No, she's really busy . . . making these lists of names. It's kind of obsessive."

Megan frowned.

"I'm sort of hoping she'll get bored of it and, like, stop. I mean, bossing people around is fun, but clerical work isn't that cool."

"That'd be good," Megan said.

We ate in comfortable silence.

When the bell rang, signaling the end of lunch, Megan reached into her bag and pulled out a paperback book with a purple cover. The title was *Things That Go Bump in the Night*.

"Take this. It might help," she said.

I took the book and made a move to lift the necklace off the table.

"Look," Megan said, pointing at it with a carrot stick. "It says *SHAME*."

SHA, ME. Shame.

"I never thought of it that way," I said, scooping it back into my pocket.

"Funny," Megan said, not smiling. "That's what the whole damn thing is. A shame."

After the final bell rang, I went to my locker.

Carter was waiting for me. "I'll drive you home?" he asked.

I nodded and followed him out to his car. I made a conscious effort not to notice the curious stares in our direction, but that made me notice them that much more.

"You all right?" Carter asked as we pulled out of the lot.

I nodded again, looking out the window at the throngs of kids happy to be done with their school day.

"If you need to talk about anything, I'm here," he said, his voice gentle. "I felt so bad yesterday. I can tell there's something going on."

No. He was just too nice. I could not let my horrible life leak inky black misery all over what he'd managed to rebuild for himself.

I never thought I would say this, but Pepper was so right.

"Carter," I said, before I could stop myself, "I can't go to the dance with you."

"What? Why?" There was a hint of nervous laughter in his voice, and he shot me a bewildered half-smile as he reached forward to turn off the radio.

"I just . . . can't," I said, taken aback by the sudden shock of disappointment I felt.

"You mean you don't have a reason?" His smile seemed plastered on, like this was just one more amusing example of Alexis's bad-girl antics.

"I *do* have a reason," I said. "I just . . . you wouldn't understand."

He laughed. "Try me. Listen, I don't care. We can skip the dance. We can do whatever."

"No," I said. "It's not about the dance. We can't do anything."

"Alexis . . . ?" His voice trailed off, and the smile faded from his lips.

"You should take Pepper," I said.

He gave a confused snort. "Why would I take *Pepper?*"

"She really likes you."

"Alexis . . . I don't want to go to the dance with Pepper Laird—I want to go with you."

Oh, this sucked. This was so hard. Every fiber of my being wanted to change my mind, apologize, say whatever needed to be said to get Carter to forgive me.

"Well . . ." I tried to force myself to sound nonchalant. "You can't."

He pulled into my driveway and braked a little too abruptly.

"I'm sorry," I said. "It's not you."

I unhooked my seat belt, and he reached over and put his fingers on my forearm. His touch sent shivers through my body, but I shrugged his hand away. "I have to go." I got out of the car and closed the door.

He rolled down the window. "There's something you aren't telling me."

"I'm sorry, Carter," I said. "Please just go."

Reluctantly, he rolled up the window and drove off.

I trudged up the walk, feeling as if there were a dark veil hanging over me that would never go away. I was trying to sort out the storm of thoughts about what had just happened—I'm a horrible person; I've hurt him; he didn't deserve that. . . .

But better now than later . . .

It wasn't until I looked up and realized I was halfway up the stairs that I paused to wonder if Kasey was home.

But the house was empty, and wherever she'd gone, she'd taken all of her research materials with her, so I had nothing to snoop into. Instead, I sat on my bed with Megan's book and the one I'd stolen from the library in front of me.

Megan's book looked like it was written for middle school kids, maybe even younger than that. The cover art was a cartoony picture of a ghost. I looked inside the front cover and saw, in Megan's precise handwriting: *Megan Wiley, 1026 Primrose Ave., July 2004.*

I skimmed over the first few chapters, which just gave definitions of different types of paranormal activity—ghosts versus demons versus poltergeists.

Frankly, I didn't care what we had. I just wanted to make it go away.

Chapter four, "Haunted Houses," explained that spirits often take on the emotions they felt as they died. So a person who died under stress or in pain would be more active and violent than one who died in his or her sleep. And the spirit could lie dormant for years before choosing to wake up and raise havoc, often on or near a significant date.

The day Shara died: October 15.

The day Kasey was supposed to make her decision: October 15.

Perfect.

I looked around the room again and felt the horror of what had happened in the house sink down like a weight on my shoulders. A woman had died. Died horribly.

And she was still here.

Something had awakened her. I remembered the story—my casual mention of Megan. Was that all it took? Did I remind the sleeping ghost of her murderous past? Did I wake her up and somehow instill a need to finish what she started?

The end of chapter four said that in most cases, avenging or solving a mystery or murder would cause the ghosts to move on. But there was no crime to solve—Megan escaped. Shara died. Not the kind of case that takes a lot of detective work.

I set that book down and picked up Walter Sawamura's, the one from the library. This one was definitely intended for adults. I glanced over the chapter names: "Identifying a Spirit"; "Symptoms of Hostility"; "Seeking Professional Help"; "Practical Concerns of Living with Spirits"; "Anchor Objects: The Ties that Bind." I stopped at that one. I'd never heard of an anchor object. I turned to that chapter and began to read.

According to Mr. Sawamura, some ghosts and spirits find themselves attached to a physical object. The object is kind of like an anchor holding a boat in place—the boat can drift, but it can't go too far from the anchor. Often, all their power is tied to this object, making it a "power center." The power center is a strong supernatural force in and of itself, but by destroying it, you could free the spirit and force it to pass along to another plane, wherever it would have gone if it hadn't been trapped.

Was the necklace Shara's power center? Was it evil?

Of all the possibilities I'd considered, I hadn't even thought of that.

I mean, from the very beginning, the first night in the house, I believed it was on my side. Protecting me. Comforting me.

How could something that made a person feel so safe be so *bad*?

And Megan—she wore hers all day, every day, and nothing had happened to her.

It didn't make sense.

My T-shirt and sweater were no match for the wind. Cool air sliced right through them and covered my skin in goose bumps.

I rang the doorbell again, and took a step backward off the stoop.

Mary wasn't home.

I went back home and stood in the kitchen like a watchdog, looking out the front window. A half hour later, Mary pulled into her driveway. I ran to catch her as she went inside.

"Hello, Alexis," she said, shooting me a weary glance.

"Don't worry," I said. "I'm not going to ask any more about my house."

"Oh good," she sighed. "Well, come in, come in; you'll freeze out here."

The living room was about four hundred degrees. I took off my sweater and draped it over a chair as Mary tightened a knitted shawl over her shoulders.

"How can I help you?" she asked.

"I just need your help for a school project," I said. "You've lived in Surrey your whole life, haven't you?"

She smiled and nodded. "Born and raised."

"Good," I said, unfolding the print of Kasey's lists. I chose one at random. "So do you know the . . . Pittman family?"

"Oh, the Pittmans," she said, nodding slowly. "That was old Mr. Pittman with the butcher shop. Of course, he was long dead even when I was a girl, but the shop was around until the 1960s."

"Um," I said, studying the names, "and who was Cora Pittman . . . Billings?"

"Mrs. Billings. That's right, she *was* a Pittman, wasn't she? She was a bit of a tragic figure. Her husband was killed in an automobile accident when I was very young. And it was quite sad, because she'd had a daughter who died of cancer. But there was another daughter, Jessie Billings, who married Phillip Martin, the lawyer. Their daughter Rosemary was in my class at school."

"How do you know all this?" I asked, a little in awe. She was like an encyclopedia.

"Well," Mary said. "Think about your friends; you know all about their families, don't you?"

Um, not quite. I shook my head.

"Oh," Mary said. She shifted self-consciously. "I mean, goodness, Alexis, we didn't have television back then. We just went around and visited. It was what we did for fun." She laughed. "I can't tell you what I ate for dinner last night, but I know the names of all the men who were in the chamber of commerce with my father."

"What about you?" I asked. "Who are your people?"

"Let's see," she said, scratching her forehead and rocking absently in her chair. "My mother was a Schmidt. My father was a Ridge—"

"Ridge?" I interrupted. That was familiar. I searched the list of names. "John Ridge?"

"Why no, he was Benedict Ridge. John Ridge was his brother."

"And Ivy Coleman was his mother?"

She looked surprised. "Yes—how do you know that?"

"Are you related to the librarian?"

"Delores Oliver?" She rocked a little faster. "Good heavens, Alexis, what do you have there? Yes, we're cousins, but we never spoke. Her father didn't like the family. He was very religious and she didn't approve of my grandfather's fondness for whiskey. . . . I suppose it's silly that I don't just go say hello to her."

My head was spinning.

"I have a picture of my grandmother," Mary said. "Would you like to see it?"

"Sure," I said absently, thinking I'd gotten all I was going to get out of Mary.

She shuffled away and shuffled back a minute later

with an ancient black-and-white photo in her hands. It was so old the white parts had a silvery cast to them. She handed it gently to me.

"See? Second from the left," she said.

The photo was a group of young girls lined up in their Sunday best and staring at the camera with solemn faces.

I flipped the photo over and saw a list of names:

Mildred Shore
Ivy Coleman
Patience O'Neil
Molly Saint
Cora Pittman
Mercy Bainbridge
Ann Patrick
Lucy Schmidt

"Patience O'Neil," Mary said, lowering herself back into her chair. "She became a Michaelson. That's your mother's family."

"Wow," I said. "This is amazing."

"Why don't you keep it?" she offered.

"I can't do that," I said. "It wouldn't be right."

"What use do I have for it?" Mary asked, waving dismissively. "It's a piece of your family history. You should know where you come from."

I looked at her face, creased and lined with age. Her eye shadow had been applied with too heavy a hand; the color on her lips was two shades too bright. She looked lonely and worn out and old.

"Okay," I said. "Thanks a lot. It's really cool."

She smiled, pleased.

"I'd better get going," I said. "But you've been really helpful."

"I'm glad," she said. "Now, you don't have to be a stranger. I know you have your MTV and your e-mail Web sites, but if you ever have a little time, come by and say hello."

"I will," I said. "I promise."

She made a move to stand.

"No, stay," I said. "I can let myself out."

I closed the door carefully behind me and started down the sidewalk, then stopped short.

Kasey was coming across the street, carrying a tray with a little pitcher and a box of cookies.

When she saw me, she raised her eyebrows but kept walking.

"What are you doing?" I asked, grabbing her by the elbow.

She jerked away. "Being neighborly."

"Listen to me, Kasey," I said. "I need to talk to you about your friend."

"Why?" she asked, her lip twisting into a sneer. "Does *Megan* want to ask her some questions?"

"Stop it," I said. "Leave Megan out of this."

She stared at me intently for a long few seconds.

"Megan is on my list," she said, looking me up and down. "And so are you."

"What *is* your list?" I asked. "I don't understand what you're doing."

"You are not meant to understand," she replied.

Her gaze fell on me like a heavy coat weighing me down. I felt as if my feet were rooted to the ground. She turned and walked up to Mary's door, ringing the doorbell in quick bursts.

I couldn't even move.

But as she disappeared inside, the leaden feeling dissolved, and I dashed home and into the kitchen. I looked in the trash and found an empty packet of lemonade mix.

My heart stopped pounding quite so hard. Maybe Kasey was just going to do what I'd done—ask Mary about the names.

I went to the sink to get a glass of water, and that's when I noticed the grains on the counter. For a second I thought they were sugar crystals, but then I flipped the light on to see that they had the faintest cloudy green tint.

I opened the cabinet under the sink.

The first thing I saw was a box of ant poison sitting slightly askew.

I poured a little into the sink.

Tiny green grains, no bigger than sand.

I didn't bother to close the front door behind me. I tore back to Mary's house, pounded on the door, and pulled it open without being invited. I heard Mary exclaim from the living room and found my sister pouring the second of two glasses of lemonade.

"Kasey," I said. "Stop."

"She's not causing any trouble," Mary said. "It's really all right."

Kasey looked at me. "You heard Mary," she said. "I'm not causing any trouble."

She stared straight into my eyes, but her glare didn't seem to lock on to me the way it had outside. I didn't get the same heavy, captive feeling.

"Go home," I said.

Neither of us spoke. After a long few seconds, Mary cleared her throat and stood up. "Alexis, dear, I'm so glad you came back . . . You forgot your sweater."

She hung it over my arm and then retreated, sensing that her gesture hadn't eased the tension.

"I'm sorry, Mary," I said. "My sister has to go home."

Kasey cocked her head.

I took a step forward.

And Kasey took a step back.

. . . Huh.

"Go," I said. *"Now."*

Kasey took another step backward, then turned to Mary and glowered as intensely as a lion watching its prey.

I began to move closer, and Kasey took off at a full run, down the hall and out into the night.

"I'm sorry," I said to Mary, trying to sound casual, dumping the lemonade back into the pitcher and setting everything on the tray. "She's just way behind in her schoolwork and our parents will get really mad if she doesn't . . ."

Mary was watching me, wide-eyed.

"Mary," I said, turning to face her. "Do me a favor? Promise me you won't let Kasey back in tonight. Or tomorrow. Not until I tell you it's safe. No matter what she says."

She didn't seem to hear me. She pulled her shawl a little snugger over her shoulders and shuffled toward a window. She checked the lock, and then shuffled to the next window and checked that lock.

"Um . . . are you okay?" I asked.

She faced me, and I noticed a shudder in her hands and a faint quiver in her voice. "Alexis," she said, "the last time someone looked at me like that was . . ."

My whole body went stiff with fear.

"Nineteen ninety-six," she whispered.

I sat on my bed with the photo.

Mildred. Patience.

These girls . . . they were in my dream.

They were the ones who had chased the little girl in my story. They'd thrown rocks at her until she'd fallen from the tree.

But if these girls weren't just minor characters in a story I'd made up . . . if they'd really existed . . .

I shifted my weight, and the books I'd stacked on the pillow tipped over. The Sawamura paperback fell open. Someone had written something on the inside cover.

Just like Megan, I thought, leaning in to read it.

SHARA C. WILEY, 989 WHITLEY STREET, SURREY CA. SEPTEMBER 20, 1996.

My breath caught in my throat.

Shara had owned that book. And the only reason she would own that book was if there were already something in the house—something evil.

Looking at the neat handwriting, I thought of the whispers that first night, eight years ago . . . and how they had invited me outside to play. Wasn't that what

Kasey had said to me the other night, when she came into my room? *Come play.*

I'd been starting to wonder why the ghost chose Kasey and not me.

But something *had* reached out to me.

And I might have been lured to my death the very first night we lived here, if I hadn't grabbed on to the necklace—which had belonged to Shara.

When we were inside Mary's house, near my sweater—in the pocket of which I'd left the charm—Kasey wasn't able to control me.

"Shara?" I whispered, taking the half-heart out of my pocket and holding it tightly in my fist.

Nothing happened.

But by that point I was completely, one-hundred percent sure . . .

My charm wasn't evil. It was good.

Shara was protecting me.

But from whom?

My hands shook so badly I could hardly get the microfiche slide to sit in the negative frame. I placed the slide inside and set the timer for five minutes, then hit the EXPOSE button. The light popped on.

Only about four articles at a time shone through onto the notebook paper I'd laid flat on the enlarger, and the print was so small that I had to lean in close to read anything smaller than a headline. Nothing. I shifted the negative tray so a different set of articles was in the light. Four more duds. And another four. And then on my fourth try I found it—"WILEY DEATH HAUNTS COMMUNITY." Ha. If only they'd known. I skimmed the text, but it was nothing new—mainly a human interest piece on the continuing concern of the neighbors, a week after the fact. But at the bottom was a featurette, a miniarticle in its own little box.

I tucked my trembling hands into the sleeves of my sweatshirt and leaned in close to read.

"THE UNHAPPY HOME ON WHITLEY STREET," said a line of bold text inside the box.

SURREY—It's been less than a week since the October 15 suicide at 989 Whitley Street, but many neighbors are anxious to put the incident behind them. Most residents regard the death of young mother Shara Wiley as a tragic reminder that no matter how well you think you know your neighbors, there's always something under the surface.

Several local residents declined to be interviewed for this story, but Francine Besser, 89, of Dennison Avenue, a resident of downtown Surrey in the late 'teens and early 1920s, recalls another tragedy that occurred in the Edwardian-era four-bedroom house, constructed in 1897 by prominent local merchant Robert Forsythe and his wife Victoria.

Robert and Victoria. The parents from my story. It was like the final depressing piece of a puzzle.

"It was really quite something to my mother's generation," Mrs. Besser recalls. "Mr. Forsythe even built indoor plumbing before the city provided it— you know, Surrey was just a little country town back then. They were the wealthiest family in the county."

Local records show that the Forsythes, in mourning over the death of their eleven-year-old daughter, Sarah,

. . . Sarah?

were killed in a fire that destroyed Robert's warehouse on the west side of town (near what is now the site of St. Viviana Church) in late 1902. Evidence found at the scene led police to conclude that the fire was a result of arson, likely committed by Mrs. Forsythe, whose madness was attributed to her grief, but may well have originated with the lead pipes used in the house's plumbing, which may also have contributed to their daughter's recorded behavioral and health issues.

I remembered the hazy, hypnotized feeling of the story pouring out of me, as if I were just a conduit.

It wasn't *my* story at all—it was a true story.

The house's story.

Back in my room, I picked up the photo, studying the girls' unsmiling faces, and noticed for the first time that the white border that rimmed the edge of the picture ended abruptly on the right side. A portion of it was missing.

I flipped it over to look at the list of names. Underneath the list was a black scribble—something had been crossed out. I leaned in closer.

Was that an *S* . . . ? And the second letter could have been an *A*. The third was an *R*.

. . . Sarah.

Someone had wanted to forget she ever existed. They scratched off her name and cut her out of the picture. I studied the edge of the image. Nothing was left that would indicate she'd been in the photo. . . .

Except the small elbow of an arm.

And half the face of the doll it clutched.

It was the same doll from my story, my dream.

Is that what Mr. Sawamura was talking about when he said *power center*?

Something Sarah had loved so much that she'd held it close even as she fell to her death . . . ?

The doll. What if it was in the house somewhere? And it was taking control of my sister? And what if it had taken control of Shara and sent her into the murderous spiral that ended in her own death?

Kasey's list. The names. Those were the girls responsible for Sarah's death—and their daughters and granddaughters and great-granddaughters.

It was a hit list.

I thought about what Kasey had been saying the other day, when I heard her talking to her dolls—*She's new. Think of what she's been through.*

So now I knew what Sarah's power center was. I knew *what* she was using to force my sister to help her carry out her vengeance. . . .

I just didn't have the faintest clue *where* it was.

Or how to get it away from Kasey without . . . you know . . . dying.

24

I FELT THE DAY'S EVENTS CAKED on my skin like a greasy film of badness. I desperately needed a shower. I was so worn out that I didn't hang up my clothes as I took them off. I just left them on the floor next to my bed.

I let the hot water pour over me and closed my eyes in the steam. I spent a few extra minutes just standing there, pretending everything was fine. No ghosts, no guilt, no crazy sister, no breaking Carter's heart. It was nice.

When I got out, I put on my pajamas and combed my hair, then went down to the kitchen to get something to eat. I stood in the dark with my back to the counter, eating a granola bar. When I finished, I dropped the wrapper in the trash, swept the crumbs into the sink, and looked around the room.

The front door opened, and I almost said something, expecting it to be Mom.

But it was Kasey.

Only it wasn't Kasey. She moved with a grace I'd never seen in my sister, with a poise that I had to assume was *Sarah's* poise, *Sarah's* grace. She didn't see me as she ascended the steps toward the second floor.

I thought she'd been in her room all night. . . .

I didn't have time to think because just then the garage door rattled open and Mom pulled up the driveway. I pretended to be going through the fridge when she came inside.

"Oh hi, Alexis," she said.

I closed the refrigerator door and followed her upstairs. When she was safely in her room, I sighed and went across the hall to my own room.

The blue numbers on the clock glowed 12:06. I flipped the light switch.

Nothing happened.

"Isn't this nice," said Kasey's voice from the corner of the room. She moved out of the shadows and came toward me. She cast a glance at the door, and it shut by itself. "Just the two of us together."

I stood frozen in place.

"Do you know what time it is?"

I did. It was 12:06.

"It's decision time," she said.

Past midnight.

October 15.

"I feel . . . different," she said, spreading her fingers wide and studying them. "I feel like today is going to be a big day."

The blue moonlight shone on her through the windows, the panes of the window frame drawing a grid on the side of her body.

"You should too," she whispered. "Because it's your *last* day."

"Kasey . . . you made up your mind?"

Even in the dim light I could see the green eyes burning.

"Don't call me that," she snapped. Her voice was thin and rasping. "Kasey is gone."

White-hot fear poured through me.

"I know who you are," I said, trying to keep my voice steady. "And I know you're evil. My little sister might be fooled, but I'm not. And I'm not going to let you have her."

She raised her eyebrows, like she hadn't expected me to make this connection.

"Let her go," I said, trying to sound sure of myself, but my shaking breaths broadcast how afraid I really was.

Kasey narrowed her eyes and spoke in her regular Kasey voice. "You think you're so smart, Lexi."

She said *Lexi*. I nearly passed out from relief.

"She's my friend. She wouldn't hurt me. She promised."

"She's evil, Kasey," I said. "Do you think demons keep their promises?"

"She tried to be your friend too. She would have helped you."

"Maybe I don't want to be her friend, did you ever think of that?"

"It's your fault she's even here," she said. "You're so mean to me. You pretend to like me, but you think I'm stupid. You treat me like a baby. She's the only one who cares."

"Is that what she told you?" I asked.

Kasey hesitated. "Yes, but—it's *true.*"

"You know what she's planning?" I asked. "You know all the work you've been doing for her? She's going to hurt people. And you'll be the one who gets in trouble. She's using you."

Kasey swallowed hard.

"Do you really want to hurt Mary?" I asked. "And the librarian? And *us*, Kasey, your family? We're on that list. After you do all of her dirty work, she's going to kill you too."

My sister took a moment to consider this, but it didn't seem to disturb her very much.

I took a step backward.

"Don't try to run," she said. "You won't make it out the door."

Up to that point I'd managed to convince myself that there was a separation. There was Kasey, and there was Sarah.

But it seemed like the line was blurring.

"Kasey, we're sisters. Why would you hurt me? What would you do without me?"

No reasoning worked better with Kasey than the "What would you do without me?" argument. If I ever wanted to win a fight with her, all I had to do was say something about how awful she would feel if I died, and she would immediately burst into tears and apologize.

If there was any of that codependent instinct left in her, I wanted it on my side. Maybe I could bring her back through the magic of guilt.

"The thing is, Lexi . . ." She stiffened and took a step closer. ". . . I'd be fine without you."

She put her hand on my shoulder.

Her touch was like a hundred bees stinging me at once. I tried to back away and stumbled, falling against the wall for support. Still, she didn't move her hand.

She was drawing the energy—the life?—out of my body. The world spun and my head started to ache. I lost my balance and slid to the ground, landing on my forearms and knees, like a baby crawling. Kasey knelt at my side, her fingers still locked in place.

She's really going to kill me.

I braced my arms against the rough carpet, trying to

keep my head off the floor, as the whole world moved in waves. It was like being on the deck of a boat in the middle of a storm. I couldn't tell which way was up. My hand hit the bed with a thud.

Nausea rose up inside my throat—I tried to force it back, tried to take a deep breath—

But I couldn't breathe. I tried again, opened my mouth and attempted to swallow huge, gasping breaths. But even though I could taste the air, sweet and cool on my tongue, I couldn't force it down my throat and into my lungs.

I was drowning, sinking . . . dying.

"No, stop!"

It was Kasey's voice. She seemed to swing past me like a pendulum, her wide blue eyes so close to my face, her clawlike grip still burning into my shoulder.

"Stop, you're hurting her!" she cried.

A memory flashed into my head—the cool, smooth-edged feeling of the heart charm against the skin of my palm.

The heart.

It was the only thing that could help me. My arm thrashed around like a fish out of water, finally hitting the rough knit of the sweater I'd left on the floor. I reached into the pocket and felt the silky length of ribbon.

My fingers groped for it, and my vision started to go gray. A horrible pounding sound echoed inside my head.

Finally, just as I was about to give up, my finger made contact with the smooth metal. I grabbed it and slapped it wildly against the top of Kasey's hand. She gasped and let go of my shoulder.

Air came rushing back into my lungs.

The throbbing whooshes went silent, and all I could hear were Kasey's soft sobs. She'd scooted a few feet away and was holding her hand protectively near her body.

I wrapped the ribbon around my hand and thrust my arm forward, the flat of the heart making contact with my sister's bare foot.

She jerked her head up, stared at me through shocked eyes, and then went limp and passed out, slumping sideways onto the carpet.

Every breath of air was like a piece of sandpaper rubbing against my throat. I had to call Megan and tell her. I had to call out to Mom.

But I collapsed.

Darkness washed over me.

25

I AM LOCKING THE BACK DOOR. *I am locking all the windows. I have closed all the drapes, like she told me to.*

"Mommy," Megan says, "I'm hungry."

I can't help but feel annoyed—can't she see I'm busy?

But then I turn and look at her, and something inside me warms a little. I kneel next to her and take her hands in mine. "I'm sorry, baby," I say. "I'm almost done, and then we'll have a snack, okay?"

Megan nods, but then the headache hits, and everything goes black for a moment.

I open my eyes to see Megan watching me, her thumb in her mouth.

KEEP GOING.

"Leave me alone!" I yell, trying to get the sound of it out of my head. Megan cowers. "No, sweetie, no, not you. . . ."

KEEP WORKING!

I'm like a puppet, doing as she commands, going from room

to room, locking doors and windows behind me. Megan trails a few feet back, watching me. It has never been this bad before. Megan tries to grab on to the hem of my skirt, but I push her away.

YOU HATE HER.

And for a second, I do. I look at my daughter and feel a burning hatred. But it flares out like a match, and all that's left is guilt, sorrow, fear. Horrible fear.

A few minutes later the job is done.

GO TO THE KITCHEN.

I do, although I don't know why.

GO TO THE OVEN.

BLOW OUT THE PILOT LIGHT.

No—no—

But I can't stop myself from obeying.

TURN ON THE BURNERS. ALL OF THEM. TURN ON THE OVEN. OPEN THE OVEN DOOR.

And I'm crying, and Megan is crying because I'm crying, and she's patting my back and I'm terrified because I feel pulsing hatred for her. I'm disgusted by her touch.

I shy away from her and look down at her little arm. I see the bracelet Mom gave her, the half of a heart, the one that fits together with mine. I reach out and touch the bracelet. I lift her wrist toward my mouth and kiss her hand.

Then I stand up and take her by the arm and drag her to the foyer, and she's screaming and crying and trying to get away and asking me, "Why? Why? Why?"

NO, says the voice.

But for once I'm stronger than the voice, and I unbolt the front door and push Megan outside.

"Mommy!" she screams. Her face is red and splotchy and she's crying so hard because she doesn't understand.

"I love you, baby," I say. "I love you so much."

And then I close the door and dead-bolt it and fasten the chain and crawl back to the kitchen. The air is heavy with the smell of rotten eggs. I take the stack of doll photographs from my pocket and start tearing them to tiny pieces. Close-ups of her face, her mangled hair, her chipped hands, her stained underclothes. She's hideous. Why did I ever think she was beautiful?

Megan thumps on the door and knocks and knocks, but I can hardly hear it because the voice in my head is screeching at me, cursing me.

I HATE YOU, I HATE YOU, YOU ARE NOT MY FRIEND, YOU DON'T LOVE ME. . . .

When the photographs are shredded, I crawl to the trash can and drop them inside.

I take a deep breath, and the voice gets lower and lower and finally disappears. The burning green eyes that have watched me so closely for such a long time go dim.

The last thing I think of is how beautiful Megan looked the day she was born, when they placed her in my arms for the first time, and I realized at that moment that I would lay down my life for this tiny person.

And then I take one last deep breath and fall asleep.

Forever.

26

Mom's knock.

I'm alive.

"Alexis, are you awake? You're going to be late for school."

She tried the doorknob, but it was locked.

I'm on the floor.

"Honey, time to get up."

I turned my head, feeling the carpet fibers drag against my face—but that was nothing. I had a headache that was like a thousand little mallets pounding on every part of my skull.

"Alexis?"

"I'm good, Mom," I croaked. "I overslept."

"I have to leave for work now."

I pictured her standing on the other side of the door, her hair neatly blown dry and pinned back, her clothes tidy.

"Where's Kasey?"

"I haven't seen her. I guess she's still asleep."

"Okay, love you," I said, rolling onto my back and pressing my palms over my throbbing temples. "Good luck today."

"Thanks, sweetie," she said. "Love you too."

I waited until I heard the car pull out of the driveway, and then I forced myself to get up off the floor. I had some serious time to make up. I slipped on my jeans and a long-sleeved T-shirt, and reached into my sweater pocket for the heart.

That's when my dream came rushing back to me.

"Shara," I whispered, putting it close to my lips. "I know you saved her life."

I had to find Megan and tell her the truth about what happened that night.

And I needed her necklace. If just one half of the heart had scared Sarah off, two might be sufficiently powerful to hold her at bay—at least long enough for me to find the doll.

I went across the hall to the bathroom and flipped the light switch.

Add to the list of things I never knew about almost suffocating: it can cause blood vessels under the surface of your skin to burst, forming bruises. The girl staring back at me when I looked in the mirror had disheveled pink hair and two black eyes.

I opened the medicine cabinet, took out a bottle of Tylenol, popped one in my mouth, and swallowed. It stuck in my throat, but I forced it down.

I ducked into my bedroom and closed the door. Then I picked up the phone and dialed information.

"St. Margaret's Hospital," I said, and waited for the call to be connected. When the receptionist answered, I asked for room 412. It rang three times before Dad picked up.

"Hello?"

All of a sudden there was a lump in my throat. "Hey, Dad, it's Alexis."

"Hi, honey!" he said. "Thanks for checking on the old man. When are you gonna make it over here?"

"Um, soon," I said. "I just was thinking about you, though, and I wanted to call."

He was quiet. "Lex, is everything okay?"

"Mostly," I lied.

"Listen, sweetie. Being in this accident . . . I've been thinking. And I want you to know that you and Kasey and Mom are the most important things in my life. Maybe sometimes I act like I don't feel that way, but . . . I'm going to try to be a better dad."

"You're a good dad," I whispered.

"So . . . yeah, well, you should skip that stupid parade and come see me."

I swallowed hard. "I wish I could."

I wanted to go see him at the hospital, give him a hug, tell him I missed hanging out with him.

But there wasn't time.

"Hey, Dad? I better go."

"Okay, sweetie. I'm glad you called."

"Me too . . . I love you."

"Love you too."

I hung up.

It took a few deep breaths to regain my composure, but finally I pressed my shoulders back, held my chin up, and opened the door.

Kasey, her hair mussed and her eyes glazed over (but blue), stood at dazed attention, like a zombie prison guard.

"You look terrible," she croaked.

I didn't answer. I just reached into my pocket for the heart.

She didn't flinch, but she also didn't come any closer.

"Going somewhere?" she asked.

"Maybe."

"Are you going to find Megan?"

"Maybe."

Her eyes flashed green for a millisecond. "I wager I can beat you there."

I shrugged.

"Actually," I said, "you might want to stick around here."

She made a rude sound and grimaced as she stretched her neck to one side. "And why is that?"

"Just to make sure nothing happens to your doll."

That got her attention. "What *about* my doll?" she demanded.

"Nothing specific," I said. "I just wouldn't leave her on her own, if I were you."

She shook her head, her nostrils flaring. I held the heart in front of me like you'd hold a cross up to a vampire.

"You don't even know where she is," Kasey said. "I hid her."

"I found her last night," I said.

Kasey exhaled slowly.

"That's how I know that her right thumb has a chip on the fingernail," I said, trying desperately to remember details from Shara's photos in my dream. "And her eyes are dark green, but when she's mad, they glow."

Kasey's threatening face had turned fearful.

"And most of her hair is cut off, but there's one big piece that hangs over her ear."

"Stop!" Kasey cried.

"But you should go," I said. "Go to the parade. Go back to city hall."

She backed away from me and shook her head.

"You can't stay away forever," she said.

"Maybe I'll just hide in the bushes and wait for you to leave," I said.

"*Get out,*" she growled.

She followed a few feet away as I went down the stairs. As I put my hand on the doorknob, she made an exaggerated sigh.

"I hope I don't have to do anything terrible while you're gone," she said. "I hope I don't decide to punish your sister."

I looked up at her.

"The way I punished Shara."

My confusion must have shown on my face.

"Go on, Alexis," she said, her voice light. "Your sister *probably* won't be dead when you get back."

I said a quick prayer to whoever might be listening, and then I slammed the door closed behind me and ran.

27

THE HOMECOMING PARADE was already under way. Only a few floats were left in the school parking lot, waiting their turn to join the long, snaking line that twisted through the blocks ahead.

I followed the parade route, weaving through the spectators lined up along the sidewalks. The farther I went forward, the thicker the crowd got.

Maybe I should have thought to put on a little concealer before I left the house, because the looks being tossed in my direction made it clear that I wasn't blending in. Combine my raccoon face and my limping, dragging stride . . .

Kiss that Homecoming Queen crown good-bye, Alexis.

I tried to ignore the shocked looks coming from every direction, even tossing out a few smiles to make people think I was okay. *Yeah, of course I know what I look like. It's the new style. The entire Doom Squad is going to show up looking like this in about ten minutes. It's a theme. We have a float.*

The problem was that, depending on the cheerleading float's position in the parade, I didn't know if it would be faster to follow the line or to cut across town and meet the parade head-on. It could be a difference of ten minutes—ten minutes I couldn't spare.

Scanning the path before me, I saw a clump of black T-shirts and steel-toed boots up ahead.

The Doom Squad! They might be annoying, but their need to constantly talk smack made them hyperaware of everything going on in the school. They were like a gaggle of small-town old ladies. I made a beeline for them.

They were camped out in front of an abandoned storefront. Lydia hovered on the fringes like a watchdog.

"Lyd!" I said. "Have you seen the cheerleaders' float?"

She swung to look at me, and her jaw dropped. "Whoa, Alexis, what's wrong with your face?"

"Forget it. I just need to find Megan." By now the whole group was staring at me.

"Why do you even care about her?" Lydia asked. "She's a total drone."

"Please," I said. I took a step back. "Anybody? Anyone?"

Lydia sighed. "Listen, it sort of hurts your image for you to be seen with her, you know." She glanced behind her. "People are talking already. About lunch yesterday . . . ? And Carter Blume? I mean, what's up with *that* whole thing . . . ?"

I backed away, looking at all the faces behind her. A couple of people seemed mildly concerned, but most of them were watching me with curiosity.

"Bye," I said numbly. *Bye forever.*

I would just have to take my chances following the line of floats and pray that I found Megan fast enough to save my sister.

I hurried away, trying to ignore the stabbing pains in my temples.

"Hey, wait up."

It was a freshman girl with long black hair. She glanced back at the Doom Squad, who were glaring at us, and rolled her eyes. "Lydia's a jerk. That float's right at the front. It's like the fourth one."

I nodded. "Oh. Okay, cool. Thanks . . ."

"Taylor. Taylor Derry."

"Thanks, Taylor." Why was that name familiar? "Sorry, I have to go."

"But, like, are you sure you're okay?" she asked, her eyes lingering on my face.

I nodded, and as I looked at her, it hit me—

She was on the list.

"Listen, Taylor," I said. "Do you know my sister? Kasey Warren?"

She nodded vaguely. "She's a year behind me, right?"

"Yeah. This sounds crazy, but . . . go home. Lock the door. If she comes to your house, don't let her in. Whatever you do."

Taylor swallowed hard. "That *does* sound crazy."

"Yeah, but . . ." I tried to think what I would have done if someone said those things to me. "Please. I'll explain later."

She shrugged. "I mean, I'll have to miss this *awesome* parade, but . . ." She smiled.

"I seriously have to go. Just please . . . go home. And be careful. And thank you."

"No problem." She flashed me a peace sign and walked away.

One less target for Sarah.

I broke off from the parade route and cut through the deserted downtown. All the shops had signs in their windows that said CLOSED FOR PARADE.

As I came around the library building I saw the Surrey High marching band and the drum majorettes leading the procession slowly across an intersection a block away. I broke into a sprint and pushed through the thicker mass of spectators to make my way down the lineup.

I saw the eagle's nest first, looming high over the miniforest of artificial Christmas trees. Stationed all around the edges of the float, cheering and egging the crowd on, were the cheerleaders themselves. At first I didn't see Megan, and then as I drew nearer I spotted her at the back. She was pumping her arms in the air and shaking her pom-poms just like the rest of the girls, but you could tell her heart wasn't in it.

"Megan!" I yelled, but my voice didn't carry over the raucous sounds of the marching band and the cheers of the parade watchers. I pushed farther toward the street, trying to apologize as the people I passed made annoyed exclamations in my wake.

"Megan!" I called again. The float was only a few feet away. One of the cheerleaders noticed me and elbowed the girl next to her. I pointed at Megan, expecting to be ignored.

But the first girl backed out of her spot and made her way toward the rear of the float.

I stepped out into the street and heard the shrill whistle of a police officer.

Megan had seen me now; I gestured for her to come over, and she handed her pom-poms to the girl next to her.

That's when I saw it, across the street—

A shock of caramel-colored hair.

Kasey.

Three things happened at once—a few feet away

from me the police whistle blew loudly; Megan neatly hopped down to street level—

And with the horrible shriek of metal on metal, the cheerleaders' float creaked to a sudden stop and lurched violently to one side.

It sounded like everyone within a hundred-foot radius immediately started screaming at the top of their lungs. Megan stood frozen in place, staring in horror as the rest of the squad scrambled to keep their footing. A few girls went tumbling down into the street, dragging other girls with them.

I ran to her side as the float stopped moving and everything seemed to settle.

And suddenly I realized where my sister had been the previous night.

"Oh my God," I said. "Kasey did this."

Megan turned to me, pale.

The trees and benches and eagle's nest at the center of the float were starting to fall toward the girls on the ground, some of whom were crying and holding their arms or wrists or ankles. Pepper had her head in her hands.

"We have to help them!" I started to move forward, but Megan gripped my arm.

"Stay back!" she said. "There are plenty of people helping them."

She was right: the injured girls were already mobbed by spectators helping them to their feet and shielding them from the decorations sliding off the side of the float.

"Kasey's here!" I said. "I saw her!"

Megan was staring at the wreckage in disbelief. "All of it. All because of me? And your face," she said. "Is that my fault too?"

"What?" Oh God, she didn't even know. "Megan, no! It's *not* your mom."

She looked like she didn't know whether to believe me.

"She locked you outside. She saved your life. A hundred years ago, this girl who lived in my house fell out of the tree and died. All the girls from town were chasing her. And now she's trying to get revenge by killing all of their daughters and granddaughters. It's so many people, Megan. Pepper and Mimi, that freshman Taylor, the librarian—me. Kasey. Our mom."

Megan's eyes were suddenly blazing. It made me think of the moment in the hallway when she stood up for Emily Rosen. "How many people?"

"I don't know," I said. "The girls all grew up and got married—so the names are different. But there are dozens, Megan . . . And she wants to kill them all.

"So—the thing is—I'll explain later, but I need your necklace."

She glanced at the girls on the ground, then pulled me away and quickened her pace. "No, explain now, on the way to your house."

"What? No!" Oh, *hell* no. Megan was not coming back with me. "She's still after you."

"You want my necklace?" Megan asked. "You're getting *me* with it."

I shook my head and sighed. I was having a hard time keeping up with her. "Fine."

She slowed a little to accommodate me, but after one block I couldn't even speak. My half-strangled throat begged for mercy, but I kept going.

"Oh, look!" Megan cried, pointing up ahead.

I looked and saw a green Prius parallel parking.

Carter.

Lovely.

"He can give us a ride!" she said, grabbing my hand and sprinting.

"No," I said. "Wait!"

But she'd already waved him down, and I couldn't manage to say anything else.

When we got to the car, I had to bend over and put my hands on my knees. I thought I was going to throw up. It was just as well. I didn't want to have to look at Carter's face.

"Can you give us a ride?" Megan asked.

". . . Aren't you supposed to be on a float or something?"

"Yes or no? It's an emergency!"

"Yeah, yeah," he said. "Get in."

Then I felt his hand on my back. "Alexis, is everything okay?"

I looked up at him and he jumped backward.

Oh, right. The black eyes.

"Who did this to you?" he whispered.

"I'm okay," I said. "Let's go."

The urge to throw up had subsided. I climbed into the backseat as Carter went around and got into the driver's seat.

"You have to go to the police," Carter said.

"It's not like that," Megan replied. "Take us to Alexis's house."

"What's at your house?" Carter demanded.

"Please," I said. "Let it go for now."

"It's a long story," Megan said, looking out the window.

"Is it safe?"

Does it look safe? I wanted to ask.

"This isn't high school melodrama b.s.," he said. "I'm seriously worried about you."

"You're right." I looked at the rearview mirror and saw the concern in his eyes. Little flecks of amber glittered among the blue. "But I can't explain right now."

We reached Whitley Street.

"Just stop in front of the driveway," Megan said.

Carter obeyed, then jumped out of the car to open my door for me.

"Listen, if anything happens . . ." I said, "I'm sorry I hurt you."

"If anything *happens?*" he repeated. "That's insane."

Yeah, it was.

"Alexis, yesterday . . . what you did. I know you're trying to protect me, but I don't need protecting."

Megan was waiting for me halfway up the front path. I started to walk away, but Carter took hold of my hand.

"Just tell me," he said. "If nothing else mattered, would you want to go to the dance with me?"

I looked into his blue eyes and nodded. "Now, please," I said. "Go."

He got back in the car and drove away.

Megan and I looked at each other.

"Anything else I should know?" she asked.

"It's a doll."

Megan stared at the ground. "I remember a doll. . . ."

"Yeah, your mom used to take pictures of it. It's the doll from my story and my dream. It belonged to the little girl who died here, and now it's possessed by her ghost. We have to destroy it."

She nodded.

"But first . . . we have to find it." I glanced at her neck. "Keep your necklace on. My sister seems to be totally scared of them. But she keeps getting stronger, so I don't know. . . ."

We'd reached the front porch. As I extended my hand toward the doorknob, the door swung open all by itself.

Let the games begin.

28

THE SUNLIGHT POURING THROUGH the front door lit up the foyer, but the hallway faded into darkness. Someone had lowered the kitchen shades and closed the drapes in the living room and the sitting room, leaving the house shrouded.

The front door slammed shut behind us.

Megan stared at it and swallowed hard. "Who did that?"

I looked up at the ceiling of the foyer as if there might be a ghost floating above us. Then I squared my shoulders and focused ahead. "Probably the ghost. But you can't let it get to you, okay? Try to stay focused."

Megan gave a minute nod. "All right."

"Follow me."

We might as well start, I figured, in the obvious place—my sister's bedroom.

Kasey never stood much of a chance against an evil ghost who used the power of dolls to lure her in. Come to think of it, maybe that's how her fascination with dolls began in the first place. Could evil seep through the walls of the house, plant a seed of obsession in someone's heart?

And what about me and my photography? I was just like Shara.

Dozens of pairs of doll eyes stared at me accusingly, but none of the dolls levitated up from her perch with glowing eyes. I scanned the rows but didn't see one that was half bald.

"What do we do now?" Megan breathed.

If we couldn't pin down exactly which doll was the evil one, we'd have to destroy them all. I grabbed one from the top ledge and hammered her porcelain head on the edge of the dresser. Her face cracked like an eggshell.

"How destroyed is destroyed?" Megan asked. "And how will we know when it's done?"

"I don't know," I said, pulling on the head of an antique rag doll until it detached from the body with a *rrrrrrip*!

One thing was certain: we had to get rid of the ghost before Kasey got home. Because if she saw this carnage she would kill us both on sight.

Megan opened a display case and grabbed one of Kasey's Grande Dame dolls, the fancy kind you order from catalogs with monthly payments. I held my breath as she wrapped her hand in the hair and slammed the doll headfirst onto the surface of the desk. The doll's face imploded.

"What was that?" Megan asked, suddenly looking up.

I glanced at the door.

I didn't see anything, but . . . something was wrong.

I took a half step out into the hallway, and before I had time to look, something barreled into me, sending me flying to the ground.

I propped myself up weakly on my elbows and looked around.

Kasey stood at the far end of the hall.

"You like that?" she asked. "Want another one?"

She held the flat of her hand up in the air and moved it toward me, just an inch, and the impact hit me like a bowling ball. My head slammed into the carpet.

"Megan, run!" I shouted.

But of course Megan couldn't run. She had nowhere to go.

There was silence.

"Come on, Megan," Kasey said. "Come on out."

Megan stepped haltingly out of my sister's room. I looked up at her, but I couldn't find the strength to move.

I expected another long-distance strike, so when Kasey came marching toward us, I knew something was wrong.

I watched from below as Megan pulled on her necklace and held the charm out in front of herself. Kasey paused a few feet away, then lifted her hand.

"Duck!" I yelled. If she didn't get close enough to feel the effects of the necklaces, they were useless.

We were powerless.

All I could see was a flash of red-and-white cheerleader uniform tumbling to the floor and the charm flying across the hall.

Before Megan could stand, Kasey had reached her. She put one hand on Megan's throat, under her chin, and hefted her to her feet, slamming her against the wall.

"Your mother should have killed you when I told her to," Kasey said. "But I guess I'll just do it myself."

Megan whimpered as my sister's hand tightened against her neck.

"Stop," I said, but I was frozen in place. I tried to move my arms, but they were paralyzed.

A few terrible seconds passed, and I heard Megan's hands slapping the wall helplessly.

"Hello?"

Kasey spun away toward the voice, and Megan went crashing to the floor next to me.

The heaviness faded from my body, and I managed to sit up in time to see Carter at the top of the stairs.

"Carter, watch out!" I screamed. He saw my sister

and turned back to retreat down the stairs, but Kasey had already raised her hand.

"Alexis," Megan's shaky voice said from behind me, "the heart . . . where's the other heart?"

Kasey pushed the flat of her hand toward Carter.

"No!" I cried.

Megan had pulled herself over to me and put her hand on my arm.

Carter seemed to balance in the air for a split second.

And then he fell.

I glanced up at my sister, who, like an angry bull, had already turned back to face us.

"I won't let you do this!" I said, grabbing the heart out of my pocket.

"Got it!" Megan cried. She dove for me, raising her half of the heart toward mine.

Just as my sister held her hand up, the two pieces came together perfectly.

A flash of brilliant blue light filled the hallway and then faded slightly into a giant blue sphere of energy. It pounced on my sister, lifting her off the ground while she clawed and kicked against the air.

After a moment the whole house shook, and the blue light exploded in every direction, absorbing into the walls, the ceiling, the floor.

Kasey collapsed.

The house kept shaking.

"Alexis," Megan whispered, pointing to the ceiling. "Look!"

I saw a smaller, greenish ball of light moving frantically around the ceiling. It glowed, but the glow was almost sinister. It seemed to move like a rodent, scurrying away from the blue sparks leaping around from wall to ceiling and back. Finally it disappeared into the ceiling. The tremors stopped, and the house was still.

"Carter," I said. "Go check on Carter."

Megan slowly climbed to her feet and limped down the hall toward the stairs, while I pulled myself over to Kasey, whose skin was a dull gray. For a horrible moment I thought she was dead, but then I saw the minutest movement of her chest.

"Carter's alive," Megan's voice called up the stairs.

Thank God.

I went to the top of the steps and looked down at them. Megan sat leaning over Carter's motionless body. A tiny blue lightning bolt jumped from the railing of the stairs to the carpet, where it smoldered, leaving a blackened spot.

Megan's eyes met mine. "There's too much energy," she said. "It's like a circuit overloading."

Suddenly I had an image of our enormous wooden house as a giant pile of kindling.

"I have to find that doll," I said.

I turned back to my sister crumpled on the floor. I grabbed her by the shoulders and shook her violently.

"Get up!" I roared. "Wake up, Kasey!"

After a moment her eyes opened. They were blue. They jumped away from me to look at the sparks overhead.

"What?" she whispered.

"Tell me where it is!" I shouted, still shaking her. *"Tell me!"*

"Where *what* is?" she said. "Ow, Lexi, stop!"

"The doll!"

"I don't remember!" she sobbed.

Then she glanced at the attic door.

I jumped to my feet and ran to the top of the stairs. The door to the attic was in the ceiling. Usually there was a string hanging down that you could grab and pull, but it was half broken and out of reach.

"I'm sorry, I'm sorry," Kasey repeated. "I'm sorry, Lexi, I'm so scared."

My first instinct was to snap at her, but something stopped me.

"Kase," I said, trying to keep my voice steady, "look at me."

She raised her tearstained face and stared right at me, like a scared cat that might bolt at the slightest misstep.

"I know you're scared. But I need your help."

She sniffled.

"Please come help me open this door."

"Alexis, what are you doing?!"

I looked down the stairs to see Megan crouching next to Carter, who was looking up at us dazedly.

"Don't trust her!" Megan said. She started to climb the stairs but stumbled and fell, grimacing.

I turned to my sister. "Megan's hurt. You *have* to help me."

Kasey took a few steps forward.

"I need a leg up," I said. "I just need you to give me a boost."

"Oh God," Megan said from the bottom of the steps.

Kasey knelt with her back to the wall, making a stirrup out of her hands.

If she wanted to, she could flip me down the stairs.

"I love you," I said. "I trust you."

"Hurry," she whispered, staring up at the ceiling.

I took a step back and put one foot in her hands.

"Go!" I said, half expecting to fly backward into the air over the foyer.

But I went straight up and grabbed the string from the attic door, and in the next second I was safely back on the carpet.

I grabbed my sister in a tight hug, burying my face in her messy, sweaty hair.

"Good, Kasey!" I said. "Now go, get outside. Call Mom. And stay out. Whatever you do, don't listen to Sarah. You're stronger than she is!"

Kasey scampered down the stairs and pulled the front door open.

"Help me get him outside," I heard Megan say.

"Lexi!" Kasey shrieked. "The kitchen's on fire!"

"Just go outside!" I yelled.

"Kasey, grab Carter's legs," Megan said.

I looked down the hall and caught a flicker of yellow light coming from the study.

But I couldn't concern myself with that at the moment.

The ladder to the attic slid down and landed on the carpet with a soft thud.

I had bigger fish to fry.

29

A PUTRID, SKUNKY SMELL FILLED THE ATTIC.

The smoke alarms in the hallway below me erupted into eardrum-piercing shrieks, one after another.

The whole house was going to burn down.

Couldn't I just go outside and wait for the fire department to show?

No. It had to be done. Now, by me—or it might not get done at all.

The rotting smell grew stronger and mixed with the heavy smoke. My "flight-or-fight" response leaned heavily toward flight, but I forced myself to cross the room, feeling heat radiating up through the floorboards.

"Where are you?" I demanded.

For a moment all was silent, and then a bouquet of blue sparks flew upward from the far corner like a mini-fireworks display.

I froze.

What if the sparks burned me? What if they were

just luring me over there so they could shoot up into my face, leaving me blind and helpless?

Something stung my leg, and instinctively I reached down and slapped the spot as if I'd been bitten by a mosquito. But then I felt the sting again, and then again, and I reached into my pocket and pulled out the two pieces of the heart necklace.

They glowed blue, surrounded by a thick mass of tiny blue flickers.

". . . Shara?" I asked.

Another spray of blue light exploded in the corner.

She was helping me.

I clenched my jaw, closed my hand around the hearts, and started climbing over and around the eight years' worth of junk between me and the far corner.

The rotten egg smell acquired a sharp hint of dead fish, and I fought the urge to gag, especially as I drew nearer to the corner.

Then I saw a box that didn't match the others in the attic; it was the clean, white kind for file storage, the kind we hadn't used when we first moved in.

I grabbed an old baseball bat and slid it under the corner of the lid, then jerked it upward. The lid went flying.

And there she was.

The doll.

Just like she'd been in Shara's photographs in my dream—bald. Chipped. Undressed.

Her eyes were closed, rimmed by a few threadbare eyelashes.

As I leaned over her, her eyelids popped open.

The eyes glowed vivid green, as if they were lit from within.

I held my breath as I stared down at her.

Then I lowered the bat and reached down into the box.

I lifted her into my arms and smoothed the few strands of hair still stuck to her head.

Yes, she was ragtag.

But in a weird way . . .

She was beautiful.

I stared down at the deep emerald eyes. There was something so comforting about the way they seemed to look right into me.

I felt a burning in my hand and realized I'd been gripping the necklaces so tightly that they'd left a red mark on my palm, like a bad sunburn.

But why, it occurred to me, should I listen to Shara? She'd nearly killed her own daughter.

The burning in my hand faded from my consciousness.

What I really needed to do was get the doll to safety.

Yes, yes. To safety. I hugged the doll close to my

chest and ran back to the ladder, but beneath me the hall-way floor was on fire.

All that mattered was protecting the doll. If I could have saved her by jumping down into the flames, I would have done it.

I wove my way back through the attic, to the small window that looked out over the very top of the tree.

Of course, once we got outside it would be hard to explain my change of heart. Megan, Kasey—they'd blame the doll for the fire. For hurting us.

I'd have to hide her and keep her hidden until I could think of a way to convince the others that she was my friend. Just for a little while. I was sure that once they met her, they'd understand.

And if they couldn't be convinced, I could always find . . . other ways . . . to deal with them.

Wait.

I shook my head, trying to clear my thoughts.

I knew I had to protect the doll. I clutched her closer and felt warmth fill my body.

But no . . . wait.

Something was wrong.

My sister . . .

"You were mean to my sister," I said.

But Kasey was so *weak*. She needed to learn to stand up for herself.

"No, but . . . you didn't have to make her do those things."

But who was to say all of those horrible things weren't Kasey's ideas? She'd been lying so much lately. Who was to say that she wouldn't try to steal the doll back? After she'd left it to burn here in the attic?

My feet were growing hot, but I felt stuck, lost in the maze of my thoughts and the doll's horrible, wonderful voice and how much I cared for the doll and how I would do anything for her.

And then the solution hit me:

If I killed Kasey, she couldn't take the doll from me.

I cried out as an explosion of sparks came flying from my jeans pocket.

It was as if a layer of gauze had been slowly wrapping around my face, so gradually that I didn't even notice it until it was ripped away.

The doll . . . the doll had convinced me to kill my sister.

"No, Sarah!" I said. "You're not going to hurt anyone else!"

I threw the doll to the floor, grabbed the baseball bat, and smashed her face to smithereens.

The glow in the eyes faded.

And I was free.

The house was free.

We were all free.

Except the part where I was trapped in a burning attic.

30

THE OAK TREE WAS A FOUR-FOOT JUMP from the house. If I missed I would fall thirty feet and land in the burning bushes.

The tree itself wasn't on fire—but some of the branches brushed against the roof, which would be burning soon enough. And then it was just a matter of time.

I gathered my strength, chose a sturdy-looking landing target, and leaped.

Surprisingly enough, I made it. It took a little doing to swing my legs up, but after a second I was scooting toward the trunk of the tree.

I scanned the branches, searching for a way down. Not an easy task—the tree was almost as big as the house, and by that point embers had drifted from the big fire and started little fires among the foliage.

"ALEXIS!" Kasey screamed. She was just an ant of a person down in the yard, flanked by Megan and Carter.

A fire truck came screeching down the street, but I

didn't have time to wait to be rescued. Flames licked at my feet.

I had to get to a new branch. The closest one was six feet away.

Could I do it? I had to.

I took a deep breath and jumped.

Just as my feet propelled me off the branch, I realized that I'd left the heart inside. I'd left Megan's only connection to Shara in the burning attic. It was going to be caught in the fire. It would melt.

I spent a millisecond too long staring regretfully at the attic window.

When my thoughts returned to my present position, I felt for a moment like a cartoon character, hanging in midair for a moment before the plunge. Everything was in slow motion.

Then time sped up, and I fell.

Seven Months Later

The property at 989 Whitley Street was on the market for four days and sold for well above the asking price. Land is too valuable these days for people to pass up a house just because the ground beneath it, for the greater part of a century, teemed with unsettled spirits. Besides, there are spirits everywhere; you can't avoid them. You just try to avoid the ones who want to kill you.

Mom, Dad, and I moved across town, to a condo— really a very nice little place; three bedrooms: one for me, one for them, and one empty, waiting for Kasey. We'd ditched the shadowy hallways and gone for the brightest place we could find. The walls were white, the counters were white tile, even the furniture we picked out was white and shiny. It was as though we couldn't get enough light.

Dad bought me a darkroom pass at the community college and promised to pay the fees until I graduated from high school. So that was cool.

It took Kasey a few months to start talking again, but now she's doing really well at the treatment center. She's not having catatonic episodes or waking up screaming in the middle of the night anymore. The doctors tell us that in a few months she should be able to come home.

The official diagnosis was psychotic schizophrenia, and we all went along with it because the insurance company won't pay for "made friends with the wrong ghost."

She even has some friends, girls her own age. I've seen them when they didn't know I was watching—they sit and giggle and make dumb jokes like all fourteen-year-olds do.

Leave it to my sister to come out of her shell at a mental hospital.

The police never even got involved. One thing I've learned is that there really *is* a group of government agents out there who wear long gray trench coats and don't look at you like you're crazy when you talk about ghosts. They hung around for a couple of days, scoured the remains of the house, took our statements, and left as quietly as they came.

They found the heart charms in the rubble, fused together, and gave them back to Megan. But there hadn't been any more sparks.

Shara had come back to help us . . . but she was gone.

All of the complicated explanations we'd been cooking up for the police turned to dust, unspoken.

So anyway, life is good. I can't believe seven months have passed. Sixteen (still no car!), broken ribs, wrist, arm, collarbone, and ankle pretty much healed, with a best friend and parents so attentive that I occasionally have to remind them not to smother me.

Not to say I don't have drama in my life.

"No," I said. "No, no, no, *no.*"

"Alexis," Megan commanded, "sit down."

I sat.

She set the tiara on my head.

Mom squealed with delight and clapped her hands.

"You're not helping," I said to her.

"Hush," Megan said. "Stop complaining and look at yourself."

"Strawberry Shortcake," I said, and then let her turn me toward the mirror.

Hmm. It was pink, all right, but not exactly Shortcake pink.

"You look incredible," Megan gushed.

The same pink dress Megan had taken from her closet last October. Shorter haircut (but still pink). Pink shoes (Mom's treat).

And, of course, the tiara.

"Oh my God, you love it," Megan crowed. "I can see it in your eyes! You looooove it!"

"Yeah, right," I said. But secretly I did kind of love it.

"Oh, Megan, you'd better get ready!" Mom said,

glancing at the clock. "The boys are going to be here any minute."

Megan cast one more extremely triumphant glance at me and disappeared down the hall.

I pushed my lips together. I was going to look in the mirror again, and I *did not* intend to smile. There . . . turn . . . look . . .

"You have such a pretty smile," Mom sighed.

I glanced up at her. She was smiling too, and her eyes were a little watery.

"Don't cry," I ordered. "I'll never go to prom again if you can't keep it together."

"I know," she said, sniffling and flapping her hands in a failed effort to dry her eyes. "I know, but I just . . . you just . . ."

I gave her a kiss on the forehead. "Listen, I'll wear more dresses, if it makes you feel better. But if you cry, I'm going to cry, and then my makeup will run, and Megan will kill us both."

Mom laughed. The lump in my throat dissolved.

"Ready," said Megan, stepping into the room.

"Oh, Megan, you look amazing," Mom said. The choked-up sound returned to her voice.

Megan did look amazing. She was wearing a black dress with spaghetti straps, the simplest little thing you ever saw. But somehow she made it completely elegant.

She wore her hair in a bob that came right to her chin.

"That's the doorbell!" Mom said, and scrambled away to answer it.

"Forgive her," I said to Megan. "It's her first prom in twenty years. She's a little nervous."

In the living room, we found Mom swooning over Carter (just a good friend . . . we all needed a little time to cool off after my sister, you know, tried to kill him) and Luke Birmingham (Megan's trophy date—"strictly eye candy," to quote her). Dad hovered on the sidelines and took photos while Mom watched the boys to make sure they admired us enthusiastically enough.

Carter came right over to me. "You look incredible," he said.

Big smile. "You too," I told him. He did look pretty nice. He was wearing just a plain black tux, but he was starting to get that old Carter thing back—was it just confidence? The way he walked and held himself.

"I brought you a corsage," he said. "It goes on your wrist. I didn't want to be a cliché and spend fifteen minutes trying to pin one on your dress."

It was a very nice corsage. I held my arm out, and he slipped it over my wrist. Our hands touched for a moment, and I got a shiver (but hid it).

Megan waited patiently as Luke tried in vain to pin

a corsage to her dress. She smiled through what was probably a frightening amount of random pin-sticking.

"Megan, did you talk to your grandmother?" Mom asked. Mrs. Wiley was off merging a few corporations in the UK. "She said to call and wake her up before you go."

Megan slipped away and flashed her date a smile. "Sorry, Luke, just be a second," she said. As Megan dialed the phone, Mom took the corsage and pinned it to her dress with zero effort.

"Hey," Carter said, nudging me, "let's go outside for a second."

I shrugged and followed him. He held the door open for me. The air was chilly, but there's a chance I would have shivered anyway.

The sun was setting below the row of trees, and a few stars were already out and twinkling. It was lovely and clear.

"So how about this," Carter said when we'd reached the sidewalk. He turned toward me.

Shiver, shiver. It's just cold, I told myself.

"How about we don't do the 'just good friends' thing tonight?" he asked.

I blinked. After we both got out of the hospital we'd made a mutual decision that, given what we'd been through, it was probably best not to jump into a relationship too fast.

"Too fast" had basically translated to "at all." And it was cool—cool to have someone to hang out with, to joke with, to talk about architecture and photography and cheesy sci-fi movies.

But let's be honest, it was still Carter. And he still had the softest blond curls and the bluest eyes and the best-smelling laundry detergent of any boy I'd ever met.

He might have expected me to talk, but I couldn't, not at that moment.

"I'm not . . . I mean, Alexis, I don't want to be just your friend. Not even just tonight. Every day. Every minute. I mean, maybe you don't feel the same way I do, but I have to tell you. I can't stand the thought that you might find someone else and never know how I—"

I put my finger to my lips. *Shhh.*

He shushed, then looked at me helplessly.

Once upon a time, I thought I knew a handsome boy named Carter, who always had the right answers and knew everything about the way the world worked.

I don't know him anymore.

I guess he never really existed.

"I ruined tonight, didn't I? I didn't mean to," he said. He shook his head, annoyed at himself. "I'm sorry."

"Don't be sorry," I said.

And then I kissed him.

And it was perfect.

He took my hand and held it like I might run away. "Really?" he asked.

I smiled. "Really." Then I kissed him again.

The front door opened, spilling light on us. Megan and Luke came out the front door, followed by Mom, who waited on the porch, camera at the ready.

"I'll be right back," I said to Carter.

I ran back to Mom.

"I have a boyfriend," I whispered to her.

She smiled. "Watch, I'm not going to cry."

"Don't you dare. I'll be home by midnight."

"Come say good night when you get in."

"Love you, Mom."

"I love you too, Alexis," she said. "You're a good girl."

I kissed her on the cheek and walked back to the car, happiness overflowing out of me and spilling up into the starry sky.

A *good girl*.

I can live with that.